A Lady of Independence

A Lady of Independence

HELEN ARGERS

DOUBLEDAY & COMPANY, INC.

GARDEN CITY, NEW YORK

1982

With the exception of actual, historical persons,
all of the characters in this book
are fictitious, and any resemblance
to actual persons, living or dead,
is purely coincidental.

11. 82 Baker 7.10

Library of Congress Cataloging in Publication Data

Argers, Helen.
A lady of independence.

I. Title.
PS3551.R416L3   813'.54
AACR2
ISBN 0-385-17476-4
Library of Congress Catalog Card Number 81–43264

First Edition

TO THE REAL ASTERA . . . AND OUR MOTHER,
CALLIOPE-CAROL

A Lady of Independence

CHAPTER 1

"My lord, it is an honor I should prefer to decline."

The perfect features of society's most sought after beau registered the shock he felt at the rejection of his proposal.

"It was my understanding," the Viscount sputtered, "that is . . . your guardian and I have settled . . ."

Astera smiled at the ego evident in the degree of his surprise. She herself was able to view him with tolerable composure, secure in her decision that she would never marry—certainly not somebody who negotiated a marriage contract with the guardian before ever meeting the lady in question! Every feeling must be offended!

"I intend to have a career," she finished defiantly.

"Good God," he ejaculated. But that was all the reaction his civility allowed him to express—immediately his face reverted to its usual mask of ennui. "Then, I daresay, you should certainly pursue that . . . notable ambition." And bowing, he turned to leave.

Opening her eyes innocently, Astera allowed that he gave very little evidence of having a "fighting" nature. At which point the Viscount Weston's lips were slightly drawn into a cold smile. "It is not my habit to engage in combat with members of the weaker sex."

Astera's eyes twinkled like the stars she was named for. "Indeed? I expect you'll live to regret that assessment."

"I think not."

Furious now at her composure and challenge, he could only bow again and attempt once more to depart.

"Upon my word, I wonder if I should accept you, after all? It would do you a world of good to be taken down a peg or two." She deliberately extended her pause, as if reconsidering, while he grew whiter and whiter with suppressed rage. He could not, as a gentleman, draw back if she consented, but it was obvious that now it had become his most sincere object.

"No," she said finally. "No, it wouldn't be worth my while . . . no matter how edifying it would be for your character."

"Then your original rejection stands?" he asked stiffly, but with a certain amount of hope.

Astera toyed with him a bit longer, deliberately rearranging the lace cuff on her sleeve, and then when it finally suited her, she resolutely looked up, as if finding the perfect pattern for her lace prepared her to solve her life.

"Yes, it stands," she said, amused. "And you . . . my lord, are dismissed."

"I shall speak to Lord Winthrop and explain the results of our meeting," he threw back hurriedly on his way out. He was so much in a hurry to be gone, Astera could no longer keep up her attitude of hauteur and she committed the solecism of giggling.

"Relieved?" she asked gently, now bestowing on him the smile that had melted her guardian's most outraged moods. It did not have the smallest mellowing effect on the Viscount. Indeed, he stopped and allowed an ungallant response—particularly out of keeping for such a noted Corinthian whose manners were known to be as incomparable as his sporting skills.

"Not relieved, ma'am, rescued."

Alone Astera was momentarily disconcerted by the insinuation that she had "rescued" him from the danger of marrying her, and indeed, might have been on the point of taking offense when her sense of humor came to her rescue too, and she laughed aloud. In truth it had been a narrow escape for both of them. Thank God she hadn't allowed herself to be influenced by Lord Winthrop's determination to inflict on her the "splendid match" that was his interpretation of her parents' wishes. Certainly she had no desire to marry at all, and if she ever did, it would most assuredly not be a union with *that* stranger with his cold gray eyes.

Dear Guardy, she sighed, he'd never understand her. He'd

been her father's and mother's closest companion and never understood them either. So it was not very surprising that a record so unblemished should be continued by this latest effort. Astera had refused when the offer was first broached to her, but Lord Winthrop had not taken her seriously—as, indeed, he had not taken any of her remarks or previous desires to heart—counting on her superior breeding to nudge her at the last moment to do the correct thing.

As usual her breeding had not nudged, and as usual, she had acted as she had said she would. Astera sighed, "You'd think Guardy would be used to me, by now!" But he was always shocked—no matter how many times he had been shocked by her before. And for a while she would really be in the suds. Well, it just meant she would have to work extra hard to turn him up sweet, but she would do it. For it was not that she was headstrong—merely that she was in a position to please herself. For although the bulk of her fortune was under her guardian's control until her marriage or his death—whichever melancholy event first occurred—her parents had left to her own use an independence. Whereupon she very obediently acted independently, to the extent of refusing even to have a season and instead taking a grand tour, traveling as did the young men of her acquaintance. And now after her return from the capitals of Europe, she was determined to write. She had faithfully kept a diary and embellished it with events she'd wished had happened, so that little by little it became a most sensational volume. Lately, under the influence of Lord Byron's *Childe Harold's Pilgrimage*, she had attempted to switch her traveling impressions into poetry, sketched in a sketchy plot, and even came up with a bang-up signature: "By a Lone Lady Traveling Across the European Continent." Its deliberate omission of any reference to her dear, harried Aunt Minerva, who had accompanied her, would give rise to all sorts of delicious rumors. Yet the next minute, not wishing to out-and-out lie, she made a hasty amendment. She would simply sign herself "A Traveling Lady of Means." For in her brief acquaintance with the ton, "means" was by no means ever despised. In fact, "means" was the most meaningful attribute a lady could have; and certainly more of a lure than *depravity*—which, after all, tended to be rather common—in all its meanings.

The one problem remaining was the sustained writing required. Just attempting the first canto necessitated giving up a score of pleasant divertisements, such as riding, sketching, reading. She had some talent on the pianoforte and had composed her own sonatas, an elegy when her parents had died and two or three nocturnes when she had felt overcast. Still, every kind of pride must revolt at a public performance—not to mention her guardian's revulsion. So that was ruled out.

It would have to be the poetry after all. Something her father would have been devilishly proud of—at all events he'd always been so whenever she'd presented him with one of her sonnets. Then too they'd often played a game called "Limericks," where each had tried to outdo the other in inventing the most nonsensical last line, and he had relished her every effort. Astera closed her eyes at the sharp pang of that memory and forced herself to go back to thinking of her recently rejected suitor. Perhaps she'd dedicate her epic to the Viscount, she thought playfully. That would assure his indicting her as lacking in all delicacy. Recollecting him, Astera could not help but recall the impression she had had at his first entry into the drawing room. For a brief second she had lost a shade of confidence concerning her chosen course of life. He was without a doubt a gentleman of fashion!

His coat was obviously cut by a master—at least Nugee if not Scott himself. His Hessians were blindingly shined and molded to his muscular calves. His neckcloth had the precise folds of a waterfall. No fobs or seals dangled from his waist. Just a quizzing glass hung round his neck, through which he had given her several quelling glances. The only other ornamentation was a signet ring. So all in all he was nothing in excess. And Astera knew what excess in men's dress was, for she had seen a great many macaroni merchants in her travels . . . and the Viscount was not aping them. There was no excessive height to his collar, nor, while his clothes were well-fitting, did it appear as if a deep breath would split the seams—as a true dandy would rule de rigueur. So he was as elegantly attired as God had elegantly featured him. Like the statues she had seen in the Greek museums that always turned out to be either Dionysus or Hermes. She was strongly considering naming her hero after the latter. For Hermes' characteristic of being so light on his winged feet inevitably made him a great traveler, ergo, the ideal choice for her journeying journal.

This very morning she could not but admit having seen a mortal man with the same lightness and ease-of-manner when looking out the window and witnessing the Viscount Weston springing from his curricle and effortlessly running up the long flight of massive marble steps leading to Mayberry's imposing entrance. And, indeed, when she first came face to face with him he gave her no small shock, so much did it seem that he had walked out of the pages of her very own heroic poem—in progress. Later, she was undecided whether her impression of him began to vastly deteriorate the moment she saw the expression in his eyes on seeing *her* . . . or whether it came about *afterward* in the course of their stilted conversation. He was civil but with a degree of hauteur in his manner and commonplace in his subject that could not but give offense. Indeed, he never ventured beyond the most trivial matters as if he assumed she was totally unable to comprehend anything beyond that.

After exclaiming politely on the floral arrangements in the room, for which he gave her credit and she politely demurred, they went on to the state of the roads, which had seen a sad alteration due to the succession of rains they had so recently enjoyed. From there it was a smooth step to his lordship's matched grays—"high-steppers," which, he allowed, were "not a bit winded on the drive down to Mayberry," her guardian's estate. There ensued directly a painful pause till he roused himself to inquire about the extent of Mayberry's grounds and she informed him that circumventing her guardian's lands would be a journey of more than ten miles. "A pleasant little drive," he responded condescendingly, and she was annoyed and allowed another pause to continue so long that he had recourse once again to his quizzing glass. Astera remained unaffected by this trial as well.

The more toplofty his manner, the less attractive his very features seemed. Odd. But it was so. And consequently the happier Astera became. For though she had planned to refuse him, she had expected to feel a certain discomfort in disobliging him, but his manner was making her eagerly anticipate the moment when he would make his offer and she could, as the young men of her acquaintance—and no young woman but herself—were wont to say, "throw him a leveler."

So much was she anticipating the moment that she resolved to push matters forward a bit by resorting to unhelpful monosyllabic replies.

His eyebrows rose a bit at her withdrawal, but he gamely carried on. After a bit he resorted to flattery, obviously assuming women would always succumb to that.

"Lord Winthrop tells me you have a way with your instrument."

"Which instrument?"

"Why . . . the pianoforte."

"I am accounted to be tolerable on the harp as well—that's two instruments."

"A most accomplished lady," he said in a voice that clearly was overlaid with unconcern. Astera couldn't resist using the same exact tone and words back to him.

"Lord Winthrop tells me you have a way with your cattle."

His eyelids fluttered a bit as if he momentarily suspected something. But he merely bowed.

She was getting more and more impatient.

"I have heard much of your talent with the needle."

That one momentarily stopped her, for she had no talent in that area and was unsure whether it had been her guardian's fulsome praise running over . . . or just that the Viscount assumed all women were proud of their handiwork and had simply treated her as "all women," and not a person in her own right. In either case she was chagrined enough to try the same ploy with him.

"I'm told you are singularly adept at whist."

His surprise could not be camouflaged—so either she had hit on a secret talent or been totally out, as out as he with his needlework remark!

Decisively, he put down his cup and stood up. Something had moved him along! Joyfully she rang to have the tea things cleared away. When the servants were gone she assumed he would now speak. She leaned forward.

"You have been on the continent," was all he said, and she was fuming so much she was almost unable to reply in the affirmative.

There was now a most obvious flush of annoyance to his countenance.

"Italy?" he persevered.

"Yes."

"Greece?"

"Yes."

He stared at her and breathed, "Ah, yes." Impatiently he was drumming his fingers on the mantelpiece. Yet another attempt at gallantry. "That is a most becoming color, Miss Claybourne." And he gestured somewhere in her direction.

"The gown or the hangings of the room, my lord?"

Now he could not doubt her attitude. Now his beautifully sculpted mouth was in a tight disapproving line. "Both, of course," he responded, biting off his words.

"You are too kind to notice. And your waistcoat is in the same becoming shade of . . . ecru, isn't it?"

"*I say!*" he ejaculated, striding about and at a loss, but she kept her face blank and innocent as she asked, "My lord doesn't care for compliments?"

My lord was confused and vexed. Whether she was just a peagoose who said the first thing that came into her head or a brass-faced impertinent chit was now immaterial. In either case, he was seriously displeased.

Looking down in what she hoped was a shy demure manner, Astera tried to restore the conversation to its original course, momentarily feeling a very definite qualm that she'd finally over-done it and he would never now declare himself.

But it seemed that either she had not been as obvious as she feared or he was much less discerning, for after looking at the ormolu clock on the mantelpiece a few times and exclaiming how much time had gone by, the Viscount set upon finishing his business there. With a sigh, he straightened his already ramrod body and grimly put the matter to the touch.

"Miss Claybourne, I collect you are aware of your guardian's consent to my making you an offer."

And he sat back as if completing a tiresome task, but Miss Claybourne was not to be cheated.

"Then make it, my lord."

Nonplussed, the Viscount stared a second, choking back his annoyance at her insisting on a full-blown proposal, and coldly began again.

"My dear Miss Claybourne, I have the most profound honor to ask for your hand in marriage."

Astera, triumphant, sighed in relief, and, giving him another one of her incomparable shining smiles, refused him.

Yes, it was pleasant to recall that moment. Not so gratifying was recollecting his "Not relieved, ma'am, rescued." And all ease deserted her at the thought that there was now Guardy to face . . . and her Aunt Minerva. Astera's previous · actions, which her aunt had dubbed Astera's "latest starts," had necessi-tated an immediate recourse to her vinaigrette. This refusal would leave her aunt not just momentarily prostrate but so to-tally overcome by spasms that not even the usual asafetida drops would suffice. Obviously, Astera concluded with anticipa-tory dread, something stronger should be waiting, for neither lavender nor even vinegar-soaked hankies would answer. Ah ha! the young girl exclaimed, remembering, and jumping up, she went quickly in search of the never-fail, all-purpose, cure-all—*burnt feathers*—before marching bravely forward to inform her aunt of this morning's occurrence.

CHAPTER 2

At the exact time Astera was reliving her morning and preparing for a difficult afternoon of explanations, the Viscount himself was also suffering a variety of emotions brought on by that morning's scene. The principal emotion—although relief and anger came strong seconds—was astonishment. He, the most sought after catch on the Matrimonial Mart, *had been refused!* Who would credit it! He was pushing his horses at a speed which was in no way called for by the destination—merely a pleasant visit to his friend Lord Cuffsworth's shooting lodge. A much-anticipated divertisement yesterday, the promise of the prime Cyprians that Cuffy was to have waiting (to ease the blow that Weston was soon to be leg-shackled) could not now lighten his lowering mood.

Perched up behind him in his curricle was his groom, Andrew, who had been in that position for many years and never had had the occasion to question his master's handling of the reins. If Andrew were ever to permit any emotion to show on his face, it would be now, at the feverish way his master was pushing his blood-cattle. For the Viscount had always treated his horses with the respect their perfection deserved.

Murmuring to himself all the while, Andrew tried to come to the nub of the mystery. "He ain't blue-deviled for nothing . . . I'll take my affy-davy he's in no way to be buckled."

His lordship was in such a brown study he didn't hear the old man's muttering, nor his louder remonstrating for the spanking clip at which they were going.

The puzzle grew more complex as Andrew wrestled with it and tried to clutch the edge of his seat at the same time—while the curricle lurched ahead. No one knew more than he how susceptible women were to his lordship—even way back when he was in shortcoats. Since then he'd seen a procession of them—from the prime bits of muslin to the most respectable beauties.

But, dash it, those black looks didn't come from just not being pleased with his intended—even if she wasn't up to snuff and even if he'd felt he'd been taken for a flat, he'd still never treat his proper prime 'uns like this, jobbing their sensitive mouths as he was now.

"Give over, m'lord," he murmured again, and when that had no effect he said at the top of his lungs, "Beggin' your pardon, but was you thinkin' of sticking our spoon in the wall?"

A slight grin from the Viscount indicated he'd been brought back from his ruminations, but only long enough to allow a short reining in to a fast trot. In five minutes' time his whirlwind thoughts descended on him again and had him racing ahead as speedily as ever and even, at one point, featheredging a blind corner. A sharp remonstrance from Andrew resulted only in his getting his head bitten off, so thereafter the Viscount was allowed to fume away undampered.

What was particularly eating away at the Viscount was that he could not decide whether his intended was an out-and-out peagoose or too needle-witted for her own good. That was important to determine—in order to ascertain whether the girl was to be pitied or horsewhipped!

But what had been obvious at first glance was the girl's lamentable lack of style. Her dress was something no lady in London would have ever considered as suitable for such an occasion. The lace on her right sleeve, which she kept toying with throughout that blasted interview, was definitely *torn*, and it was not due to lack of funds. She herself had an independence and certainly her guardian could afford to dress her in the best. No, obviously her turnout was the result of her own slipshod ways and deplorable taste. He shuddered as he thought of the bright orange-red bows down that brownish-beige dress that indeed had only been matched by the brown-beige hangings of the room. And after he'd been kind enough to compliment her on it, she'd had the nerve to bring attention to the fact that his waistcoat was practically the same color. Of course what was suitable for a gentleman was not for a lady.

Not that she seemed to see that distinction!

Moreover, the dress was silk! And as an unmarried girl, she should have worn muslin. But she was just not up to snuff!

It was his father's fault! The previous year the Earl of Castlewick had sent a message to his heir, requesting a visit—at which he'd point-blank asked what Weston's plans were for setting up his nursery. The Viscount had demurred in his usual not-to-be-intimidated manner and his father had dropped the subject. Relations between the two had always been of the best, and the Viscount was surprised that the Earl would do anything so uncharacteristic as a direct interference in his life. He had always been an easygoing parent and since the Viscount had inherited a minor fortune from his grandmother over ten years ago when he had first graduated from Oxford and went on the town, he had never had to please anybody but himself as to his pleasures. This changed only after his mother, an equally gentle woman, took her son aside and let slip that his father's health was declining and that that was the reason he had felt the need to speak to his heir before he lost all chance to see the succession assured.

Thereafter, the Viscount had made an effort to choose from the diamonds that he had been setting up for flirts, but, whether because he felt his hand now forced or whether because there was something lacking in this year's crop of debutantes, he had given up in disgust and returned to his parental estate and frankly asked his mother's help in choosing. She was delighted to do so. She proposed her dear friend's daughter—the Duchess Volton's eldest girl, Cissy. She was beautiful and docile and in every way would make the perfect wife for her dear son. The Viscount stipulated that nothing was to be said till he met the young girl, and a party was arranged which both were to attend. After half an hour with her, the Viscount was assured he could not possibly spend even another half hour, let alone his entire life, in her constant bland presence. But his mother was not discouraged; she had another bosom-bow who also had a daughter,

Clara. Clara turned out to be so much a horsewoman, the Viscount was assured he'd have to spend his life in a ménage à trois —which might have been amusing if the third party had not been her horse, Dolly.

At that point his mother either ran out of girl friends or the Viscount just changed his mind, for nothing was proposed by either side for several months till his father had another setback and now, newly roused to action, the Viscount agreed to accept the very next suggested girl—sight unseen. It happened that his father was fond of reading and had on his shelves the volume of moral tales by Astera's mother as well as the poetic effusions by Astera's father. When the problem was presented to him by his wife he happened to be standing in his library right next to the Cs and his eye hit on the couple's literary efforts, which he took as a certain sign. On such chances does life oft tend to spin.

To make it even more inevitable, it appeared the Earl had known both Claybournes slightly and generally admired them, and further, he was even better acquainted with Lord Winthrop, who was guardian to the Claybourne's only child— the lively, irrepressible Astera. The Earl instantly suggested her to his wife, who was dubious—a daughter of bluestockings would not be right for her son—but she had run out of bosom-bows with daughters, and so Astera was hesitantly proposed and, surprisingly, immediately accepted by the Viscount—with the stipulation that this time he not meet the girl before the marriage settlements had been drawn up all right and tight so he could not draw back! Knowing his nature, he realized if he were to marry at all, it would have to be a fait accompli. Lord Winthrop was consulted by the Earl, and between them the matter was quickly settled over a glass of port. The Viscount was duly informed and correctly arranged a personal meeting with Lord Winthrop, which soon became two, as the guardian had a great many stipulations. But eventually, after the combined efforts of the Earl, his lady, Lord Winthrop and himself, the marriage was fully and finally arranged, and in not above three-and-twenty minutes that young chit had disarranged all!

Further, she had done that at just about the time the Viscount had begun to acknowledge that at nine-and-twenty and after a good many years on the town, society was beginning to pall. The same ceaseless breakfasts, balls, routes, race parties at Ascot, gatherings at sparring and fencing saloons, evenings at Watier's. He long ago had given up nights at gaming houses—preferring to put his money in horses and women. But his stable was the envy of all his friends as were his opera singers and other high-steppers—although lately neither had seemed worth the amount of money or time spent on them. And the beautiful young ladies of his acquaintance always came equipped with eager mothers. But neither the bluest eyes nor the most determined maternal maneuvers had brought him up to scratch. Indeed, up to now so many lures had been thrown his way, he'd begun to feel like a very slippery trout. Or if he were to put it in the vernacular of his favorite sport, the truth was he was more the hunted than the hunter . . . and now he wanted to run to cover. Dash it, perfect lips and blond curls under the same high-domed bonnets were beginning to blend into each other. So in that state of ennui and with the incentive of his father's health, and considering his need of a change—any change, even one for the worse—Weston had begun not only to be ready but eager to make the sacrifice—only to have the entire sacrifice and all his plans thrown back in his teeth.

With such a guardian (Lord Winthrop was in every way a gentleman) and with parents so respected, it was impossible for him to have imagined that the girl in question would not at least be a "lady!" But what had greeted him was an outspoken, almost brazenly antagonistic girl—no longer at her first flush of youth, either. Three-and-twenty if she was a day! Perhaps even four-and-twenty! Obviously her salad days were long past, and it was impossible to comprehend her reaction. At the very least she should have shown gratification at having been offered what even he would not be flattering himself to call "a splendid match." Yet instead, she had out-and-out rejected him . . . and without a legitimate excuse. That "career" remark was obviously a hum—something a woman with such lamentable high spirits would concoct at the spur of the moment.

At first sight, despite her lack of clothes sense, he'd been relieved to find she was *presentable*. In fact, when she smiled, she was downright enchanting. Her eyes were dark and lashed so profusely and with so much of a lively sparkle it was no wonder that her mother and father (both noted scholars of Greek) had named her Astera—the Greek word for star. Unquestionably, she was starry-eyed.

But that was the end of her good points. Her golden-blond hair was worn in a fashion not accepted anywhere outside of the schoolroom—loose and long over her shoulders. Hadn't she ever heard that fashion insisted on curled hair worn high in Grecian knots with the fascinating tendrils on neck and cheek that kept inciting a man's attention whenever a beautiful woman moved her head? Obviously not, for there hadn't been either a single loose curl or Psyche knot there. Then, as to her figure—who knew whether that was to be praised or tolerated, for it was totally hidden under that beige bag of a dress! But what could not be hidden was that she was too tall to be called *petite*, as were the usual women who attracted him.

Still, while hardly a dasher, something could have been made of her so she would not have shamed him. He would have taken her straight to Paris and had her totally outfitted. Indeed, he had been thinking that very thing when, as a test of her taste, he'd remarked on her clothes—only to have her, rather than blush in embarrassment at her own lack of clothes sense, comment upon *his!*

But, upon his word, what could you make of a girl who'd had the audacity to act as if she were merely being polite to praise his driving, when it was well known that his reputation was justly earned. Not that he enjoyed seeing younger men try to emulate his way with the whip, any more than he cared for their trying to duplicate his latest neckcloth creation. For today he'd himself designed "The Bridal Fall" in honor of the occasion, and now it had wilted as totally and irrevocably as had his spirits. His blood was up at the thought that she probably hadn't sense enough to appreciate *that*, as she obviously didn't have sense to appreciate him.

"Good God!" he ejaculated, looking about him. He was almost at Cuffy's lodge and he had not yet prepared an explanation. They'd all be waiting to wish him happy! That was another score he had to settle with that damned girl!

But later when he and Lord Cuffsworth were sitting alone in the study and Cuffy insisted on being told all the news, the Viscount, always an honorable man, instantly confessed that he'd been turned down flat.

Cuffy choked on his drink and then began to laugh. "Coming it much too strong, dear fellow, I'm not a total gudgeon."

"I say she refused me without a blink of her eyes. Steady as they come, she let fire. It was an honor she 'should prefer to decline.'"

"No, Wes, *no*, I say. Don't try to gammon me. Astera would never do anything that shabby. She's just not that kind. Well, dash it, I mean she's kind. She's the kind that's *kind*, if you know what I mean. Wouldn't do that to a fellow—let him get the marriage settlements all right and tight and then turn him down to his face! Did you quarrel?"

The Viscount's eyes narrowed. "How do you know what Miss Claybourne would or would not do? And how do you have leave to use her first name? What is this, Cuffy? Are you trying to gammon me?"

"Haven't seen her in years . . . but knew her when she was a child and I was a mere stripling. Neighbors, you know . . . well almost. We grew up in each other's hair. A real game girl. Nothing missish about her ever. Could climb trees with the best of us and throw her heart over the jumps. She'd hardly hurt a fellow on purpose. Soft heart, you know, for birds . . ."

"Ah, that explains it. Since I'm not of the ornithological branch of my family, nor, indeed, avian in any way, I expect I don't incite her sympathies."

"No, dash it, Wes, don't mean just for birds. Just mentioned them because I remember her taking care of a baby bird. . . ." Cuffy paused. His large blue eyes were troubled. "Can't recall whether it was a lark or a sparrow. . . ."

"Does it signify?" the Viscount asked resignedly.

Cuffy grinned. "No, only to the bird, I should imagine. All in all I just meant she was a good-hearted sort."

"Well, then, it must be an aversion to me personally."

Cuffy was even more horrified by this conclusion and refused to accept it as the Viscount's most loyal friend and admirer. "Impossible," he exclaimed. "Ain't ever been a girl that didn't make a cake of herself over you—even before hearing you're in line to be an Earl!"

Weston was amused by his friend's tribute. "You move me, Cuffy . . . as far as the decanter."

But Cuffy was still trying to figure it out. A faint recollection caused him to frown. "There was that, of course."

The Viscount turned back instantly. "What?" he asked in a casual voice, but his eyes were intently interested.

"She was always a bit of a bluestocking, you know. Comes of having scholars for parents. Always could think circles around me. I had to cuff her whenever she got too literary—you know, Shakespeare and such. Used to try to get me to play Romeo to her Juliet while she hung over my head on a branch of a tree. Unnerving. Come to think of it . . . lots about a bird in what she used to recite then too . . . something about a tassel bird on a string . . . which I didn't relish above half . . . so when she called me 'Cuffy,' she had good cause. Not that I did cuff her one but always threatened to when she got above herself."

"Are you implying that the lady is too intelligent for me! Good God, I thought you were a friend!"

"Not saying you're not smart, Wes. Just saying she's smarter. Anyway was when she was a child. Course, I've noticed women who start out just as smart if not smarter than us get widgeon-witted when they come out. Maybe that's it! Maybe she was too overcome by the honor you were doing her?"

"She declined the honor in no uncertain terms and very certain, *unawed* tones!"

"There's no explaining it then."

"Then do stop trying to," Weston snapped, and Cuffy looked long at him.

"You're really blue-deviled, ain't you?"

"I am a trifle annoyed . . . rather humiliated and anxious never to hear or see that particular young woman again . . . or talk about her!"

"Won't say another word. Lotsa flowers in the garden, fish in the brook, birds on the wing . . . if you get what I mean?"

"Perhaps," his friend snapped. And then sitting down and turning the glass in his hand round and round he finally said calmly, but with a hint of menace, "Nevertheless, she's the woman who shall be my wife—whether she desires it or not. The only question is—how do I go about getting her?"

"No go!" Cuffy exclaimed, alarmed. "Told you. Know her. Once she makes up her mind, hard to get her to change it. Never would stop reading Shakespeare at me. She said no, she meant no. My experience: it's devilishly hard to get a girl if she don't want to be got. You've never had that experience though you're older. Might do you good to experience it. Had things too long too easy—especially with females. Learn your lesson . . . and go on to other girls. No use beating a dead . . . eh . . . nail into the ground. What?"

"I tell you, whether she wants to be gotten or not, I'm going to get her."

"Might as well reach for a star."

"Precisely what I shall be doing. Contrary to what the lady believes, I never have and never shall accept defeat. Not when I've been so obviously challenged."

But Cuffy continued to shake his head. "Didn't want a season when all the other girls had to go through that . . . and she didn't have one. Wanted a grand tour when *no* other girl has that . . . and she got that. Very definite girl, that. If she said *no*, accept it."

The Viscount was now on his feet. "I do not accept it. I accept only the challenge. And I will lay you odds she'll be going down the aisle with me before the year is up." He was smiling—already sensing and relishing his victory, when Cuffy burst out.

"I'll take that bet and add my own. That she will be walking down the aisle but . . . with me."

"*You* . . . where do you enter into this!"

"Where do *you*? Always fond of Astera. Waited for her to grow up. Now, I fancy I'd like to see her again. She's got one weakness and I know about it and can use it—like I always did when I got her to do what I wanted. And what I want now is to save her from you. If that means marriage, by Jove, then marriage it shall be."

"Cuffy, you're a lunatic. You can't compete with me. Not in swords or riding . . ." He was laughing now almost uncontrollably. "Not even for women I didn't really want—and *this one I want!*"

Cuffy was unafraid. "This girl's different, and I'll win because I know she is . . . and you'll lose because you think she isn't."

"Damn you, Cuffy, stay out of my way in this!"

"It's my way now too," Cuffy said softly, but with enough quiet conviction that the Viscount was surprised at last into believing him.

"Well," the Viscount smiled. "I expect it shall be an interesting autumn after all."

CHAPTER 3

The interest of the season was assured when the Viscount wrangled an invitation for a fortnight's visit to Mayberry for himself and a party of his friends.

Lord Winthrop, totally overset by his ward's insult, not only to Weston but worse, to his father, the Earl, rode, without stopping, to London to make his apologies in person the very next week. Considering the papers being signed and the unexpectedness of Astera's refusal, he was dreading the encounter—only to be met with, not an affronted young buck, but a gracious, understanding host who would not permit a word of apology. Indeed, he implied an obligation to Lord Winthrop rather than the other way round, and even went so far as to keep him there three days during which he was so feted and so enter-

tained that Lord Winthrop was almost desperate to hit on a way of lifting a particle of the obligation.

A return invitation to Mayberry for a fortnight's stay was the least he could do. Upon the Viscount's smoothly inquiring who else would be of the party, Lord Winthrop was at a loss and much relieved when Weston offered to bring the entire group with him! "A sole arrival would tend rather to single me out, would you not say, my lord?" Weston asked, smiling warmly. "Yet within a party I might not seem so singular, and thus, less of an embarrassment to Miss Claybourne . . . and her inclinations."

To that her guardian could not but agree and, even more, be impressed with the young man's tact and thoughtfulness, while wincing at how little of either of these qualities his own Astera had shown.

So the Viscount was to make all the decisions, not only where and who but when. All that remained was informing Astera of the forthcoming fortnight of guests. Of that responsibility Lord Winthrop could not divest himself. He did put it off the first night of his return home, but the very next morning he nerved himself and told her straight out.

So astounded and unprepared was Astera for the intrusion of the Viscount Weston again into her life, she had to instantly excuse herself and retire to the grape arbor for a vigorous pacing before she could feel herself sufficiently collected to return for the particulars of the proposed scheme.

The blow was what the young bucks called a leveler, and again and again she knocked aside a heavy bunch of grapes hanging just above as she paced beneath.

Was it possible that the Viscount still retained hopes in her direction?

No. Quite impossible. From the furious expression on his face when she'd last seen him, *that* idea was totally out of keeping with her estimation of his character. Obviously, since he could not reach her, he would conclude she was as sour as the grapes in the fable and not worth his effort.

Concerned by her distress, Lord Winthrop had followed her

into the arbor and made every effort to make the proposed visit sound like a treat.

But Astera would not be deflected. "All strangers—not only to myself, but, most shockingly, to the host himself! It is unheard of! It is a gross imposition!"

He stiffened at that, basically because he knew her to be essentially correct—one did not generally allow a guest that freedom, but this case was different. Actually, he was not clear how it was different, but *he*, who had never been called upon to have to explain himself, even to himself, was not going to fall into such weak habits at his time of life; and he said as much!

And Astera, to avoid seriously displeasing him, for he was already beginning to redden alarmingly, forbore and remained silent.

Her silence weighed more with the lord than her words and he began again to attempt to put a better face on the visit, assuring her that the Viscount accepted merely to be polite . . . that it was just the "civil" thing to do . . . and she was just being called upon to do the "civil" thing as well . . . and then that would be that!

"Very well, he is to come," Astera sighed, "but one last point," she pleaded. "What necessitates *my* remaining here? Certainly there shall be some degree of awkwardness which both of us should wish to avoid? And if you are under obligation to him, sir, I am exactly the reverse! There can be no better time for me to visit my father's publishers, for I have already incorporated some of the travel poems written over these last few years into the beginnings of a narrative, and I should like to see his reaction—whether he would encourage me with my idea for eventual publication or not."

"There can be no possibility of your not being present!" Lord Winthrop exclaimed in alarm. "The Viscount Weston's party shall include two very elegant ladies, and that alone necessitates there being a hostess to receive them—I assured him of that point before we parted!"

"Did you indeed?" remarked Astera with a smile. "Then *he* insisted *I* be here?"

"Certainly not! Stab me, if I can see why you're taking such a pet! He merely suggested *a lady* be present as hostess to entertain the *ladies* he is to bring . . . along with the two gentlemen."

"Any lady . . . or myself?"

The good lord was beginning to perspire in the arbor. Wiping his brow, he concluded decisively that a hostess had to be here and that meant Astera herself. The suggestion that Aunt Minerva would suffice he would not even consider. The ladies coming were young—not ones who would wish to discuss various ailments. In fact, these ladies were of such impeccable standing in society as to honor his home by their presence! One he had had the pleasure of meeting already in London, and he could only say that as charming as his ward was, even *she* would have to use all her resources to keep such elegance suitably entertained! And the sister of that young lady was Lady Marvelle, who was an intimate of none other than Lady Sefton, the renowned patroness of Almack's! So Astera was please not to do anything . . . that is . . . she was to try to be as respectable as her dear mother would have wished!

And with an expression that suggested he did not think Astera would quite achieve that exalted state, my lord made his escape, leaving Astera to pace the arbor in anguish.

So many questions presented themselves: from why such "distinguished" ladies should wish to come to her guardian's estate, where the ton had never been known to congregate . . . to what their relationship was to the Viscount . . . and lastly, how she was going to entertain them all . . . and, further, how she could bear their being here at all!

If the Viscount was seeking a way of punishing her, he could not have found anything more appropriate. For Astera was certain this entire visit had been maneuvered by him. What his object was beyond revenge, which seemed petty, also kept her occupied between her rushing about to prepare Mayberry for the honor it was about to receive. Her aunt, of course, had had a spasm at the news, and the entire management was left in her hands—extra servants had to be hired for the occasion, the rooms prepared, menus planned, entertainment devised—and all for strangers whose likes and dislikes she could not possibly know . . . or want to know!

It could not have come at a worse time. For Astera, as she had explained to her guardian, was deep into her poetic novel— *Idyll in the Isles*. She had decided that while her hero was ideal, he should be based on reality to give her adventures some measure of verisimilitude. Therefore, she modeled him, most suitably, on a sculptor named Andreas Jason she had met in Greece during her grand tour. Dark curly hair, deep, smoldering, snapping, olive-dark eyes and a chiseled face—he looked his occupation. He was exuberant and voluble and wily. While pleased by his attentions, Astera had been too aware that his pockets were "to let," which she adjudged to be the principal goad for his pursuit and she never allowed their relationship to advance beyond a flirtation. But, in memory, his eyes lost the calculating gleam and took on a lover's true ardor—to which she found herself particularly susceptible—especially at a distance. All in all, his improvement in retrospect was of sufficient sweep to make him quite suitable for use as her hero. She obviously needed not the slightest bit of alteration to be the heroine. Yet all names and times were changed to save her blushes. Following common practice, she transposed her narrative to a tale of ancient Hellas. Since anything occurring that long ago was bound to be viewed less censoriously—people assuming those dead for ages could hardly benefit from moral lessons at this late date. Also, using gods and goddesses would give her narrative an easy flow, for whenever she reached a gap, a goddess could conveniently pop up and bridge it. The plot concerned a sculptor (Andreas/ Hermes) falling in love with a goddess (Astera/Artemis) and creating a statue to her perfection. The goddess then finds the sculptor's efforts so pleasing she rewards him by appearing in the flesh. The love affair ensues, inspired by Byron's uninhibited cantos. So far Astera was uncertain how it would resolve itself. Her sense of humor leaned toward making the sculptor find life with a real goddess so intolerable as to make him deeply regret ever having prayed to her! Yet at other times her sense of romance wished to have it develop into an all-out *doomed* love affair—for nothing could be more delightful than that! However, whatever the denouement, the tale had to be suspended, for the Viscount and his party were intruding on her creativity. In the midst of her versifying, she would begin thinking of the smoking chimney in the second guest room, and how the "elegant" lady would react to dark smoke billowing into her face, which set her to laughing, and that would sufficiently do in the most passionate poetry!

Aunt Minerva, after a few days taking to her bed, recovered sufficiently to follow Astera about and bewail all the decisions her niece was making. "What *was* she thinking! A lady could not be happy in *this* chamber—it was decidedly stark . . . flowers would not help, for there was always the chance that she might be afflicted with hay fever! . . . Further, a chaise longue had to be brought in for moments of repose as well as a hanging from the attic to soften . . . time must be made then! For no lady could be sufficiently comfortable in its bare . . . Well, if there was so little time, why were all those beige hangings from the drawing room being put in the Viscount's chamber! How is it possible he had requested them!" And many more such helpful asides.

So much had to be done that some had not to be done. The rose and apple-green Sèvres china was brought out from the recesses of the cabinet, but not the gold plate. The inside marble stairs were scrubbed, but not the outside. And while the windows—many to the floor (which afforded such magnificent well-wooded views)—were cleaned and sparkling, the crystal chandeliers were simply dusted. Thus, by cutting here and improvising there, and further, by keeping the maids in good humor with little bonuses, and lastly, by approaching Burton, the butler, with just the right amount of cajolery and appeal to his pride in the Winthrop establishment, Astera had the house tolerably prepared.

As for the elder Miss Claybourne, her outrage finally resulted in her taking over the planning of the meals, for Astera's orders were "so meager as to be shameful!"

"One course and only three removes!" she had cried. "Why, it is positively nipcheese! And nowhere near suitable for Lord and Lady Marvelle; not to mention the consequence of the Viscount and another lord accompanying him, nor that elegant young lady your guardian cannot stop praising for her beauty and taste! You shall be shaming him and me . . . and yourself! There must at least be *two* courses. . . ."

"I shall explain to them that since I am a Philhellene and you the sister of the most famous Philhellene, our ways are necessarily Spartan!"

Her aunt paled at the thought of such a statement and would have argued its merits till she noticed a twinkle in her niece's eyes and demanded, "Astera, you shameless child, what *are* you planning!"

"Simply to make their stay as short as possible!"

So after that, Aunt Minerva bestirred herself to get together with cook and handle the management of the menus. Astera's only recourse was to plan unending evenings of whist. And since both her aunt and guardian were quite addicted to that game, they did not find that plan amiss . . . nor, indeed, her recommendation that they invite the Reverend and Mrs. Smallward, who were known to be quite impassioned by the game themselves and could further enliven the party by inserting an uplifting sermon or two!

Astera's dress on the morning when the guests were due was the same ecru sack with the orange bows that had so impressed the Viscount on their first meeting. When her aunt vaguely asked if she had not worn that dress before, Astera had joyfully claimed she was wearing it out of sentiment to call to mind the many compliments the Viscount had made her on it; and her aunt was pleased that the dress (which, in fact, she had chosen) had found favor, and further delighted that Astera should be civil enough to consider the Viscount Weston's feelings on the matter. But while agreeing on the dress, she insisted the lace cuff had to be mended.

Minerva Claybourne actually preferred the beige dress to the puff sleeves and high-waisted muslins being worn now, which she could not help but decry as "paltry." In her day, voluminous silks and full-bodied brocades in strong colors with elaborate undergowns were the vogue. And hair was never cut, but worn in curls to the waist with puffs over the ears—all slightly powdered, to give it a gray cast. Total elegance. In fact, she'd kept a blue Italian taffeta that had garnered her more than her share of pretty compliments from many gentlemen and poetic allusions from her brother's friends—one of whom in three weeks' time had made her a declaration, and all matters were joyfully arranged between them when he was stricken by lung sickness! His doctors ordered him to Italy, where he died in a sennight—alone and in quarantine in the port of Naples. There, his last letter was written to her and found clasped in his hands along with a miniature of her in that selfsame blue taffeta dress. They were returned by the authorities, and ever after kept in a music box on her dressing table. Since then, *illness* had been Minerva's terror, for she knew how it could break you just at the moment of your greatest happiness and blight all your future to come!

Astera took time from the preparations to once more hear the story of her aunt's aborted love, for however many things had to be done, relieving her aunt's feelings on this subject whenever they boiled up needing relief was to Astera always of prime importance. So she sat respectfully silent and, though having heard the particulars countless times, once more was profoundly moved—even joining in her aunt's tears, which gratified and lightened that lady of her burden enough to enable her to revert to her generally brisk ways and carry on till the next time the memory seized and laid her low!

There was a prodigious number of gowns in a trunk up in the attic that contained not only the famous blue Italian taffeta and other of her aunt's gowns but her mother's things as well. Astera was wont to go up there and hold the sable capes and cherry taffetas and yellowing ermine-trimmed billowing bombazines and remember some, laugh over others, but generally come away concluding how simple it would be if she could wear those, rather than having to go through the tedium of having new dresses and gowns made by the local dressmaker, Mrs. Elton. That somewhat talentless widow was very efficient in repairs but had no eye for style. Nevertheless, she was a friend of her aunt's—being a joint collector of nostrums and symptoms. Even Mrs. Elton herself when she finished an outfit for Astera would stand back and wonder if it were "quite right." Reluctant to disappoint the dear lady, both Astera and her aunt would always assure her it was "just the thing." And, indeed, till Astera had gone abroad she had not been aware how very far from right her wardrobe was, for neither she nor her aunt were subscribers to *La Belle Assemblée* nor did either know such a periodical existed!

But Astera had not allowed her unfashionableness to interfere with her joy in traveling, for there were so many important things to see that how she was *seen* seemed vastly unimportant. Bon ton was decidedly not for her. Presumably she had avoided it by not having her season, yet now it was unobliging enough to be coming to her!

In retaliation her only weapon was to appear unconcerned and attempt to feel that as well. And there she composedly stood, atop the long row of Mayberry's marble steps, flanked by her aunt and her guardian, the sun full on her beige dress with the orange bows as the two carriages drove up.

The Viscount was out first, quickly running up to greet his hosts. Face to face with Astera he immediately perceived the orange bows and his eyes narrowed—revealing he remembered not only the gown but the discussion, and was uncertain what the reappearance of it signified.

Immediately she glanced at his waistcoat, but, alas, he was not as sentimental as she, for he was wearing one in shocking lavender. They had no more time than to exchange a brief commonplace during which their eyes met. Each received a clear message of challenge. Each instantly accepted it. But all further silent messages and any verbal ones were aborted by a loud cry of "*Astera!*"

Miss Claybourne turned in disbelief! A young lord dashing out of the curricle seemed familiar. "Cuffy," she whispered, and then, nearly tripping as she ran to embrace him, shouted, "*Cuffy!*"

He, almost knocking over Lady Marvelle, gave Astera a jolly good hug. There was much to exclaim over, heights to be measured, changes noted and remarked on, joy expressed. "Good heavens, if I had known *you* were to be of the party I should have arranged things differently," Astera confessed in unwary delight.

"Really?" the Viscount interposed. "I begin to fear that this fortnight will seem a great deal longer."

Astera, recalled to the challenge, answered archly, "A visit may seem as long or as short as the guests have wit to make it!"

"Actually, the success and failure of any gathering has always been the responsibility of the *hostess* . . . and the measure of *her* success or failure," he replied languidly. "It shall be rather interesting to see how *you* rate. Eh, Miss Claybourne?"

Astera colored at the thought of the evenings of whist planned, but recovered enough to answer, "A willing hostess, perhaps!"

But all conversation came to a stop when Lord Winthrop handed down the "elegant" lady herself—Sybil Farnshorn. She wore a striking blue velvet hat trimmed with a single ostrich plume over her flaxen hair. Her pelisse was in a similar blue velvet, as were her eyes. An ermine muff completed the attire. She moved gracefully to the top of Mayberry's stairs and turned round slowly, as if to survey the surroundings—thus giving onlookers a chance to view her from all sides. Behind, almost as an extension of herself, came an abigail with a blue parasol, which she held out at the correct angle—no matter which direction her mistress moved or stood. Still Miss Farnshorn paused. At last, feeling the right amount of time had elapsed, she turned toward Astera and her aunt and acknowledged them.

Lord Winthrop rushed to make the introductions. Polite exclamations were generally exchanged. Then Sybil was escorted into Mayberry by her host as if she were visiting royalty. The rest followed in her wake, Astera and Cuffy far to the rear.

CHAPTER 4

Astera did not have time the first day to think out either the nature of the Viscount's clear challenge or her own reaction to seeing Cuffy again . . . or even the cold wave of dislike she felt
from both sisters, for her guests were making too many unexpected demands. To begin with, she had expected both ladies to
bring their maids, per course, but they had in addition each
brought a *dresser!* And Lady Marvelle's, Miss Puce, had airs almost as elegant as her mistress', demanding a sitting room as
well as a private chamber. She was only out-hauteured by Lord
Marvelle's valet, who made so many demands of Burton, Mayberry's dignified, usually unflappable butler, that even he was
kept running to Astera with complaints. Cuffy and the Viscount
brought only their grooms, whose total demands were satisfied
by a tankard of ale.

"Good heavens!" her aunt cried, wondering where to put
them all. Astera however, had ruthlessly declared that the ladies' dressers should be satisfied with one of the many chambers
(without sitting rooms) on the third floor—and that Burton was
in full charge and would decide on all requests on the basis of
what extra time and help he could spare and what *he* deemed
necessary. Burton, puffed up by being made the ultimate authority, vowed to put them all in their places and proceeded to
do so. Thus, things seemed to be working themselves out when
Lady Marvelle and her spouse further added to the compli-
cations by demanding separate suites. Cuffy saved the day by
giving up his and willingly putting himself in the only available
suite on the floor above, which was once a governess' apartment
directly adjoining the schoolroom. Rather than standing off,
Cuffy joined in and made an adventure of moving, encouraging
the maids with sallies and praises as they turned out the unused
chamber, so it was all over in a short, happy time.

Examining his accommodations, Astera was delighted to find he appreciated the view more than he mourned the lack of hangings.

"I say, you can see the stables! What luck!"

Astera's eyes twinkled as she responded, "Even luckier yet, on a good stiff breeze you can even *smell* the stables!"

"By Jove, can you? Nothing I like better than to smell horse! You can keep all your pansies and other posy sniffs, there's nothing as satisfying as a good stiff sniff of stable!"

"Pansies do not have a scent," Astera put in; but he waved her quiet and opened the window, taking in a deep, satisfying snortful.

"Ahh! Makes you think of good clean runs . . . of . . . of sweaty gallops . . . of soaring jumps . . . of . . ."

"Of muddy falls!"

Cuffy whirled round. "If you're going to start about that *one* time!"

"One time!" Astera exploded. "You slid off as often as you got on . . . a more cow-handed, slippery-bottomed rider I never saw. You were always coming up covered with dirt!"

"Speaking of dirt, who went looking for some dashed imaginary lady-in-the-lake . . . and fell flat in it and was *all over mud* . . . and who . . . who . . . got me to fall in pulling her out! And we were not just dirty but fully mud-caked as we walked into your mother's tea—trailing weeds. . . ."

Astera was convulsed with laughter. "And she looked at us—all wet and slushing all over everything, our clothes clinging to our bodies—and calmly said, "Astera, that reminds me, Mrs. Jenkins here tells me Thomas Bowdler, you recollect him, is purifying Shakespeare by eliminating all mention of the word 'body.' Think of that!"

Cuffy guffawed as he added, "And you calmly sat your wet body down on the settee and chatted away with her and that old lady with all those books over her lap, while I edged *my body* out of the room, hoping she wouldn't punish me as well by making me listen to all that stuff! By Jove, I'd rather have been whipped, as my father would have done!"

"Nonsense, she wasn't punishing me for getting my clothes wet, it was just not as important as the topic my wetness called to mind—you never understood my parents."

"That's right. Talked Greek. Dash it. And you *answered in Greek!*"

"Certainly. Ancient Greek was our common private language. And you could say all sorts of naughty things in it and just get praised for your fluency!"

Astera took one last look at his room and, finding it would do, started to lead Cuffy downstairs, when on entering the hall she thought to ask softly, "Why did you come, Cuffy? Why did *he* bring you?"

Cuffy was uncomfortable, and by the way his eyes couldn't meet hers, she realized there was something he was in an agony to tell her, and that just at the last moment, some code of secrecy held him in check, for he bounced away and opened the adjoining schoolroom.

"I say," he exclaimed, changing the topic none too smoothly, "here's a place we could explore!"

And she had enough kind feelings for him from the past not to push that topic and joined him in searching the place.

Cuffy was disappointed to find just books. The way he kept reacting to the discovery of one after another had her laughing again.

"What did you expect to find in a *schoolroom?*" she began, but was silenced by Cuffy's insisting she reveal where the exciting things were hid. Shaking her head, Astera reminded him that she was past her school days when she'd moved to Mayberry—just after her mother and father died within weeks of each other of the same slow fever.

At that, Cuffy was instantly, awkwardly silenced, knowing her loss must have been acute, for he recollected how dashed fond she'd always been of her parents—as "unusual" as they were. He'd been at Eton at that time, and then Oxford, and when he came back to Derbyshire where they'd had neighboring estates, Astera was long gone. And thus, through the distance and years and Cuffy's disinclination toward correspondence, their friendship had dwindled to dim acquaintanceship.

"Well," Astera continued philosophically, "when I was alone Aunt Minerva was kind enough to give up her horses and come live with me—to give me 'consequence'—but Guardy wanted us both to move in with him, so there was no point in trying to keep up an empty estate, particularly since for me . . . it would never again be filled. . . ." Here, her eyes teared and, annoyed with herself, Astera sniffed them away, continuing quickly, "Ever since Guardy and my aunt have been prodigiously kind, but I never again felt the understanding I had from my parents."

"Lord no, who could understand any one of you!"

Astera grinned, acknowledging it, and turning aside the depressing topic, she questioned him about Oxford. Had he come across other people interested in the classics?

Cuffy recollected with a groan the scores of "blue" people there, as devilish strange as she, but he'd long ago learned to deal with that sort by simply throwing in an occasional "by Jove," and that always made those gudgeons think he was making a "classical" allusion, and they'd be good for fifteen minutes on the gods, during which he would make his escape.

Laughing at that, Astera was surprised to have her hands clasped and to hear an earnest Lord Cuffsworth claiming he'd often thought of her laughing face and wished he could see it again, especially when she'd gone off to Europe—then he'd worried she'd get herself into a "devil of a fix with one of those foreign coves who dash well don't understand that though you are . . . eh . . . 'spirited' . . . you are still a *lady!*"

Moved by his concern, yet amused by the conclusion, Astera assured him she was now rather genteel; but not, however, as genteel as the two ladies he'd brought with him.

"Oh, I say, don't blame *me* for them!" Cuffy objected. "That bunch of stiff-necked, toplofty gudgeons. Especially that peagoose Sybil—she's Wes's last season's flirt, you know, and ain't likely to give him up, though I'll be dashed if I know why he brought her if—"

Cuffy broke off—his face registered alarm. And looking about for a way out of his dilemma, he spotted the cupboards, which

he flung open till a cry of triumph indicated he'd discovered
something beyond books. Indeed, a set of spillikens spilled all
over the floor, and he blithely stepped over them to victoriously
produce—a cup and ball!

Instantly he was at it, catching the ivory ball on its point
twenty consecutive times and challenging Astera to meet *that!*
Delighted to do so, she completed thirty before he could blink
an eye.

"I say," Cuffy objected. "We're dashed near back to the same
old relationship! All that's needed is for you to bring out the
foils and that will foil me for certain!"

Astera instantly recollected that incident. Cuffy had "bor-
rowed" his father's foils and taught her to fence in secret, only
to discover he was being disarmed by his budding pupil. In retaliation, he greased the handles; then both kept losing their
grip. Their match from that point became a farce neither could
sustain without laughter . . . and thus ended the fencing lessons.

"If you grease this as well!" Astera threatened with a laugh,
and Cuffy assured her that that was his very next step—if she
did not noticeably decrease her points. But on the final challenge Cuffy had improved to fifty straight, and Astera grimly
set about topping him . . . forty . . . forty-seven . . . forty-
eight . . .

But on forty-nine, she was down flat on the ground, and the
culprit Cuffy with her.

"*Unfair!*" Astera protested heatedly from her undignified position.

"Unworthy, Cuffy. One never trips a lady when she's winning
—one merely defeats her."

Astera and Cuffy turned in astonishment at the Viscount's
voice. He was observing them on the schoolroom floor with a
decided calm. And taking the cup and ball, he nonchalantly and
without a single miss caught one hundred on the point before
putting the game down and bowing in Astera's direction. Then
turning to Cuffy he asked if he should prefer to share *his* suite
rather than being out of the way up here, but Cuffy, laughing at

the Viscount's one-upping them both, insisted nothing could be better than being away from all those "fashionables." And Weston, though smiling at that, continued seriously to question whether this floor was fit for habitation for someone accustomed to the elegancies of life and illustrated that complaint by running his hand over the dust in the room, leaving a telling mark. To which Cuffy replied airily, "Oh, dust-snuff! Living in London gets one used to a dashed sight more dust than that!"

Remembering her position as hostess, Astera coldly assured the Viscount that Lord Cuffsworth's suite, *adjoining*, was perfectly *clean*, and Weston, as if not trusting her word, turned in that direction to examine the accommodations himself. Astera had to pause to contain her temper before following the gentlemen. When she entered, Cuffy was eagerly showing off his chamber, pointing out the major attraction—the view of the stables! To which Weston responded, "Quite. I was aware it was in *that* direction the instant we entered. The stables are situated rather close to the main house, are they not?" He turned to Astera.

"Ah, now I begin to understand the reason for your sudden return. You are interested in buying the estate, my lord?"

"I am interested in buying something in the estate, yes," he concluded calmly, giving her time to read what she would in that remark, before finishing. "Your guardian tells me he has some interesting horseflesh he would be prepared to part with!"

"I was not aware that anything was for sale. Perhaps putting prices on living things is a practice more common in London . . . but *not* here."

"Why, whatever do you mean, Miss Claybourne?" the Viscount asked with a small smile which grew larger as Astera seemed more intimidated.

Trying to recover she added quickly, "Tattersall's, of course. Is not that where one buys horses? Certainly not here. Any horse my guardian wished to be sold I shall buy from him to keep things *just as they are*."

"Status quo, Miss Claybourne, can be quite static . . . one must be willing to accept change. One can't remain in a stall all one's life—a thoroughbred would wish to break free and gallop to greener pastures."

"It is extremely vulgar to speak like a jockey, if that is not your profession, and certainly vulgar to allude to another person in such a way as to suggest she is a horse."

The Viscount smiled and allowed that she did rather remind him of a frisky filly one would wish to *"bring to bridal."*

So enraged was she at his stressing that last phrase and his delight in his pun, which recalled a connection between them best forgotten, she forgot herself enough to raise her voice. "I repeat, there is no flesh-peddling going on here—especially not *to you or any of your crowd!"*

"I say," Cuffy interjected, alarmed. "Why are you in such a huff over a few horses! I mean, dash it, if you don't want to sell any of your nags, then don't. No need to come on so strong . . . to . . . *all of us!"*

Astera colored deeply, and the Viscount smiled at her discomfiture, continuing smoothly, "Yes, extremely uncivil, isn't it, Cuffy? But I am certain Miss Claybourne has been *mis*understood?"

Cuffy relaxed. "That's what I was telling you. There's no understanding her, but she's a devilishly good sort. Never takes a pet . . . for long, does she?" he said grinning, turning to Astera, who, recovering a bit at this tribute, assured him she did not, and gave him a flashing smile that always weakened him . . . and did again.

"Cuffy," she whispered, "you know I cannot be angry with anyone who did me the good favor of bringing you." And turning to the Viscount, she said warmly, "For that I must thank you sincerely . . . and further, I do hope, since you have considerately brought your own entertainment from London with you, that with a little effort on both our parts it will seem, to you, as if you had never left there, and to me, as if you had never come."

The Viscount laughed at that conclusion, admiring her deft jabs under the cover of graciousness, but Cuffy had only understood the welcome and was thanking her and exclaiming at her sweetness, and she smiled indulgently at him and gave him her hand, which he kissed with much fervor—half in humor and half in earnest. About to lead them down, Astera turned, just in time to see a flash of anger in Weston's eyes and was puzzled, for she'd assumed they had just concluded a truce—but immediately that expression was replaced by a blank indifference that made her doubt her first impression.

Dinner that night would have done a more demanding woman than her aunt proud. Nothing went amiss. No attention was missed. No servant was remiss. As well as the two main courses she'd insisted on, there was quail and duckling and fish as a remove. And when it came time for dessert, the dining tablecloth was lifted to reveal her aunt's pride—the intricately embroidered dessert cloth underneath, which was the elegant setting for the mousse and fruits and jellies.

Planning to make no unusual effort for her appearance that night, Astera had been rather amused to hear from her own abigail, Marigold, that the two ladies were spending near to two and a half hours, assisted by their dressers and maids, on their *toilettes*. Therefore, Astera agreed to wear a different dress (the beige having made its point). She chose a green and yellow satin striped gown, also rather baggy but without bows, and even added a string of pearls given her by her guardian on her return from Europe, and felt the results were tolerable. Then on the staircase she came face to face with the two ladies and knew what perfection was . . . and how far she'd fallen from the mark.

Lady Cicely Marvelle was all in lace—from her delicate mauve gown to her lace mauve cap—that made her appear to be an exquisite piece of handiwork. But it was Sybil that caught everyone's breath. Obviously she was what was described as "a diamond of the first water." But there was more than perfection of features and coloring to Sybil. More than her elegance of dress. It was there in her movements and carriage of head. She was all grace—so much like a swan, she made every woman around her feel like an ugly duckling! Her dress tonight was appropriately white with flounces that gave the illusion of wings and helped promote the swanlike impression as she glided from gentleman to gentleman with a word here, and a word there, till they were all standing back quite breathless. At the table she had been seated next to Lord Winthrop at his own request; and it was embarrassing to Astera to see the old man acting so unlike himself, trying to make witticisms and elaborate compliments. Astera was seated between Lord Marvelle and, on her insistence, Lord Cuffsworth, with whom she'd hoped to have the pleasure of conversing throughout the evening, but that hope was overset by Lord Marvelle, who demanded an attentive audience. Between the soup and the first remove, she learned he had been one of "Prinny's" set at Carlton House. He was also inordinately proud of his corpulent figure and dandified dress, since he felt it made him resemble the Prince Regent himself—"Now our good King George the fourth."

That Lord Marvelle was a dandy was made evident not only by the amount of fobs and seals and golden chains he wore, making him clink whenever he moved to get his plate refilled, but by the points in his shirt, which were so raised above normal height as to make it necessary for him to stretch his neck whenever he wished to look at the person with whom he was conversing—in this case, Astera. Somehow, with the fish came the snuff—a topic that could not long hold her attention, but one in which nevertheless she was fully instructed: from the various kinds, to how to prevent its "catching cold" or drying up, and lastly, a strong admonition never to soak it in scent as some ladies had the habit, till she assured him she would not; and only when he began with a list of other helpful instructions did she tactfully explain that neither she nor her guardian kept snuff, and thus his injunctions were not essential to their comfort. Much surprised, the lord sputtered and responded severely that *every lady* must know how to handle a gentleman's snuff— if she were at all concerned with pleasing her gentleman! Only Cuffy's breaking in with a story about a man who gave snuff to his horse finally shocked Lord Marvelle into silence and ended the discussion. Astera gave Cuffy a look of pure gratitude, which he returned with a conspiratorial grin that was not lost on the Viscount.

When the ladies retired, it was only a few seconds before Cuffy joined them and he was sitting next to Astera assuring her that he had not been funning and giving her the particulars of the horse-addicted-to-snuff story, which had her in high glee when the Viscount entered.

Since Cuffy had always amused him, the story repeated for his benefit had him laughing too. Astera suggested they try the experiment on Cuffy's own horse, which Cuffy, taking the bait, heatedly refused, whereupon the Viscount joined Astera in wondering how Cuffy could suggest something and then be unwilling to put it to the test. Thus the two, teasing in concert, were beginning to feel somewhat friendlier, when Sybil appeared before them like an apparition. One minute she wasn't there, and the next she was—a pure white column, staring straight ahead, breathing significantly. It reduced them to an abrupt silence.

Astera could not resist. "Ah, the silent Sybil, what doth it portend?"

Trying to hide his smile, Weston rose quickly, followed somewhat more reluctantly by Cuffy.

Sybil spoke softly. "My lord, I would speak to you about a subject. . . ." A long pause ensued while all waited, and then Sybil concluded, ". . . *my dress!*"

"How deflating," Astera sighed, and the Viscount coughed to hide his grin, as he seriously assured her he could think of no more beautiful topic than any apparel that graced her.

Did he not recollect, Sybil pouted, the last time they had been to feed the swans, he had likened her to one of them? *That* had inspired *this very dress*, which she had specially made; and now, he had not even noticed the results of his . . . inspiration.

The Viscount was effusive in his apologies and compliments and Lady Marvelle, taking tea across the room, wanted to know whether the Viscount had been pleased, which necessitated the

Viscount's leading Sybil toward her sister and repeating a good part of his compliments, with the result that Sybil had the pleasure of not only hearing them twice herself, but having everybody join in with *their* appropriate remarks and allusions as to her resemblance.

"What's that all about?" Cuffy demanded in disgust.

"She wants everybody to compliment her on dressing up like a goose," Astera concluded, and Cuffy did not trouble to hide his laugh.

"By Jove, she does look like a goose, and sounds as silly as a goose . . . well, will you look at that part there, is that supposed to be a tail?"

"That," Astera assured him, closely observing a strategic flounce, "must be a wing"—did he not think?

Weston, who had left Sybil to Lord Winthrop's struggling efforts at pleasantries, returned in time to hear a good part of that exchange and remarked coldly that a beautiful woman could never be made to look less beautiful by an unkind tongue, to which Astera responded lightly that a beautiful woman did not have to spend twenty minutes of a company's time soliciting remarks on her beauty unless she resembled a swan mentally as well as physically.

"No, dash it," Cuffy objected. "Swans are pretty needle-witted. Throw 'em some bread, they always come back to the same place. Now a goose looks a little like 'em, but she waddles around honking for everyone to notice. I'd say 'goose' is closer to the lady."

"And how far from a gentleman are you, Cuffy?" the Viscount said coldly, causing the grin to die on Cuffy's face and be replaced by a shame-faced smirk.

Astera decided to draw the Viscount's fire her way. "Cuffy was merely speaking privately to a close friend. How much of a gentleman are you to overhear a private conversation and call anyone to account!"

The Viscount looked as if he were ready to turn his censure

on her—going so far as to raise his quizzing glass at Astera, as if implying a questioning of her right to speak of any woman's beauty, when Cuffy hastily jumped in, taking Astera's hand affectionately. "Easy there, Twinkles, Wes ain't my father. You don't have to save me from a trimming!" And turning to the Viscount, he confided happily, "Ain't she full of ginger? Dashed if she isn't still trying to protect me. Always had my father at point-non-plus. Just when he was ready to ring a peal over me for overheating the horses or some such, she'd be there with a long story that made me come out like a dashed hero, and the old man wouldn't know which way to look!"

"Miss Claybourne is under some misapprehension if she suspects me of chastising you, Cuffy. You, I sometimes suspect of not being quite the perfect gentleman, as I have pointed out to you before; but there is never malice in your statements unless it has been inserted by other means."

"In other words," Astera demanded, "Cuffy is a fool, and I, a malicious mastermind?"

The Viscount merely bowed politely. "As you say, ma'am." And he took his leave. Cuffy laughed good-naturedly, but Astera fumed—totally overset.

The remainder of the evening had more trials for Astera. The pianoforte was opened and, urged by Lord and Lady Marvelle and, after this reminder, hastily by Lord Winthrop, Sybil agreed to seat herself directly at the instrument. She had the satisfaction of seeing the Viscount draw a chair near to her, and her joy swelled her song with a sweetness no one could deny. Indeed, she could not fail but please: her voice, though small, was generally in tune; her airs, a bit languid (a natural characteristic of hers), were effective for the lovelorn songs chosen; and her appearance was always charming—though she opened her mouth too wide to encourage a louder sound, yet that flaw was overset by her opening her eyes equally as wide, resulting in an appearance of animation which she generally lacked. On concluding, the results were all she could wish. The Viscount was enchanted. Lady Marvelle, triumphant. Lord Winthrop, de-

lighted enough to drum along with her, Aunt Minerva, to
hum along. Astera, determined to be polite, was all attention.
Only Cuffy's constant shifting of position and relieved expression
at the conclusion interrupted the flow of general delight.

CHAPTER 5

Total triumph was the only way Miss Farnshorn and Lady Marvelle could describe the evening. No attractive lady was present
to compete. (Miss Claybourne was obviously not even to be
considered.) Weston seemed more attentive to Sybil than he
had been *all* last season; and since it was known that he was, if
not eager, at least no longer reluctant to consider matrimony,
this invitation had lit Sybil's hopes to a fine glow! The admiration of the dear Lord Winthrop was also satisfying. Thus, neither sister complained about the fact that no important
members of the ton were present.

Indeed, in the next few days little occurred to disturb them.
The food was excellent, and the attentions never lacking. Only
Miss Claybourne, while civil, was not completely obliging, for
she was not sufficiently impressed with their consequence—being often inattentive to Lady Marvelle's descriptions of her
court triumphs—and as their stay progressed, she showed ques-
tionable breeding by spending long hours either alone in her
room or off riding with Lord Cuffsworth.

When Lady Marvelle's curiosity and desire for news finally
overcame her reluctance to discuss any other female but herself
or her sister, she pressed Lord Winthrop for a reason for his
ward's being remiss, and was deeply shocked by the reply!

Miss Claybourne retired to her rooms—to *write!* Lord Winthrop, not aware how much his pronouncement had astonished
the lady, further explained that Astera was following in her
father's and mother's path. It was no idle indulgence but
a determined effort toward a career. In fact, just two days since,

she had received a letter from her parents' publisher, who had read the beginning of her poetic epic and was pleased to encourage her with a promise of publication—even urging her to forgo anonymity and continue the Claybourne name; perforce, Astera had to spend as much time as possible at her pen—leaving him with the pleasure of spending more time with the two most gracious ladies (he bowed in her direction) he had ever been honored to meet.

"A bluestocking!" Lady Marvelle was shuddering to herself as the old gentleman continued, unaware of how he was damning the girl with each added word. Now he was questioning what the ladies would wish for entertainment while the men were busy shooting?

The warm weather, both ladies felt, was not conducive to elegance of person, and thus they had remained as languid as possible so as not to put themselves to the necessity of changing their attire above the three or four times required by fashion. Accordingly, they had previously refused Miss Minerva Claybourne's offer to mount them and have them join her and Lord Winthrop in their daily gallop. Several other suggestions were also found to require a more than acceptable level of activity, till the lord hit on "a nice leisurely ride around his entire park in a carriage and ponies." The offer was pronounced "delightful" and immediately agreed upon. Whereupon Lady Marvelle departed as quickly as the gentleman's garrulousness allowed— all impatient to inform her sister and husband of their hostess' fatal preoccupation!

This fact was soon spread by Lord Marvelle to the Viscount and Lord Cuffsworth on the very next day's shoot. Neither was sufficiently outraged to suit Marvelle. Cuffy, expecting as much from his knowledge of her parents, merely asked whether the work was to be "in English or Greek?"

Uncertain whether he was being hoaxed, Lord Marvelle coldly allowed that he was not privileged to have seen the lady's efforts, but he'd be dashed if he wanted it known he was visiting a "bluestocking," and that his wife, too, felt it "very keenly"! The Viscount, at whose invitation they had come, soothed him with the reminder that they were visiting Lord Winthrop, who was not known for any literary inclinations, that the lady would not desire "her efforts" to be read while still in progress, therefore, they could all be tolerably at ease. Thus persuaded, Marvelle allowed himself to relax, albeit continuing to look suspiciously at Miss Claybourne whenever she approached with a volume in her hands, but, as she did not open it in his presence, all was well.

As for the Viscount, while soothing others, he, himself, was vastly displeased.

His intention on arriving was to bring Astera to the point of wishing for a renewal of his offer and then consider whether *he* wished to do so or not. Also, it was imperative for his own self-consequence that Cuffy be there and be given every opportunity to make his own moves and fail—then watch with awe how, almost without effort, Weston would prove the winner! For the Viscount never could permit a challenge to go unmet—whether from foe or friend.

His campaign tactics were to include such time-tested devices as jealousy and a bit of address. He had planned no further. He had never had to plan any further with any woman—lady or Cyprian.

And up to the present he had been congratulating himself on some measure of success with Miss Claybourne, for he had judged the incivility of her long absences in her room as pique and a tribute to his maneuvers with Sybil. Also there was her "preoccupied air," which he had read as an indication of her sensing her "loss." Now both could be more properly understood as being an absorption in her own creative world! And further, there was the possibility that not only was she not being affected by him, but that she was not even fully aware of his presence! Nettled, he swore to jolt her into full awareness! For the rare times she was totally alive to the people around her occurred only when either Cuffy was present or the once or twice when the Viscount himself sufficiently probed and jabbed to get her indignant attention. An instance of the latter was when he'd made a point of thanking her for recollecting his pleasure in the beige hangings and thoughtfully placing them in his own private chamber! Astera had not looked the slightest bit shamefaced, rather her eyes had positively twinkled. "It was my most earnest desire to give you every pleasure, my lord."

"And thus the unending evenings of whist?"

"You recollect I mentioned having heard of your talents in that area, and since it so exactly corresponded with my aunt's and guardian's desires, I felt certain, with the beneficial addition of Reverend Smallward, your evenings would be exactly what one would wish."

"Ah, would *one* indeed? You are too good, Miss Claybourne, and I collect I have you to further thank for the inestimable Mr. Smallward's efforts. We have Proverbs for the deal . . . Psalms for the play and Revelations for the tally!"

"You have not then heard *his own sermons!*" Astera asked in consternation.

"That pleasure has been denied me . . . but little else," the Viscount said gravely.

"Yet it is my opinion that with the addition of Miss Farnshorn and Lady Marvelle in duet, the evenings can scarcely be improved upon!"

"Which explains why you are so careful to avoid them? But that is not your lone mistake. I should inform you that you have been *misinformed*. Whist is not my passion. Nor is loo. Nor any other game of *cards!*"

Astera's eyes widened in mock dismay. "You surprise me, indeed! But how noble you must feel—at long last earning your title of nobleman!" And as the Viscount's eyebrows shot up, she went on eagerly, "Ah, think—why the less you enjoy, the more *noble* your sacrifice! This entire stay may do wonders for your character!"

"It is of course edifying to find you so concerned about my improvement, but I feel I have been sufficiently ennobled during my stay and request that tonight you bestir yourself *as a hostess* and plan some *other* kind of entertainment to which you'd be gracious enough to lend the honor of your presence."

Astera merely smiled, and if the Viscount assumed that was

acquiescence, it only indicated how little he knew her. For that evening Astera was again not in attendance. However, nor were the cards brought out. Instead, Lord Winthrop announced that he had been informed there was a general desire that neither cards nor the pianoforte distract from the Reverend Smallward's discourses—and so tonight that revered gentleman was to have their total undisturbed attention!

The Reverend was in his moment of glory as he reviewed several of his most successful and most edifying sermons and picked one after another choice excerpts till they were close to having heard the entire repertoire. As his audience was stunned into a silence, no objections were forthcoming to stem his flow. At the conclusion, the Reverend flattered himself it was the overwhelming impression he had made that had them rushing to retire to their rooms to compose themselves. Indeed, the Viscount himself, after thanking him profusely, had claimed that this evening's entertainment would result in *his* altering *all* his future actions! That was praise indeed!

The Viscount's decision was just one of that evening's repercussions. The next morning all his guests carried their complaints to the astonished Lord Winthrop. What with Lord and Lady Marvelle's barely polite protest and the Viscount's suggestion for an alteration and Cuffy's loud and indignant descriptions of his sufferings, the good host could hardly remain in ignorance of their wishes. Thus, the Reverend Smallward's dream of mixing with nobility came to an abrupt end. Henceforth, he was excluded from all future evenings! He reconciled himself with Lord Winthrop's excuse—the company, the ladies especially, had been so deeply affected they needed a sennight at least to recover!

The following night, directly after dining, Sybil was applied to by Lord Winthrop. Someone near and dear to her had whispered that she was as proficient in the harp as she was the pianoforte, and he had the harp brought down from the attic and prepared in the hopes of a recital.

Further, after a discussion with the Viscount, Lord Winthrop was made so conscious of the incivility of Astera's not appearing in the evenings that he promptly made a special request for her presence, and Astera promised more regular attendance—on occasion. That night was one of the occasions.

Astera sat through the harp recital with good grace and didn't even blanche when the Viscount kissed Sybil's fingers in tribute to their talent . . . although she did permit a small smile.

When Weston asked later for an explanation of the smile, she was surprised that at that moment of such tribute, *her* reactions had been observed, but she had not the smallest objection to explaining. She had been considering including that gesture in her poem, but feared it might be somewhat "overblown" for the gentility of her hero! And with another such smile, she retired for the night.

The Viscount was now furious! Never had a woman so deliberately challenged him, and then tossed him away. His every action was either of no importance to her or fodder for her writings! And Cuffy was becoming a decided bore with his "Astera this" and "Astera that." Up to now Weston had been trifling with her, but now he was determined to use the same ruthlessness and determination that had made him such a champion boxer at his club. While frequently he would pull his punches for an opponent not up to his weight, when well-matched, he never hesitated to leave his opponent properly floored.

Coincidentally, this new-found determination of the Viscount's came at the exact same time that Lady Marvelle learned a second shocking fact about Astera from Lord Winthrop. This young person, this *dowd*, had actually had an offer from Weston and refused it! Quickly this news was brought to Sybil and the two spent the entire afternoon trying to discover its meaning and the effect on their plans. That Weston should have offered for that shocking bluestocking was surprising enough, but that she had refused him left both ladies momentarily speechless. They recovered in time to send for Lord Marvelle to join them in his wife's chamber—a summons he hastily answered, being much awake to the novelty of such a summons during a time when his wife was accustomed to being in bed. His appearance in a golden brocade dressing gown without his corset was such that both ladies might have been alarmed if they were not already accustomed to his massive phenomenon.

To their astonishing news, he could, however, merely utter an unhelpful, "Lud." The two sisters patiently waited for more . . . which at last was forthcoming. "Probably all a hum! Not likely Weston would so forget what's due his consequence!"

A coincidence of feeling on this point was quickly discovered and afforded real relief to all. Lord Winthrop must have been confused. This probability assuaged them for half an hour before Lady Marvelle unfortunately recalled that Lord Cuffsworth was present at the time of their host's revelations and had not been a whit surprised. The impossible must be thought of. Then Lord Marvelle mentioned Weston's sense of whimsy, but Lady Marvelle could not believe he would ask for a lady's hand in jest . . . although if he wanted to set the entire bon ton to laughing he could not have chosen a more fitting object.

Lifelessly, Sybil, whose pale face had turned parchment white, signaled that she would speak. Solicitously, they waited while she gathered her thoughts. In her heart, she began softly, she feared the story was true, for Wes was often impossible to understand. At least she had always found him so. There was that amused look in his eyes when complimenting her that often left her more uneasy than gratified. And, heavens, if Miss Claybourne had refused him, he would want her more than ever!

Did not her sister recollect the time Baron Manners had those matched grays that Wes wanted, and how he'd spent almost an entire season trying to get them, till they'd finally passed into his hands after a bruising horse race where the Viscount had won not only the grays but the reputation for preferring long odds—having made his chances even longer by tying one hand behind his back and even giving the Baron a head start, and the Baron was no slow top? And yet, yet, Wes had won!

Lady Marvelle was shaken by these stories, but allowed that neither she nor her sister were to be defeated by a country girl who had not even had a season, who was known to ride astride and, finally, who was at the very moment writing a poetic effusion! All feelings must revolt at the thought of such an ineligible connection.

Sybil, after all, was the daughter of a baronet and while Miss Claybourne's guardian was a lord, neither of her parents were *noble.* Lady Marvelle had never heard them referred to by a title! And as to connections, that chit could not suppose herself equal to *Sybil,* for it was well known *they* had an uncle who was a marquis and a second cousin who would have been an earl if his ancestors had not lost the title by supporting Cromwell. In conclusion, Miss Claybourne would bring no blood, no alliance, and no name—or rather one associated, whether the commodity was wares or words, with *trade!*

It was clearly their duty to save the Viscount by revealing Miss Claybourne as the unimportant nobody she was.

That decision was put into operation that very evening during dinner. Lady Marvelle looked for an opportunity, but the conversation was veering into an unrelated direction. Weston himself regaled them with the latest on-dit about the Earl of Malsworth, who, lost in the London fog, appeared at Almack's after twelve o'clock and, as was the rule, was not admitted by the patronesses, so he sent messages to several women within and danced with them on the stairs, causing so much commotion the patronesses relented and allowed him to vault the rules and enter!

"What else would you expect from a man," Lady Marvelle added, "who fathered a child with each of the daughters of his neighbor, Squire Danvers, with the exception of the twelve-year-old, naming each offspring according to the alphabet and was presently up to the Fs!"

Lord Marvelle followed by eagerly introducing several oddities of their friends, concluding with the Duke of Amshire, who paid a "prime article" *not for silence,* but to link his name with hers and thus build up his reputation with the ladies. Awkwardly, trying to blend in, Lord Winthrop asked if the present king really had "a way with the ladies"—which naturally delighted Lord Marvelle, giving him the opportunity to launch into the tales of Prinny—then the Prince of Wales and the first gentleman of Europe. Perceiving that once this topic took hold there would be no other for the remainder of the evening, Lady Marvelle stayed not for tact but immediately broke in with, "Speaking of our gracious majesty, so many poems have been written to him, and Miss Claybourne is quite a rhymster herself, or so we've been informed. Could she not honor us this evening with some of her effusions?"

Miss Claybourne, who had not been attending to the entire conversation, looked up in surprise at the sound of her name. Lord Winthrop, to whom this remark had been ostensibly addressed, agreed he would certainly ask her, but that authors were, from his acquaintance with her divine mother and equally . . . eh, divine father, not likely to read anything from a work "in progress." "Not that I'm familiar with the completed versions either for, dash it, never could get beyond the foreword in either of the Claybournes' work. Nevertheless, Astera's mother read aloud very prettily, perhaps . . ." He gestured in Astera's direction, but Astera merely colored and murmured something about not being prepared, and the matter would have been dropped but for the sisters who, seeing how discomforted Astera was, pressed the matter.

The Viscount was pleased enough at this sudden development to properly not interfere. However, Cuffy, a misguided friend, urged her on, and before the meal was over, the evening was anticipated by all but Astera—who could hardly finish the small amount of duck and asparagus she had on her plate and had to totally pass on the fruit after attempting a grape and discovering it felt like a cantaloupe going down her fear-constricted throat.

Reading her own work would be impossible, she explained when the ladies were adamant on that, as they all seated themselves for her recital.

She would, if they insisted, read some of her favorite lines from Cowper, Pope or Shakespeare—whichever was the ladies' preference. Lord Marvelle quailed at the mention of Shakespeare, and that was heartily supported by Cuffy, who had once had to sit through an entire evening of it . . . and what with all those fairies and Pucks . . . and suffering such a severe shock that anyone would pay to have an ass's head bray at him, he put his foot down on Shakespeare forever after.

Astera suggested quite a lovely piece by the new poet Keats who had recently died.

Here the Viscount put in the objection that Lord Marvelle might be adverse to any writer from the Cockney School promulgated by Leigh Hunt's *Examiner*. To which Lord Marvelle, a respected Tory, gratified to have his feelings acknowledged, exclaimed, "By Jove, yes! We won't have anything by *one of those!*" He'd never heard of that "Kit" fellow, "but as for the *Examiner*, it ain't a fit periodical for ladies to read!"

They were at a standstill, till Lady Marvelle concluded in her no-nonsense voice that only poetry by a member of the peerage would be acceptable, which left Astera a limited choice—till she hit upon Lord Byron.

Lord Marvelle, it transpired, was personally acquainted with Lord Byron, he had been in a group introduced to him at one of Prinny's extravaganzas when Lady Caro was making such a cake of herself over him, and tried to stab him or herself—which, he couldn't quite recall but it was prodigiously interesting. "Nothing else was talked of for weeks—why some ladies still cross themselves at just his name . . . and especially since his last affair with his sister when . . ."

Quickly Lord Winthrop announced that the ladies present would certainly not wish to hear those particulars, and though the ladies did wish it, they, of course, agreed they did not; but eventually they allowed that a *poem* or two from Byron would be "unobjectionable."

Astera had a low voice but she read with expression and feeling because she was reading things she loved; and after an awkward pause in the beginning, she was soon in the world of the poet and had forgotten the ladies' sharp glances, the Viscount's ironical gleam and Cuffy's tragic distress, plunging deep into

Byron's *Childe Harold's Pilgrimage*—which was by now her bible, for she'd read it so often, not to imitate but to inspire her to like effort. The descriptive passages caused nothing but yawns from the ladies and Lord Marvelle, but when she reached Byron's eulogy to the Spanish women and softly recited the canto expressing how Spain's maids were "form'd for all the witching arts of love," she had all their attention!

Her golden hair lit by the firelight and her eyes lit by the poetry released a passion in the room that had never been acknowledged openly by any of the people present—not the ladies, to whom it was shocking, not Lord Winthrop, who was unaware of what was being said, for he and her aunt had long since dozed off, not Lord Marvelle, who loved the talk of passion but not the essence of it; no, not even Cuffy, who was embarrassed by the hot flash of it. Only the Viscount grimly faced up to it and even reached out further by moving in closer to the young English maid who seemed to feel the passion of that disgraced lord and let it loose among the civilized representatives of society. On the words:

> Her lips, whose kisses pout to leave their nest,
> Bid man be valiant ere he merit such:
> Her glance how wildly beautiful!

Astera's glance, rising, met the hot eyes of the Viscount and faltered, but she was too deep in her journey to pause or hold back Byron's indignant cry against women of the northern clime:

> Who round the North for paler dames would seek?
> How poor their forms appear! how languid, wan, and weak!

At this point, it was inadvertent but somehow appropriate that her eyes should seek out Sybil's; and for a brief beat or two there was a silence while all realized how much Sybil represented the despised, languid, pale dames; and then Astera, coloring, was plunging ahead:

> Match me those Houries, whom ye scarce allow
> To taste the gale lest Love should ride the wind . . .

Abruptly Lady Marvelle's voice finished the recitation. "Shocking!"

Lord Marvelle was quick to second that opinion. "I say, is *this* the kind of thing genteelly reared young ladies should even be reading, let alone reading aloud! Whories, did she say? Stab me, but I never thought a young chit would bring me to a blush!"

Lady Marvelle was exclaiming about the "warm passages" and her fear of the effect on her sister. Instantly Sybil took the hint and claimed she felt faint. The outcry abruptly awakened both Lord Winthrop and the elder Miss Claybourne. Both were aware only that a guest was feeling ill. Sybil's maid was immediately rung for, and both ladies had to have recourse to Aunt Minerva's vinaigrette before they could be escorted out of the room. Lady Marvelle needed her husband's arm. In low, affecting tones, Sybil asked for Weston's, but he stepped aside to permit the host to have that privilege, and Lord Winthrop eagerly escorted her out . . . followed by a frantic Aunt Minerva, who ran from one fainting lady to the other, and soon only Astera, the Viscount and Cuffy were alone in the room.

An explosion of laughter from Cuffy was the appropriate finish to that scene, but neither Astera nor Weston joined him. Astera was too stunned and confused, totally vulnerable at this moment—a fact which Weston, as a gentleman, took into account and forbore to strike. In fact, still moved by the past reading, he even attempted a, for him, awkward consolation.

"It was rather well read," he said softly, and Astera started, just then aware of his presence. She opened her mouth to explain and could not.

"Warm passages!" she repeated finally. "Surely not!"

Cuffy, still laughing, was no help to her distress, allowing that "it was warm enough for him." "In fact," he continued, "it built a nice fire and got them all the blazes out of here!"

She turned unconsciously to the Viscount, who with great nobility continued to pull his punches. "It is not generally read—"

"But . . . *Childe Harold* was on every lady's bed table a good many years ago. I mean, everybody knows it."

"It's not generally read *aloud*," the Viscount explained. "What ladies read to themselves or, indeed, whisper to each other would perhaps put a blush in Lord Byron's cheek, but not aloud, not acknowledged. To do so is rather 'bad ton.'"

He could not resist an admonitory tone to his voice at the end, enjoying her blushes and confusion, fully expecting her now to be reduced to tears by his reproof, when she turned to him with those same fiery eyes and snapped, "Oh fiddle! If you consider what is said aloud in Shakespeare's plays that all these same young ladies attend without once having recourse to a vinaigrette! What about Mercutio's description of Rosaline's eyes, lips and thighs? . . . and Hamlet's 'Lady, shall I lie in your lap' speech? . . . and so, so many descriptions of kisses—"

"By Jove, why did you not tell me all those things were in *Shakespeare!*" Cuffy interrupted. "I thought it was all ass's heads and such. Might give him another look!"

"Oh Cuffy!" Astera grinned, but her attention was all on the Viscount now, determined to persuade him, but he only raised his eyebrow and said, "You have a remarkable memory for the warm passages!"

Astera was discomforted again. "They just came to mind now because of the topic. I mean . . ."

But now that she was fighting back, the Viscount would not retreat. "Yes, I see that you have a decided predilection for them, perhaps I could call a meeting of the young bucks and you could give us a choice selection, it would be . . . very well received, I assure you."

Astera started. "You are mistaken, sir! But if that's what you think of me . . . well . . . then . . . I see no reason for either you or your party to remain in my polluting association a day longer."

"You cannot have been thinking, Miss Claybourne. If we leave now under 'these circumstances,' the story of your shocking exhibition shall be all over London in a very few days. A very mistaken opinion of you will indeed be abroad."

"I don't care what you and your narrow-minded, empty-headed friends think of me. . . ."

"Or what is said about Lord Winthrop and your aunt, upon whom your conduct will reflect, bringing them into general censure!"

Astera began breathing hard in her dismay. "Well, of course I should not wish *them* to be in any way—"

"Then perhaps we had best say you were reading merely the descriptive selections and were unaware of the passages that followed."

"That would be a lie! I know the whole thing, each canto. I read that . . ." she stopped and blushed.

"Deliberately . . . to show your opinion of Sybil and her sister."

"*No*," Astera insisted, but she was sufficiently honest to wonder if that were not, indeed, the reason she had picked those parts—feeling more disgraced by this thought of her "pettiness" than by the previous general declamation on her immorality.

Abruptly she bowed her head. The Viscount had his triumph and laid out his conditions of surrender: "I shall explain away the matter to the ladies and Lord Marvelle *for you*, and, subsequently, I daresay, we shall be seeing you *regularly* in the evenings?"

Astera nodded in silence, but the Viscount, recalling a time when she had demanded a full proposal from him—not satisfied unless he used every formal word—now insisted on her *full capitulation*.

"Then you wish *me* to explain the matter away for you, as I suggested?"

Understanding, and flaring up at his condition, Astera nevertheless had to comply, for the thought of her aunt's and guardian's humiliation was too alarming to allow. "I should be very grateful, my lord," she coldly enunciated, "if you would indeed . . . do . . . as you *suggested!*"

He bowed. And with a singularly intimate smile, whispered, "I shall be delighted to comply with such a 'gentle' request.

And perhaps, in turn, some day, you shall give me a *private* reading?"

And with another amused glance at her now outraged face, he exited—more jubilant than at any time since his arrival at Mayberry.

CHAPTER 6

That very night Astera learned she was in disgrace with her guardian who had heard a highly exaggerated version of Astera's behavior from Lord Marvelle. And as a result Lord Winthrop was actually too embarrassed to even see her—he sent an order through her aunt that she was to cease reading all poesy stuff and devote herself henceforth totally to their guests! Having already promised as much to the Viscount, Astera could not but agree—but it would mean getting up before dawn to continue her writing while the honored guests slept.

But there was no sleep for her that night as Astera relived that scene again and again. She finally concluded that she'd underline the passages in question and ask her guardian if he could *really* be affronted by those lines! But by morning she knew it was best to accept things as they were, for whatever Lord Winthrop's verdict, the point remained that guests in his home *had been* offended, and not only the ladies but even Lord Marvelle! She wondered, indeed, if there were something wrong with *her* that she had never thought to collapse over the reading of those lines!

Before breakfast Lord Winthrop had a meeting with the Viscount, and, after that, was able to greet his ward at the table with a tolerant smile, acknowledging that the fault was "as the Viscount so rightly said, not in your lack of taste, little puss, but in your lack of knowledge."

Astera winced, but remained silent. Indeed, there was a general silence around the breakfast table till Lord Marvelle leaned over toward Lady Marvelle and Miss Farnshorn to comment on the "very poor meal" they were making—at which point his wife eagerly let it be known that both she and her sister were still suffering from the effects of last night's occurrence!

Effusive apologies were once again forthcoming from their host, who once again favored his ward with such a cold look, her head began sinking in misery. Yet she had the additional humiliation of hearing for herself Weston's explanation of her "ignorance," which was not only unnecessarily long, but was obviously affording him unnecessary enjoyment. Grimly, she acknowledged that she should never have allowed him to handle the situation—not only because he was *deliberately* making it worse, but also because she was now beholden to him. And that really chafed! But it was done. She must bear it. Though one more "innocence," one more "delightful naïveté," and she would repudiate him and all agreements!

He said the one-more: "Obviously the poem is too advanced for such a naïve—" and she spoke!

Only to be drowned out by Lady Marvelle, who, concurrently, was becoming just as annoyed with the explanation. "Forgive me, my lord," she exclaimed, "but one might not be aware of a line or two, but beyond that, it would be evident to even a child! And as far as the tone it was read in, I shall not speak of *that*, but surely it was done in such a way as to suggest approval . . . if not *enjoyment!*"

The Viscount exchanged a smile with Cuffy on that which roused Sybil to unwisely press the point. "Certain words," she maintained falteringly, "certain nomenclatures of women . . . especially one"— "Houries," Cuffy put in, but not loudly enough for her to have to admit hearing, as she breathlessly continued—"was such that would be unsuitable to the *ears* of any well-bred female, let alone to her *lips!* The thought, I fear, is making me quite ill again—"

"Balderdash!"

All eyes turned in surprise to Miss Minerva Claybourne. As an expert in vapors, she knew when other people were counterfeiting. During the previous evening's contretemps, her initial concern for the health of the ladies distracted her, but upon observing that neither sister had need of her vinaigrette the moment they were out of sight of the gentlemen, she abruptly left them to sleep off their "ill-humor." As to the cause of their distress, Miss Claybourne, who had accepted hearing her brother's description of Medea's acts, could hardly be overcome by Byron's mention of lips and kisses. Obviously the ladies were exaggerating their *ill health deliberately*—an act which, especially when she remembered her fiancé's death, she found *most reprehensible!* "It is my opinion," she pronounced coldly, "that there is more objectionable matter in a single one of the on-dits with which we have been inundated since the start of your visit than in all the books read by that innocent child!"

Lady Marvelle's response was muffled by a muffin; Sybil's wadded by a wedge of ham. Only Lord Marvelle spoke up, and rightly so, since he was the most frequent disseminator of those stories, insisting *he* had certainly said nothing that would "cause a lady to blush," that it was all "*implied,* madam, nothing explicit!"

"Then it is just hypocrisy as well," the elder Miss Claybourne calmly concluded and placidly continued her tea.

The Viscount ended the matter by saying a soft, "hear, hear," and promising on his part to watch what he would say in the future.

Astera hugged her aunt in private, once more, as so often on her travels, grateful for her sense and presence. Yet it was a curious quality in Aunt Minerva that she could take things calmly that would totally overset others . . . and *yet*, minor matters, which would by others be generally taken in stride, often caused her acute discomfort . . . if not collapse. A case in point: Lord Marvelle's calling for jugs of vinegar. She was decidedly exercised over that . . . wondering what he could want it for . . . was it a snub on the housekeeping? . . . or was he, worse terror! suffering from some contagious disease which *she*—or perhaps her precious *Astera*—might contract! She could not rest till Burton had discovered the cause. Then, to her intense relief, Lord Marvelle's valet came up with the answer—his lordship *bathed* in it, apparently as a restorative. It was, in his set, "all the crack"! That had soothed her, and even so intrigued, she determined to try the effect on herself and further urged Astera to do the same. Astera declined.

Meanwhile, Lord and Lady Marvelle had need of a restorative themselves, and they met in private and allowed they did not have cause to congratulate each other on the results of last night's affair. Having the Viscount turn out to be that "dowd's defender" was not what had at all been intended!

After much ratiocination, Lady Marvelle hit on the solution. Rather than stressing Astera's immorality, why not extend the Viscount's very argument of her as a naïve country bumpkin. Point out her lack of sophistication and knowledge of the world. For since the Viscount Weston was such a noted Corinthian and leader of the haut ton, this must seem a fault indeed. Further, there was much in Astera that would support this conclusion. Her shocking clothes! Her childish ways with Lord Cuffsworth! And her total disinterest in the doings of the Viscount's and their set! Had not Miss Claybourne, the other night, evidenced surprise on hearing that certain newspapers printed in detail everything particular members of the ton were engaged in—from where they dined, what evening party they attended and so forth. Her passing remark that she could hardly imagine those facts being of interest to other people was given a sharp set-down by Lord Marvelle, who read those items religiously, insisting one would find more of interest in those periodicals than in the blue and buff one she had in her library—referring to the *Edinburgh Review* in its shameless Whig colors—but Astera had merely blinked in her stupefied way and was silenced. Nor did she know any anecdotes of the great actors of the stage (a favorite pastime of the Viscount's) or even the names of the great boxers, nor did she contribute to the general praise of Weston's last speech in the House of Lords, and even professed ignorance on the topic. And though on-dits were ruled out of order, certainly conversation about "mutual friends" must, of necessity, rule Miss Claybourne out.

Appeased by this conclusion, both husband and wife ran to

inform Sybil, who had retired to her room in reaction to the scene at breakfast and the Viscount's disinterest in her lack of appetite. These new plans roused her enough to begin her toilette for the afternoon's outing . . . and the results did not fail her usual standards of pure perfection.

Lord Winthrop was to take all his guests to see his pride and joy—the pheasantry located two miles from the flower garden. All were to come. Astera as well, for her guardian had been overheard to be reinforcing his orders for her appearance.

They crossed over wet grass to an ivy-covered little building where Lord Winthrop himself opened the door to reveal pillars covered with the last roses of the season. Passing through a large aviary filled with a prodigious quantity of parrots, canaries and goldfinches, they reached an open grassplat surrounded by evergreens. In the center the keeper stood calling, and the pheasants came forth—the golden ones and the silver-pied—followed by the tame rooks and even pigeons. Near five hundred was the count. They fluttered as the ladies and gentlemen approached, resulting in a great many exclamations: some of delight, by Sybil . . . and some of distaste, by Lady Marvelle. Lord Marvelle had another reaction: "By Jove, I wish I had my piece!" Cuffy was entranced, moving again and again among them and getting them all a-flutter. Astera hung back, and was surprised to see a look of disapproval on the Viscount's face.

"Yes," she agreed.

He looked at her in astonishment and realized they were of a mind. "I am accustomed to seeing them flying—loose and free."

"I have repeatedly asked Lord Winthrop to cease the practice of cutting one wing as soon as they are hatched, but having them here is such a pleasure to him! Yet it does quite break one's heart to see them so . . . forever grounded."

"I should not say my heart would shatter that easily, but every feeling must revolt at something so against nature!"

Precisely at that moment Sybil ran out holding a golden pheasant against her own pale golden hair and the Viscount was momentarily thrown from his position by seeing what a beauty of nature the two made. The Viscount made the appropriate comparison and Sybil was satisfied enough to return the bird to its companions.

Astera found his hypocrisy even more censurable than Cuffy's pleasure in the birds' inability to quite escape him, and said as much when ordered by the Viscount to explain her look.

"As usual, Miss Claybourne, you judge too hastily. Cuffy is as much a child of nature as the pheasants and should be appreciated for that quality . . . and for the beauteous Sybil, sympathizing with the birds' plight does not preclude one's ability to see her beauty—which together with the golden pheasant was, as you must admit, quite . . . eh . . . picturesque."

"She studies the picturesque," Astera said coldly.

"Indeed. But why should she not? That is her main attribute in life. She strikes attitudes and postures as if she were a participant in a charade, as indeed most ladies *mime* their way—using their persons to express themselves, rather than words . . . or even deeds. Which is how it should be, for we all have our fit position in the sphere of things. On the other hand, certain 'literary ladies' who could never successfully achieve such entrancing postures, not having the splendid 'instrument' required, can only censure others *who do*. Is that not so?"

Instead of getting incensed as Weston had hoped, she merely looked steadily at him and continued, "But, do you not see— Miss Farnshorn is as unnatural as a *person* as are these *birds!* Her wing has been clipped at birth, and she must always . . . always prance around . . . *grounded* and imprisoned."

"While you are free?" asked he, amused.

"I am free. I have traveled. I have the funds to allow that and the training. I guard that freedom . . . that independence. She would too, if she had tasted of it, and because she has not, I am sorry for her with all my heart!"

The Viscount had received another shock from Astera. That she would sympathize with the woman he'd brought there to challenge her was not at all how he'd planned it. Nor indeed had he planned to find himself more and more interested in Astera with every conversation. He would hardly congratulate himself if his wife spoke as Astera did just now. Freedom or love of it was not exactly his idea of the complaisant wife. Nor was he pleased at her showing him so graphically that his idea of the perfect wife had been unnatural—with one wing off. Yet if Sybil were his ideal, it was strange he had not availed himself of the opportunity to achieve that ideal during the previous season.

"The devil take that girl," he whispered and thankfully saw her arriving all disheveled and mud-splattered from a run back from the outing with Cuffy. The Viscount was nice to a point over his attire, and the one main point in Sybil's favor was that she was the epitome of taste. No matter how many times Astera could move him with her insights and feelings, she mainly moved him to fury and, at times like this, to disgust. Totally ramshackle. He would never allow even a distant relative of his to appear like this in private, let alone before a group of the most respected members of the ton. Her petticoat when she raised her dress to jump the marble stairs was thickly covered with mud; her hair was totally windblown and looked as if it could stand a thorough brushing.

As she passed by, he looked all the disapproval the ladies expressed.

Lady Marvelle rolled her eyes. "Surely it is that aunt of hers. The simple rudiments of good breeding are sadly lacking."

"Ragamuffin ways," Lord Marvelle loudly agreed. "Not at all the thing!"

Sybil expressed her sympathy. "It certainly is a good thing she never had a presentation. I understand from her guardian that she is *more than* four-and-twenty! If she had come out in the ordinary way, this would be her *fifth* season and she would unquestionably be thought of as ineligible by any but those who had given up all hope of making an eligible connection."

The Viscount, aware that not only had *he* made the young lady in question an *offer*, but been refused, was doubly chagrined at all talk of her ineligibility. For while it was odious to be refused by any lady—to be refused by one judged so inferior to him was what had driven him into a frenzy of revenge—and just as he had begun to see new qualities in the girl, he was shown what a fool he would have been thought if she had accepted. In a way, her refusal should have been a relief. He told himself that time and again, and could not understand why it always needed repeating.

"Don't you agree, Wes?" Sybil was asking.

He started, coming out of his grim reveries and strategies. "There is quality in her," he finally was forced to answer as Lady Marvelle too continued to press on Astera's ineligibility.

Both ladies and the good lord were horrified by this pronouncement. Indeed, they could not see anything in her but a rather vulgar streak that allowed her to give free rein to every thought and emotion and inclination.

"A lady," Lady Marvelle opined, "must be able to hold back her feelings. Servants can give in to whoops of laughter . . . can, indeed, give in to passions, and thus be subsequently turned off without a character—but a lady keeps her character by keeping her place and her opinions to herself."

Both Sybil and Lord Marvelle loudly agreed. If the Viscount wondered whether, by her own definition, Lady Marvelle's decidedly putting forward her opinions had ruled her unladylike, he merely thought it and outwardly graciously nodded his head.

That evening at dinner—which Astera was having a hard time in eating, since the first remove was a variety of pheasant—it seemed to both Cuffy and Astera that for the second night in a row all had contrived to make Astera the object of their conversation. Bombarded from all sides, she scarcely had time to fully answer a question. "Never had the pleasure of meeting the King . . . no, nor the Duke of Wellington . . . unfamiliar with the science of craniology . . . must have merit since Lord Marvelle's dome was thus read . . . distressed to hear my cranium gives such an impression, especially from such a distance across the . . . yes, indeed, one observed the dent in Miss Farnshorn's skull almost immediately upon meeting her and could only congratulate . . ."

And so forth till Lady Marvelle began narrowing in on more personal accomplishments and had Astera admitting that she could neither paint tables, cover screens nor net purses. "In fact,

I am known to be very remiss with my needle," she said and looked pointedly at the Viscount, wondering if he remembered their initial discussion on that topic. He showed he did by smiling and inserting, "Not as remiss as I am at whist!"

Astera and he shared a laugh over that, and while the ladies were distressed to sense some kind of private understanding, the mention of whist had Lord Marvelle recollecting a win he had had a few days back from the Reverend, which turned the topic.

Yet shortly Astera found herself in question once more, this time by Miss Farnshorn: Since Miss Claybourne was so fortunate as to have such a first-rate instrument, how was it possible she had never availed herself of it?

Lord Winthrop answered for her. "Oh, she plays all right and tight. Makes up her own études. Very pretty voice. Minerva and I have come in from a hunt with a megrim and Astera can sing them away for us!"

"Indeed," Lady Marvelle continued. "Most young ladies have 'very pretty' voices . . . only a few have *excellent* ones." And she bowed in her sister's direction. Lord Marvelle seconded that and allowed some ladies were a positive punishment to hear, which had Lord Winthrop insisting that they hear Astera if they really wanted to be soothed.

"Perhaps when either of us gets the megrim," Lady Marvelle dismissed, and then continued ruthlessly, "but a really accomplished lady, besides knowledge of music and drawing and dancing and all modern languages must have a certain air of elegance . . . in her way of walking . . . in her way of *dressing*."

The last word hung heavy in the air around as everyone pointedly looked at Astera's plaid silk in the most unbecoming shades of gray and ginger. Even Astera caught herself looking down at the offensive dress.

Lord Cuffsworth leaped to her defense this time. "What would you say to a lady so accomplished that she not only knows all modern languages but fluently converses in ancient Greek!"

This attempt at puffing her up fell rather flat.

"Ancient Greek!" both ladies shrieked as if they'd discovered she wore patched underclothes.

Lord Marvelle was bristling. "I daresay that's all a hum . . . even those dean fellows back at Oxford could only read in it . . . and if you mean modern Greek—then that's not much, lots of people who live in Greece do, even children . . . and they wouldn't be accepted in society for all that . . . certainly wouldn't have been accepted in Prinny's day!"

Cuffy insisted she show them, enraged by the old man's questioning his veracity; Astera tried to change the topic . . . Aunt Minerva tried to change the topic . . . Lord Winthrop finally did, asking the ladies how they'd enjoyed their outing today, and after receiving enough compliments to be gratified, he asked Miss Farnshorn if the sun had not been too much for her, for he'd heard she was a bit disconcerted that she had not brought her maid with her parasol.

Sybil agreed that it had been a mistake on her part. "You must understand, sir, for a lady of my delicate complexion, the sun is monstrous disagreeable! I was all a-fright I should be tanned. Indeed, I detect a shading here on the tip of my nose that I fear shall make me unfit to be seen this age! I can only say, my lord, that I shall never, ever allow myself on any future outings without my abigail to hold my parasol! Only think if I should break out in—freckles!" She whispered the last word with a shocked tone that could not but totally convey her horror at such a possibility.

Astera tried to sink further down in her seat. Not only was she in the habit of going out without a parasol-bearing abigail, but, indeed, without a hat as well, and she was unquestionably rather tanned—but worst of all, right across the bridge of her nose marched several of the dreaded freckles!

Lady Marvelle looked so pointedly at them, they could scarcely go unobserved by anyone else! Not satisfied with that, she brought it out in the open by offering to lend Miss Claybourne a special lotion she had made up by her dresser in case such an unheard of possibility occurred, for if she were not mistaken Miss Claybourne had quite a few brown spots all over her face . . . and even beginning to appear in her décolleté.

All turned to examine her décolleté, but Astera blushed so red, it was impossible to distinguish them.

This time it was the Viscount who took pity and asked Lord Marvelle if he'd heard the shocking news about Sir Thomas Lawrence's losses at billiards. This was a topic that could not help but deflect all interest away from Astera till dessert, when Lord Marvelle, reaching for the decanter, slopped some wine on Astera's dress and though he mumbled his apologies, he seemed rather pleased with his clumsiness. In fact, when Astera excused herself to change, Lady Marvelle almost congratulated her husband, whispering that that splotch gave the dress an air of distinction it had previously lacked. This sally was greeted by such a burst of laughter from both her sister and husband that even the Viscount began to frown, although he did not quite join Cuffy in swearing under his breath.

When it was time for the ladies to leave the gentlemen to their cognac, Minerva excused herself from the sisters' presence and sought out her niece. She found her agitatedly walking up and down in her room.

"But why are they all making me the object?" she cried out on her aunt's entrance. "I have tried so hard to be accommodating to them for Guardy's sake, though they are all strangers to me in fact and in soul!"

Miss Minerva Claybourne explained that she feared Lord Winthrop had inadvertently let slip the fact of the Viscount's offer and her refusal. "I imagine they want to make certain he does not renew those offers," she sighed, "by pointing out your . . . defects."

"Then it is *deliberate cruelty!* How can Lord Winthrop allow them . . . oh, of course, he is not aware . . . he is so often not aware!" she agonized and not for the first time since she had come to live with him. "If only they would leave . . . and take Viscount Weston with them! Did you see the way he looked at my *freckles!* With such positive distaste!"

Aunt Minerva smiled and once again tried to urge some lotion of Denmark on Astera, but she refused to attempt to please him or them—especially since they'd made such a point of it. "I shall ride without my hat and become one big freckle if I care to! And let him and his friends go to . . ."

"*Astera!*" her aunt warned, reaching for her vinaigrette.

"London," Astera finished lamely. "Oh, I wish they would."

But the next day the Viscount only went as far as a walk to the pond for a private conversation with Lord Cuffsworth about his intentions!

"I say, Wes, what do you mean?" Cuffy demanded, surprised in the midst of throwing a pebble to disperse the slime skin.

"I mean, you have been very pointed in your attentions to Miss Claybourne, has she encouraged you?"

"She has not," Cuffy admitted ruefully, dropping his stones and looking morosely in the water. "She sees me very much like the Cuffy of old—to laugh with and play with, and when I put my arms around her yesterday when we went berrying, she merely thought I was trying to steal her berries! I put one in her mouth and she in mine, and, dashed, if I could resist kissing her . . . and, by Jove, you know what she did!"

"I am breathlessly waiting to know," the Viscount said grimly.

"She kissed me back."

"Did she, indeed!" Weston fumed.

"Very sweet were her lips . . . and very, very sisterly. And she said, 'You're so sweet, Cuffy!' and flew off for more berries."

"I see." The Viscount relaxed. "Then you are not progressing well in your suit?" he challenged with a grin.

"No better than you, dear boy."

"You feel I am making little progress?"

Cuffy went into whoops. "Progress! I feel you have decidedly dashed well fallen back a peg or two. Though how far can one fall from an out-and-out rejection! Sybil is not helping you, Wes. She is only pointing out how much you two '*elegants*' are well suited . . . which, indeed, you are."

"Those are your conclusions?"

"And Astera's. She told me you two look exactly like a 'matched set'! And dashed if she ain't right!"

"But you are both right, Cuffy, my boy. And I acknowledge it. Miss Farnshorn and I are obviously a 'matched set.' You can rest easy that I shall no longer challenge you for the impossible Astera!"

Cuffy was instantly relieved. "Oh, I say, Wes . . . you can't think how happy I am to hear that. Told you you'd never suit. She's a rare bird that soars . . . too high for me, but, by Jove, I've been fond of her for so long, giving her up would be almost like giving up . . . riding! Trouble is, may not ever notice me."

"But of course she notices you!" the Viscount soothed. "And Cuffy, my boy, is it not delightful that we can be together as friends again instead of challengers?"

"Oh say, ain't it? Have to give it to you, Wes, there were times when you had me in a quake. When you told her you'd read all of that Greek fellow and even quoted some in the library the other day, I thought I'd been given a flush hit, for certain. And when you admitted to having read her father's work . . . and understood and admired it. That was a brilliant stroke. No faster way to get her than to praise those she loved and lost so suddenly. Still suffers from it. Went into a quake when I thought you'd deliberately memorized that stuff. Thought to myself, 'By Jove, if he'd do that, he'd do *anything* to get her.' Lost all hope. Especially when she gave you that special smile when you'd finished. Remember?"

The Viscount did remember. Astera was always jolting him with that smile . . . as she had then, looking so moved by what had been a deliberate maneuver on his part, that he'd even been shamed.

"Sybil's the gal for you, Wes. She'd never give you any trouble. Everything would be so serene with her, what?"

"Yes," the Viscount agreed grimly, "serene is exactly the word. But since when have I ever struck you as the kind of man who sought that?"

Cuffy was alarmed. "I thought you said . . ."

Weston retrieved his slip smoothly. "I mean there is more to her than that," he amended, and Cuffy was reassured. The Viscount then proceeded to question Cuffy on how he planned his quest of Astera. "I recollect you said you were aware of certain qualities in her which you would use to your benefit. Now that I am no longer in the contest, perhaps I can be of assistance to you?"

Cuffy was delighted to tell him: Astera's main flaw was very similar to the Viscount's. The Viscount was affronted by that remark, but not wishing to distract Cuffy from his answer, he simply raised an eyebrow and urged him on.

"Both of you can't refuse a challenge. Only way to get her to pay attention! Her father used to challenge her to get her to excel. Could she learn this or that passage in so short a time? And she'd be determined to do it . . . no matter if she had to give up riding with me! Told her girls couldn't fence, and she was determined to learn . . . beat me, too, so I had to drop that. Thing is, can't think how to challenge her to love me . . . I mean, dash it, can't say, 'I challenge you to care for me as much as I do for you,' can I? Wouldn't be the thing."

The Viscount agreed it would be difficult, but he urged Cuffy not to fall into the blue dismals, assuring him he would concentrate on the information and shortly come up with a solution.

Cuffy was very effusive in his gratitude.

CHAPTER 7

The next day brought no relief for Astera. It began with Lady Marvelle volunteering to lend her the services of her dresser, Miss Puce, as a peace offering. Astera declined. She was urged to accept her once more. Astera again declined more coldly. Lord Winthrop, when appealed to, had allowed that no one had more style than Lady Marvelle, and he could see nothing but a kindness in her wishing to help out his "little puss," but, unfortunately, Astera wasn't much for fashion and such!

"But you are remiss to allow her to so neglect herself!" Lady Marvelle continued, shocked that the dear girl should be so deprived. She, she exclaimed, was determined to do all in her power to remedy that situation! Lord Winthrop effusively thanked her for her kindness and accepted the services of the respected Miss Puce on behalf of his ward.

Both sisters were delighted. Hurriedly Aunt Minerva tried to claim that it was hardly necessary. Cuffy, grumbling, allowed he thought she looked "dashed good enough" as she was! And the Viscount merely sat back and watched it all, his eyes glittering at Astera's confusion. She happened to catch his amused glance and felt him to be a party to this additional humiliation and had one more mark against him. By the time breakfast was over, the ladies had totally taken her over and short of deliberate rudeness to not only them, but what was more impossible, to her guardian, Astera had to acquiesce to their strategy.

As both sisters were anxious to consult their wardrobes and dressers and fashion plates, they urged Astera to follow them. In one last attempt Astera claimed she had promised Cuffy a ride. Cuffy, quick to follow her lead, insisted he would never let her off from their appointment.

Lord Marvelle, however, spiked that by reminding Lord Cuffsworth that he was pledged to Lord Winthrop and himself for a spot of fishing that very morning! Long a fishing enthusiast, Lord Cuffsworth had been looking forward to being shown the best spots in that tempting lake that ran through Mayberry. They were all at a standstill till Cuffy claimed that a *gentleman* must always honor a commitment to a *lady* before one to even *several gentlemen*—especially as this was a sporting occasion, it being a challenge to a horse race between the two! Instantly the gentlemen saw the force in that argument, and Astera was moving gleefully toward the entrance, when the ladies spoke. "Could not Miss Claybourne simply release him from his promise, for surely she would not wish to inconvenience both her guardian and her guests! All would be settled if Miss Claybourne simply *cried off*."

Astera watched grimly while all were busy arguing the disposition of *her* time and thought again how difficult trying to be kind to Lord Winthrop made her life. If not for him, not only would she be able to say no to every suggestion, but she would not have to bear with their presence in the first place, nor would she have to do all her writing in the dawn before the servants were up, precluding even a reviving cup of tea . . . and indeed, if not for Lord Winthrop, she would never have had to suffer the embarrassment of Viscount Weston's invasion of her life at all! And with such thoughts, her eyes darkly fastened on the elegant culprit, who, sensing her feelings, raised an eyebrow in her direction and stepped in to solve the situation all round.

"The ladies cannot want Miss Claybourne immediately, for they must wish time to look through their patterns and plates and gowns and fripperies and make their peace with the formidable Miss Puce; as to Lord Cuffsworth, he is in quite a dilemma for he must not wish, in all conscience, to renege on either appointment. Would not the perfect solution be to have someone else—by name, myself—step in and take Lord Cuffsworth's place in the horse race? For, as all who know that lord's riding ability would agree, he could not offer much of a challenge to Miss Claybourne! Thus, the ladies could make better preparation *without* Miss Claybourne's presence till closer to this evening, Lord Cuffsworth and Lord Winthrop and Marvelle here could enjoy their sport . . . and myself and Miss Claybourne could enjoy . . . eh . . . our sport!"

Thus put, none could disagree, although the ladies attempted once more to insist on Astera's total presence, for a "great deal had to be done," but the Viscount had a way of sweeping all objections before him, and before anyone could say another word, they were each sent off to their appointed tasks.

Keeping his Corinthian tradition of sweeping all obstacles before him, the Viscount also easily won the race. Under the eyes of the ladies, Astera had had to dress in the accepted narrow habit and hat, which she did not usually wear while racing, and though she wished to ask him how he would do if *he* had to ride sidesaddle, she, instead, grimly acknowledged another defeat in a string of defeats.

They stopped to rest their horses by a stream in the woods and Astera was brimming with such anger toward him and his whole party, she could hardly reply to his conversation.

"One must learn to take defeats as well as victories," the Viscount chided softly when her silence became pronounced. "Or are you not up to competing with anyone of more weight than childhood friends and *poets!*"

A flash darkened her eyes as she stared at him with feelings close to loathing.

"Yes, you have remarkably beautiful eyes, Miss Claybourne, but that is not sufficient means of communication. If you are to continue so silent, I shall assume I am no better off with you than the divine though brainless Sybil."

Astera removed her riding hat and let her long golden hair hang free. "I do not choose to enter into verbal combat with you, my lord. To do so would be what *you* wish, and what *I* do not wish. I thought I'd made clear that I preferred the least possible connection with you . . . or your friends!"

"Splendid! You are talking! But what possible objection can you have to my friends?" he asked innocently. "Here are two ladies anxious to aid you—to what, even your guardian must admit, would be a needed improvement."

"Was this . . . this . . . 'improvement' your idea?" she demanded.

The Viscount bowed. "You give me too much credit—the impetus for this scheme, I fancy, must stem from *yourself!* Why should you assume that it was I?"

"Perhaps, my lord, because I've noticed a similarity in yours and your friends' prime interests. Every day here you have dazzled us with your many outfits, the shine of your boots, the difference in the arrangement of your cravat each morning!"

"I'm delighted you have noticed. Each day's arrangement has a special significance, indeed. Tonight I shall dedicate it to you. I shall call it 'The Miraculous Transformation'!"

"Very well," Astera acknowledged, "and I shall dedicate this race home to you. I shall call it 'Watch My Dust'!"

And furiously she mounted her horse, using a stump as an

aid, and though her habit forced her to continue sidesaddle, she, more accustomed to it now, took off with almost winged speed. The Viscount, laughing, joyously took off after her. It began to have elements of a hunt as she streaked on; her horse, Frolic, was surprised to feel what he never had felt before, the first slight taste of a whip; but even more than that, he sensed her urgency to win, and put his heart in it for her. On the two flew—with the Viscount thundering behind, closing in, closer, his face set— but Astera eluded him, always a length or two ahead. Her hair was streaming behind her as she rode into the sun, a glaze of rays surrounded her, almost lifting her and her animal—they were as one as they blazed ahead, skimming the ground . . . forward . . . flying . . . flying . . . ahead!

She reached the stables a good five lengths before the Viscount, but didn't stop to acknowledge his congratulations nor do more than turn over Frolic to Jem, her startled groom, as she jumped off and ran on into the house.

Back at the stables Weston was smiling. It had not done her ill with him to have won, for he felt she had the advantage in knowing the turns and paths of Mayberry, but more, the spirit in her flight had so intrigued him, he had almost wanted to slow his horse just to watch her racing by. He could not recollect a woman with a better seat . . . nor one so game . . . nor . . . so impossible!

Within her rooms Astera tried to get her breath, relieved that she had at last won something and yet doubly angry at herself for so having pushed poor Frolic, shocked Jem and somehow . . . somehow, winding up with the feeling that the Viscount had won anyway. Something in the fiery look he gave her as she turned to proclaim her victory! Something in the satisfaction she sensed in his face when he watched her dismounting and whispered softly to her, "You ride like the blazes!"

That must be his famous address to women—the reason he had Sybil and even her sister dancing to his every suggestion, waiting patiently like lap dogs for a pat of acknowledgment . . . and here she was, after defeating him, instead of feeling triumphant and smug . . . feeling grateful for that look he gave her and those warm words of praise. Oh, he could go to blazes!

Just as she was regaining her composure, a knock on the door filled her with further alarm!

But it was not either of her guests—merely her aunt's maid reporting what she had so often reported to Astera and with the same round eyes and hushed voice: Her aunt was suffering from the nervous complaint and was, in consequence, in "seclusion" —for not only the rest of the evening but probably the next few days as well!

Astera shut her eyes at that pronouncement. As often as she heard it, she never could accustom herself to her aunt's sudden withdrawals from life—usually when the pressure on herself or one of her loved ones proved too much. Tonight Astera had been counting on her aunt's standing by her while the ladies proceeded with her "transformation."

Well, she would have to endure it on her own! After visiting her aunt and determining that it was nothing more serious than her usual withdrawal, and after assuring her aunt she could take care of Lady Marvelle and Sybil and was not at all disturbed by their planned transformation—in fact, she was looking forward to it!—and other false assurances that soon left her aunt eased; and after ordering a tisane for her aunt's nerves and tucking an afghan around her legs, she left, secure that her aunt was now tolerably composed.

Back in her room Astera jumped—for both sisters were there impatiently waiting. She had hoped for a moment to compose herself and accept her aunt's desertion, but she was not to have it. Squaring her shoulders and looking round at both majestic dressers entering, led by Miss Puce, and followed by both of the sisters' maids, and then even her own Marigold bringing up the rear—all laden with clothes and boxes till Astera began to sense the ordeal was going to be more difficult than she had even imagined.

The shock of all concerned on inspecting her wardrobe was soon converted to voluble protestations of dismay! There was nothing that could be done! She was bombarded by questions to which she could not respond, since at the same time her face was covered over with cucumbers, which were removed periodically and dipped in milk and then replaced on her freckles! The results were not encouraging.

"But your skin is so . . . coarse!" Sybil complained. "Touch mine to sense how a lady's skin *should* feel!"

Astera declined the opportunity.

Lady Marvelle then proceeded to go through Astera's chests and examine her linen and underclothes. She could only pronounce them clean, but her abigail, she imagined, would have more lace on hers! They next continued inspecting her closets— opening a quantity of boxes on the floor, expecting them to contain hats—and were shocked to discover they contained books and memorabilia from her travels.

It was then that Astera's sense of humor, which had sadly flagged throughout this stay, suddenly reappeared. It was probably set off by Lady Marvelle's open mouth when she held up a naked statuette of the god Hermes.

"What . . . what . . . ?" she stammered, and Astera could not really resist.

"That is a replica of a man I met in Greece. He is thought to be quite a talented sculptor and that, I expect, is quite faithful to him . . . in all particulars!"

"Indeed!" was all Lady Marvelle could permit herself to comment. Sybil looked closely at the realistic details of the statue and then rolled her eyes—almost dropping it. The maids took many a giggling glance, and somehow after that, Astera could take their poking and pulling at her . . . their private signals and public smirks. It was at last agreed that no garment that Astera owned could sufficiently make the transformation they were so wishing to effect to please their host. Therefore, on what Astera realized was a prearranged signal, Sybil's dresser, Rose, departed to return almost immediately with "The Swan Dress" itself!

Astera instantly objected. She could not possibly wear Miss Farnshorn's dress. Miss Farnshorn insisted. And further, Rose, her own dresser would arrange Miss Claybourne's hair in the exact same style as Sybil had worn that first evening—closely curled against the skull to give the suggestion of a tiny swan head.

"But we are not of a size!" Astera continued to call out fruitlessly, for the dress was forced over her head and ruthlessly snapped shut, and tied with an extra flounce around the waist to hide the opening seams. Thus, the dress. Next, her hair was brushed strictly into the "à la Swan," although perhaps in tighter, flatter curls than Sybil's . . . and she was ready. All stood back to survey the results!

There was a deadly silence . . . broken at last by Lady Marvelle.

"Quite what one should wish!" she pronounced decidedly, and her sister and the servants rushed to agree. Astera wished to look in the looking glass, but was rushed away by both sisters, who had earlier dressed themselves, a very noble sacrifice; and now all three ladies hurried down to the waiting gentlemen.

Astera was certain she did not look her best—the dress felt tight and was a bit short. The flounce around the waist, she felt, could not add to the line, but most of all she was certain that these sisters wished her ill and that if they were so pleased by the results, she must look a positive fright!

When the ladies reached the drawing room, the two sisters stepped aside for the gentlemen to have an unobstructed view of their handiwork.

Silence again.

There was a huge gilt-edged mirror at the opposite side of the room, and for the first time Astera saw herself. She looked huge and misshapen, forced into a smaller size, and the flounce at her waist gave a decided look of somebody enceinte. But the hair was the worst . . . all the golden gloss was crimped and flattened away and pulled so tightly her eyes had a permanently alarmed look.

Nevertheless, Lord Winthrop thought she looked very much as Miss Farnshorn had done; in fact, "was not that . . . the very same dress?"

Lord Marvelle pronounced her "quite an enlightening sight" . . . and did not scruple to hide his smiles.

The Viscount was furious, wondering to himself how Miss Claybourne had allowed this "transformation," but he made no audible remark, contenting himself with a polite bow in her direction. Then Astera turned to Lord Cuffsworth, glancing from his face and then to the mirror and back. Suddenly as their eyes met and held, it was too much for them, and both broke into peals of laughter—joined in a few moments by the Viscount himself.

Lord and Lady Marvelle added an uncertain smile, confused by the laughter, wanting everyone to acknowledge what a frump the girl was and how impossible it was to compare her to "the divine Sybil," but somehow not expecting *her* to be laughing loudest of all! Sybil was pouting. This had been what she assumed a "master stroke." After seeing the *difference*, any man had to pick her, and yet, yet . . . the Viscount was now going up to Astera and whispering something that had the two of them laughing again.

"More like *both wings*, my lord," Astera responded. "As a bird of any species I'm afraid I make a sad specimen."

"No, you are better as a horsewoman," he approved, and Sybil and Lady Marvelle had the discomfort of seeing Astera and the Viscount carrying on a conversation in friendlier terms than ever before.

Cuffy was saying something about her being "pluck to the bone," and the Viscount murmured something about her civility and concluded by escorting *her* in to dinner!

While Sybil's spirits were dampened, Lady Marvelle was made of sterner stuff. The next morning she volunteered to attempt another transformation, but this time Astera felt she had been as polite as possible and replied merely, "Was not one jest sufficient, my lady? Surely you realize to continue would lead simply to tedium?"

Thus, the rancor was out in the open and Lady Marvelle claimed without bothering to wrap it up in clean linen that she wished to have a word with Miss Claybourne. Astera inclined her head and invited her to her rooms. Lady Marvelle suggested they send for her sister since she was "somewhat concerned in this as well." And Astera agreed.

Sybil arrived, and after a hurried, *sotto voce* conversation with Lady Marvelle, she joined her sister on Astera's settee.

Lady Marvelle began: "A report has reached me, Miss Claybourne, that has shocked me to the core!"

"I am sorry to hear so. Would you like me to ring for my aunt and her vinaigrette?"

Bristling over the interruption, Lady Marvelle began again. "I have been informed on good authority that the Viscount Weston has made you an offer."

"Of marriage . . ." Astera put in helpfully, her eyes twinkling.

Thrown off again by this insertion, Lady Marvelle proclaimed, "I did not suppose he would be offering you a carte blanche! Or if he were I should hardly wish to discuss that with you!"

"Would you not? I should think it would make quite an interesting on-dit."

"Miss Claybourne! You are insolent! We are your guests. You owe us the civility of an honest answer."

"My dear Lady Marvelle, I owe you nothing for your incivility in questioning my concerns. I am not aware that you stand in such a way to the Viscount that you are privy to his private decisions, but you are certainly not and will never be privy to mine!"

Sybil broke through here. "Let us cease this chatter. Did Weston ask for your hand or not?"

Astera shrugged. "Why not ask . . . eh, Weston?"

Lady Marvelle's face was becoming red with anger. "I have been told by no less than your guardian, Lord Winthrop, that he made you an offer and you refused it. And *that report* I find *impossible* to believe!"

"Did you inform my guardian that you questioned his word? You would be the first in his long life to do so!"

"But to pick a girl with such brazenly unbecoming conduct . . . a *romp* in manners and a *dowd* in fashion . . . sadly lacking in all attributes of a lady . . . no taste . . . no . . . dignity! And now we discover that your lewd readings are of a piece with your lack of moral fiber! Only a woman of the most shocking lack of decency would keep a nude statue of an 'acquaintance' in her boudoir and boast of its . . . 'likeness'! I spoke of it to my husband and he informs me that not even the worst jade, the most depraved doxy would be so brazen! *You*—a girl who is sunk quite beneath reproach, to marry the most eligible man in town . . . the most gentlemanly example of taste and honor? The thought revolts!"

Sybil added she had to agree in all particulars.

"There can be nothing else then for us to say," Astera finished, trying to keep her voice calm. "Your opinion of me has been clear from the moment you stepped into my home. I have gone out of my way to be gracious to strangers, and you have repaid me with insult, and my guardian with ridicule, and have used my home for your own purposes. If the two of you are examples of *ladies* . . . then, I can only say, thank heavens I was not brought up to such a low level of standards for that term! I cannot urge you more heatedly to quickly return to where you and your like are appreciated."

"*Well!*" Lady Marvelle shrieked. "I have never been spoken to in such a way by a young chit! Sybil, come! We have much to say to Lord Marvelle. We shall not remain a single minute longer to be so insulted! In my opinion, far from anyone's ever offering for you again, after what is now known about you becomes *generally* known, I should be very much surprised if you are ever even received!"

And with that both ladies swept out.

Astera sat down weakly, unused to such open hatred and uncertain if she had handled it as she ought, but, in truth, not being able to do anything but respond after all their taunts. Well, at least the discussion had precipitated their going . . . and that must be a blessing. Thankfully Aunt Minerva was still keeping to her bed and would not have to be present when the sisters made whatever report to her guardian; Astera's only regret was that she had not been able to hold on the few remaining days of their visit to please him.

When Astera came down for dinner that evening, she expected to face reprimands and to see preparations for her guests' departure. But none was in evidence. Evidently they had decided to be silent on the topic and remain. While relieved for her guardian's sake, Astera could not but be displeased for her own!

Tonight the conversation pointedly excluded her. Kean's portrayal of Hamlet was discussed. Favorite mottos on seals were debated; an exhibition of embroidered copies of original paintings that were "most like" announced; and finally an anecdote of Lady Belvidere's disgrace was recalled. The only remark halfway in Astera's direction was Lady Marvelle's astonishment at the "country way" of grooms serving at the table "who were never quite free of the odor of the stable"—this a reference to Jem's assisting. Astera just smiled, pretending not to understand.

Not understood either, not even observed, was Miss Claybourne's one gesture. She had deliberately dressed in her beige with the orange bows to show her refusal to be changed, but the dress had gone unrecognized—even by the Viscount!

At breakfast the next morning there was still no mention of departing. They gathered at the table, the atmosphere conducive to indigestion. Lord Marvelle and Lord Winthrop and the Viscount were availing themselves of the newspapers awaiting. The ladies had not a word to say but their expressions spoke columns. The highest point of the repast was when it was passed. Why, evidently suffering such displeasure at their visit, did they yet remain!

That puzzle was solved at last when Astera consulted Cuffy during their ride together. Lord Marvelle had indeed spoken of leaving, hinting that his wife and sister-in-law had received an "intolerable" insult, but Weston had merely bid them adieu, claiming *he* was to stay. Thus, after deliberating with his wife,

Lord Marvelle decided they would graciously overlook the insult and remain as well.

In other words, nothing would budge them. Astera sighed deeply as they turned and rode home, the reins listless in her hands. So obviously blue-deviled was she that Cuffy anxiously attempted to cheer her by reminding her that *he* would still be there as well—which elicited the first smile from Astera of the day.

Thus encouraged, Lord Cuffsworth, while helping her dismount, put his arms around her and forced several kisses on her astonished face and lips.

"Cuffy!" she admonished. "What *are* you doing!"

"What do you mean what am I doing! I'll be dashed if I thought I'd have to explain that to you! You read all that poetic stuff. I'm pushing my suit, by Jove, and I wish you'd stop laughing and take me seriously!"

Unfortunately for Cuffy, the Viscount rode into the stables at just that time, and when Astera had left, he admonished his friend. "In a *stable*, Cuffy? Not the most romantic of places to press a lady? *Surely?*"

"Well, dash it, why not? Happy in a stable!"

"Yes, I daresay. But you must strive for more finesse, dear boy. And, as I promised, I have found just the thing. And if you accomplish it with some concluding words I have arranged, you shall definitely make progress!"

"*Words!*" Cuffy objected. "Don't mean I'm to *memorize*. Nearly got sent down from Oxford because I dashed well couldn't remember one thing from another!"

But the Viscount assured him this would be a very simple speech and would be enormously effective; so, glumly, Cuffy agreed, although he concluded it was almost not worth getting a girl "if you had to *memorize* . . . the next thing you'd know I'd have to be spouting *poetry!*"

The Viscount's eyes gleamed. "Exactly," was all he said.

CHAPTER 8

That afternoon before retiring to change for dinner, Cuffy made his move. They had been informed Astera was to have her publisher for a guest, and he concluded she'd be all tied up in "literary talk," so if he was to make a push it had to be now or never.

His face seemed as white as if he were standing for a *viva voce* examination. Pulling on her sleeve he whispered in a broken voice, "Must see you . . . alone."

Astera, though fearful that he would continue his advances, could not stand up to the white and terrified look on his face and instantly agreed to meet him in the library.

Once there and alone, Cuffy took out the book the Viscount had given him. Then in an odd, strangled voice, he began, "This is for you. Ready? I say, don't fidget. I've got enough of the fidgets for myself! . . . if I can ever get through this dashed dull poem!"

"A poem! Cuffy!" Astera gasped.

But Cuffy was grimly opening the book to the appointed page, and after a sigh so deep it would have moved an Almack patroness, he began in a singsong voice:

> She was a phantom of delight,
> When first she gleam'd upon my sight;
> A lovely apparition, sent
> To be a moment's ornament;

Another sigh ripped through him as he clenched his teeth to doggedly carry on.

> Her eyes as stars of twilight fair;
> Like twilight's, too, her dusky hair;

He paused and stared, a bit disconcerted. "I say, that's off, ain't it? Should be *golden* hair. . . . I don't know what that poet-fella was thinking . . . but the eyes are right."

"Perhaps he never saw me," Astera put in as seriously as possible, and Cuffy was completely thrown off.

"Dashed but he promised it would fit . . . and the blasted thing don't!" he snorted.

"Fit *me*, Cuffy? Who said that?"

"Wes said it would fit you—all right and tight—and all I had to do was read the dashed thing, but, hold on, I'm not finished yet, you're not supposed to speak till I've finished and then you're supposed to . . ." Cuffy caught himself and went back to the book with a white, desperate face, and muttered menacingly, " 'A dancing shape, an image gay . . .' "

"You're skipping!" Astera whispered.

"What? Don't tell me you've read this dashed thing before!" Cuffy exclaimed in disgust. "I thought . . . I was telling you something *new!*"

"Wordsworth, isn't it?"

"How do I know if the words are worth anything or not . . . can't get through the dashed thing without tripping all over all these dashed words it's got in it! But here's a part underlined, so Wes said I have to stick it in."

"The Viscount Weston suggested you read this poem to me?" Astera interrupted one more time, only to have Cuffy indignantly shut the book and complain.

"This stuff's bad enough to get out. If you keep putting in asides, I'll never get through it!"

"Sorry," Astera murmured cautiously, trying so hard not to betray how close she was to laughing that her face set into a deep scowl, which Cuffy perceived, and fearing she was losing patience, he rushed on, opening the book to finish swiftly, loudly:

> The wretch, concentred all in self,
> Living, shall forfeit fair renown,
> And, doubly dying, shall go down
> To the vile dust from whence he sprung,

Suddenly Cuffy's voice began to falter as some of the meaning began registering, but, shrugging, he concluded resolutely:
" 'Unwept, unhonour'd, and unsung.' "

The last line was too much for Astera, who was by now deep into laughter, and Cuffy was himself eyeing the poem with surprise, repeating the last line—as if saying it once more would alter the meaning. " 'Unwept, unhonour'd, . . . and *unsung'? I say*, that doesn't sound . . . quite right?"

"Indeed," Astera was laughing. "It seems a bit harsh . . . as does 'The wretch, concentred all in self' going down 'to the vile dust from whence' I'm supposed to have sprung."

Cuffy was shaking his head, speechless, unable to explain, and then disgusted, he slammed the book shut and exploded. "What good is all this poesy stuff! I tell you, Astera, I'd know better myself than to say *that* to a gal. I mean . . . seems a bit much . . . 'vile dust' . . ." he murmured. "What *could* the fellow mean . . . sounds like he's either a cad or more than three-parts disguised! Not surprised though, all poetry sounds like someone's more than half-sprung. Got a notion it's all a hum. Well, dash it, I read you some, didn't I? And look what happened—got you laughing instead of . . ."

"You mixed up the poems, Cuffy," Astera explained, when she could be serious. "I perceive you've got an anthology there."

Startled, Cuffy looked at the volume in his hands. "Have I, by Jove! That explains it then!"

Astera was off into laughter once more as she valiantly continued, "You seem to have started out reading one poem and finished with Scott!"

At that Cuffy dropped the book as if it were on fire! "Knew this would get me into trouble. And when you think of all the poems Wes wanted me to read . . . got them all marked, I would have been here all night. Good thing you thought to warn me off . . . I mean about its being an antithology. Not a regular churchgoer myself, but no need to blaspheme—what?"

"Indeed," Astera mused, not listening to the last, beginning instead to open the volume to see what poems were marked.

"This volume is the Viscount Weston's?" she asked casually.

"Well, you don't imagine it's mine!" Cuffy exclaimed, affronted. "Not likely I'd be as nutty as Wes to bring a thing like this along! By Jove, it's rather a good thing you saw through

it, though. Better warn Wes about it too. *You're reading it!*"
Cuffy accused indignantly.

"Just the parts underlined," Astera assured him. "There's a
name . . . rather my name, eh, Astera, in the margin here. I
collect that is not your handwriting?"

Cuffy denied it vehemently, and as Astera was continuing to
read to herself, he demanded she inform him what that fellow
was saying now! On still further urging, she read softly:

> It is my lady; O, it is my love!
> O, that she knew she were!
> She speaks, yet . . .

Astera's voice trailed off, back to reading to herself, her face
flushing at the words, till, called to order by Cuffy, she falteringly attempted another line: "'Two of the fairest stars in all
the . . .'"

"'Heaven . . .'" a soft voice from the entrance took it up,
causing Astera and Cuffy to whirl round in surprise as the Viscount approached them. "'Having some business, do intreat her
eyes . . . to twinkle in their spheres till they return.'"

Coming closer, reaching over to gently touch Astera's cheek
with the tips of his fingers in almost, but not quite a caress,
Weston continued:

> What if her eyes were there, they in her head?
> The brightness of her cheek would shame those stars,
> As daylight doth a lamp . . .

And then lifting her chin and glancing deep into her eyes:
"And . . . Astera's 'eyes in heaven . . . would through the airy
region stream so bright . . . that birds would sing and think it
were not night.'"

The silence in the room grew as if in respectful echo to his
words, and Astera and he stood immobile—inches apart, glances
touching, holding—till Weston abruptly stepped back, breaking
the moment. Then, smiling casually, he concluded, "Shakespeare might have been thinking of Miss Claybourne in that
last—wouldn't you say, Cuffy?"

To which Cuffy added knowledgeably, "Knew it was Shakespeare . . . had something about a bird in it, didn't it?"

The Viscount admitted as much, and Cuffy was vindicated. "Never heard such a bird-brained sot! And the rest of that book of yours, Wes, is the same! Don't see why you said I should read any of it! It didn't do me a bit of good—all that 'unwept, unsung' stuff got me in a devil of a fix and had her laughing just like she is now!"

The Viscount looked to Astera for explanation. "Scott," was all she could manage, but the Viscount understood. "You seem to have read the wrong one, dear fellow, that one is about a coward . . . a knave . . ."

"Thought as much when he had me calling Astera a wretch!"

"*Wretch!*" the Viscount expostulated, valiantly keeping his countenance till Astera's laughter was too much, but almost immediately he sobered and continued, "My apologies, ma'am . . . for Scott, Lord Cuffsworth and myself!"

Astera accepted them with grace and cheerfully went off to dress for dinner, stopping at the door to once more share a smile with the Viscount—the two of them more in accord than ever before.

When she was gone, Cuffy said dismally, "I don't think our plan worked, Wes."

"You are mistaken, old boy. I perceive it has been an overwhelming success!"

And Cuffy, though a bit doubtful, was nevertheless heartened by that assurance.

That night Astera took extra pains in dressing herself. Usually making an almost immediate choice, this time she spent a full ten minutes glaring at her wardrobe trying to decide which was the least offensive.

If her conscience was troubled, she instantly quieted it by claiming she was dressing strictly for Mr. Millbanke, but since she had often met her father's publisher, and never once considered the effect the color of her gown would have on his sensibilities, she was not able to sustain this fabrication.

Time and time again the image of the Viscount's look into her eyes intruded (and left her with an understanding for the first time in her life of the phrase "a speaking glance")—till she was well nigh too distracted to do more than find her own copy of *Romeo and Juliet* and reread the passage the Viscount Weston had selected for herself.

She was thus engaged when Marigold entered to chide her for not being dressed. Astera's Marigold had been as much insulted as had her mistress by the prank pulled on her by "those two," which was how she and the entire staff below stairs referred to the overbearing sisters. It was a decided shame, they all concluded, that their young mistress had been gulled, especially since Miss Claybourne, Burton pronounced—to their total agreement—"was more of a lady than both sisters put together!"

Actually Marigold felt the insult much more keenly than her mistress, for she had eagerly taken part in the transformation team—not realizing its intent. From the first moment Lady Marvelle's dresser had entered Mayberry, Marigold had followed Miss Puce about—totally in awe of that august lady and listening to her every word—in hopes of garnering some of her expertise. Thus, seeing the figure-of-fun they had deliberately made left her doubly shocked—for her mistress and for her own misguided admiration. She had wanted to cry out as Astera bravely went down to dinner without a word of remonstrance to any of them. Now she was determined to spite not only Miss Puce, but the two sisters as well! And she would do it by putting her quick lessons into effect. Further, carefully thinking back on all the dresses she'd helped iron and arrange for the visitors, she realized not one was in quite the loud prints or overlarge plaids that seemed to comprise the majority of Astera's wardrobe, so she sought and found one in direct contrast. It was sky-blue cambric, and although suffering from the sacklike, ill-fitting problem that was the trademark of Mrs. Elton's creations, at least by its simplicity it was the least likely to overpower her mistress . . . and if nothing did that, anyone but a blind person could see the beauty that was there in her face and eyes . . . and good heart! Smiling smugly, Marigold laid the dress out and approached Astera who, forgetting the time, was still reading. With the ease that mutual affection and long years together had earned, she chided, "Still mooning over those books and the ladies all dressed I'll be bound . . . and, aye, the lords waiting! Well, well, you'll stir your stumps, I expect, when you hear Mr. Millbanke arrived an hour since!"

"Has he though?" Astera declared, recalled to her duty, and instantly abandoning her book. Rushing to her closet she put on the first dress handy, which Marigold had made certain was the blue cambric. Further Marigold insisted on doing her hair a new style. While there was no time for experiments with swirls and ringlets, at least there was time for brushing her golden locks till they shone and lifting up the sides in two sweeps that were held by golden filigree clips that faded away into the gold of her hair —only to unexpectedly twinkle as she moved her head.

Stepping back, Astera could not help but be pleased. "It's not too bad, is it, Mary?" she whispered hopefully and was assured that she looked "a picture"!

On her entering the sitting room where all were waiting, Cuffy was the first to say it. "Dashed if you don't look as fine as a five-pence."

Lord Winthrop seconded it, as did Mr. Millbanke, whom she greeted with open and unguarded enthusiasm, apologizing that she was not there when he arrived. But he graciously assured her that he much preferred seeing her after he had a chance to get rid of "all his dirt," and he promised further to have a long talk shortly that would be "very pleasing to them both and very encouraging to her career," which set up Astera's spirits so high she was positively shining and looking forward to the rest of the evening.

The Viscount prided himself that he had made some very definite inroads with Astera today—her face, when she left him, had had that same degree of blushing stupefaction that most of his flirts evidenced on the point of surrender. His smug conclusion was that he needed "just a touch" more of his famous address to have her anxious for him to renew his proposal—at which point he'd next consider whether he wished to do so or not, indeed, whether she'd be worth all the disturbance she would obviously cause him.

He took as a compliment to himself the evidence of improvement in her appearance, and it further enlivened the hope that her worst faults could be somewhat ameliorated. But then Astera had ruined every good impression by throwing herself into the arms of that middle-aged, fat, unknown *man*. The Viscount could not give him the distinction of calling him a gentleman, for it needed but a few minutes conversation to decide he did not merit that appellation, that, in fact, he smelled suspiciously of trade. Listening to the man's conversation with Miss Claybourne confirmed his worst fears—that man was encouraging her to contemplate publishing! A step which would indicate a thorough lack of breeding that could never be countenanced in his wife! Every feeling must revolt at the thought of her spreading out the most private emotions for the entire society to read and comment on.

This possibility, though probably remote, incensed him—but even more oversetting was the sudden thought that Astera had not dressed up to please him after all, but rather her visitor! Once again after assuming himself to have conquered, she had eluded him. In retaliation, he felt the gnawing need to instantly alter Astera's happy visage. And he calmly proceeded to do so.

"Would Miss Claybourne favor me with her assistance?" he asked smoothly, with an innocent air.

Astera turned her smiling face toward him, happy to oblige, when he continued, "I have been struggling to find the most apt poetic description of a pair of extraordinary eyes . . . and thought perhaps you could suggest a text for . . . Miss Sybil Farnshorn's beautiful blue eyes!"

There was instant attention from all. Jubilantly the sisters fluttered close.

"Indeed," was all Astera could manage, the smile dead on her face. In one remark he had diminished the singularity of his choosing poems for her, and further showed how gullible she had been for refining so much upon that!

"Indeed, indeed," he mimicked softly. "It would be a very

noble deed, indeed, for you, Miss Claybourne, who are so addicted to rhyming, to versify those divine objects."

"A verse from me would surely be considered *objectionable* by
the *subject*," Astera parried coldly.

"Who could be adverse to a verse from you, ma'am, when
rhyme is your main *object* in life and Miss Farnshorn's eyes
such lovely *subjects*."

"Surely it would be thought perverse in you to ask a verse
from me on that subject," Astera thrust on, rising to the challenge. "Unless you had some other *objective* in mind!"

Weston, beginning to smile, had just leaned forward to advance the duel with another pointed remark, when Sybil
stepped between their swords by claiming his attention. Not
quite clear how a conversation which was ostensibly about *her
eyes* could leave *her* so aside, she testily proclaimed that Miss
Claybourne was "unfit" to assist him, and she preferred an
effort of his *own!*

Thus Viscount Weston was now forced to hurriedly devise
something—a feat which had him frowning and stammering
over "blue and true"; ignoring Cuffy's whisper, "Make it half a
verse, 'cause she squints," and coming up with something tolerably mundane. Whereupon Sybil triumphantly repeated it—first
to one person and then to another till she had circumferenced
the entire room—during which demonstration, Astera and Mr.
Millbanke retired to the corner settee for a private conversation.

Watching them from a distance, the Viscount stiffened, disturbed that his thrusts had been so gentle, but she had set the
pace by making it a challenge of words, and he, impressed, had
played along. And now there she was—unmarked, not the
slightest dent in her composure—in fact, she was even more
broadly smiling right into the face of that vulgar, encroaching
toad of a publisher! His opinion of Mr. Millbanke, he could
clearly see, was heartily seconded by Lord and Lady Marvelle,
who looked arch at everything that "man" said, and specifically
exchanged a very knowing glance whenever he reached over and
patted Astera's hand.

Determined to break into that tête-à-tête, the Viscount advanced their way. Astera, back on her guard since Weston had earlier reverted to his old tactics, was warier still when he approached with such a stiff countenance. Even so, she was not prepared for his reaction to her gracious attempt to include him in their ongoing conversation: her mentioning the poets Mr. Millbanke had published, and how it was gratifying "to know whom to thank for making those glorious voices available!"

Mr. Millbanke was *visibly* gratified by this, and he bowed and smiled and kissed her hand again and even patted her knee and raised his eyes to meet the cold hauteur of the Viscount Weston in full force and was totally confused.

"It is of course always . . . interesting to meet any successful business agent . . . but one does not usually do so at dinner."

The affable smile froze on Mr. Millbanke's face and Astera's eyes were shocked blinkless! She was on the point of remonstrating with him when the Viscount merely bowed and walked away. Rushing to extend her own personal apology to the affronted man at her side, she was assured with a sigh that he was accustomed to "these lords" and their "starched-up ways" and urged not to distress herself on his account. Those and other gentlemanly remarks made Astera even doubly angered, so much so that before sitting down to dinner, the Viscount had lost all ground he had made with her earlier, and further, all her pleasure in the evening was quite cut up. She could not comprehend the deliberate rudeness to such a man as Mr. Millbanke, whom she had known as a child and whom her father thought good enough to dine at *his* table! And, by heavens, if he were good enough for her father, he was far, far too good for that insufferable, conceited, overbearing lord! It was amazing how Weston never had to raise his voice or show the slightest emotion, and yet was able to leave his victims totally overset!

Never had a table held a group of guests more out of sympathy with each other. Both ladies and Lord Marvelle were still smarting over the Viscount's inexplicable insistence on his remaining where *they* had been insulted; the Viscount was seriously displeased by Mr. Millbanke's familiarity toward Astera and his own ambivalent feelings; Mr. Millbanke was discomforted by having been so sharply set down and feeling out of place with the rest of these high-in-the-instep gentry; and Astera was positively pale and unable to do more than stare ahead, alert for more discourtesies to either her friend or herself.

Only Cuffy and Lord Winthrop were at ease—protected as usual by their being unaware of what was happening round them. With Aunt Minerva still abed, there was no one to even attempt a harmony.

Lady Marvelle set the tone with the first course—allowing that this sauce was not as tangy as one was accustomed to, and, unfortunately, a barely tolerable attempt was very often worse than leaving food plain.

If not everyone absorbed the hidden insult in her pronouncement, Sybil helpfully spelled it out. "That's an interesting hair arrangement, Miss Claybourne; a winged effect, however, does not suit you . . . something a jot simpler would have been more . . . eh, suited to your . . . simpler appearance!"

"I'm grieved it does not meet with your approval," Astera flashed. "We are not all so complicated as yourself, ma'am."

Sybil's hairdo tonight was a maze of buns and twists; therefore, she narrowed her narrow eyes even further, suspecting an aspersion, but the new arrangement was so becoming, she could not seriously believe anyone would view it without awe, and accepting it as a compliment, she patted her coiffure and announced it was called "Winding Road to Love."

"Indeed," Astera responded. "With all those twists and turns one suspects a very disordered driver!"

Mr. Millbanke let out a laugh and then tried to hide it with a cough.

Lady Marvelle took up the response by speaking directly to the publisher.

"I suspect, sir, that it is to you we owe Miss Claybourne's semi-transformation. She would not bother to make the attempt for any of us, although both my dear sister and I volunteered our assistance, and our *example*—all to no avail. Then, the moment *you* are to appear she actually has . . . brushed her hair, or am I overly optimistic?"

Mr. Millbanke, assuming he had not understood, and indeed *not* understanding, could think of nothing to say but that Astera always looked "champion!"

"Just so," the Viscount replied with his cold, lazy smile. "She is always at her best when in a combative state."

"And some people are always at their worst then!" Astera responded frigidly, still smarting over his snub of her friend.

"But Lady Marvelle is quite correct on the influence of the esteemed Mr. Millbanke," Weston continued with the slightest bit of asperity in his generally calm tones, goaded by Lady Marvelle's bringing his own suspicions out into the open. "For none of *us* would you have made such an effort! Apparently *our* merits do not merit that distinction? And how fortunate he is that you have held back in your little childish whisperings with Lord Cuffsworth tonight. Why, one would almost assume you were, in reality . . . a lady."

"I say, W*es!*" Lord Cuffsworth intervened, outraged.

Astera was not at all daunted. "And there is a remarkable change in you tonight as well, my lord. Before one was always under the *impression* that you were a *gentleman!*"

The rupture between them was now complete. They had advanced beyond insinuations and repartee into the ultimate, outright insult of *not* being a *lady* or a *gentleman*, and after that, they could have nothing further to say to one another. But the startled exclamations from the others that followed this exchange forced even Lord Winthrop to become aware that something untoward was occurring at his table. Miss Farnshorn's "*Oh ciel, quel barbare!*" had him concerned enough to put himself to turning the topic. Naturally his choice fell on his principal interest, hunting. Unwittingly, it was more appropriate than he assumed, for all mention of "running the fox aground" and "going for the kill" became, under the Viscount's burning, unswerving glance on Astera's heated face, to have double applications that left the lady exceedingly uncomfortable. That he should still, still be allowed at her table, and she still forced to sit there under his blatantly improper stare had her white with anger. It was with relief she signaled the ladies to retire.

With most noticeable haste, Mr. Millbanke followed; and he and Astera sought the seclusion of the library, leaving the sisters to discuss the indignity of not having a hostess to pour their tea.

When the Viscount arrived and was obviously seeking someone not present, the ladies acidly explained that Miss Claybourne *and* Mr. Millbanke had secreted themselves in the library "this half hour!" But the Viscount had said all he would on the subject of their hostess and refused to even acknowledge the whispered animadversions against the absent lady. Thus, a difficult silence ensued till Weston released them to say what they would by challenging Lord Cuffsworth to a game of billiards and leaving the room.

On the two lords' return to the saloon, they were informed by Lord Winthrop that Astera had retired early for the night to look after her aunt; and Mr. Millbanke, after repeating a few general words of appreciation for the evening to the host, picked up a candlestick on the sideboard and lit himself to bed.

As if relieved of a polluting influence, both Sybil and Lady Marvelle let out sighs and fanned themselves excessively to rid their nostrils of the "scent of shop." Lord Marvelle, also relaxing, used the opportunity to suggest an Italian medley by Sybil and Cicely, and the ladies determinedly entertained till they ran out of songs.

The next-day-but-this was to be the last of the visit and Minerva Claybourne roused herself to appear, since Astera had announced that she had reached her limit and would not stay in the same room for even half an hour with *any of the party!* This was translated into "exhaustion" by her aunt and an "indisposition" by her guardian, but under either heading, she would be in seclusion for "at least a sennight or so."

Cuffy mourned that fact, if no one else did, and by the following morning the ladies, Lord Marvelle and finally the Viscount were all prepared to leave. The Viscount—who had spent the entire day pacing the grounds recollecting their conversation, trying to justify his remarks, smarting under Astera's, wishing never to see her again, yet hoping for her appearance, only to be doubly enraged by her obstinate seclusion—left Mayberry as much decomposed as he had been at his first departure from that estate—if not perhaps more.

Only Cuffy received a word of farewell from Astera, and that was transmitted through her aunt.

The visit was over. In contrast to the arrival, Lord Winthrop stood alone atop Mayberry's grand marble stairs to bid them adieu. Graciously he handed both sisters into the waiting carriages and walked back to the top step as the lords joined the ladies; the postilions took their positions, and the carriages were off!

From the window above, Astera watched both vehicles going down the path at a smart pace till nothing remained but the dust the horses had kicked up . . . and then that too settled. They were gone.

Turning back to her boudoir, Astera was surprised that she was not overflowing with the exhilaration expected at this long-awaited moment, and slowly sitting at her dressing table, she examined the flushed face in her gilt-edged looking glass. "Please God, I shall soon be myself again," she promised resolutely, "if only I never have to see him again!"

CHAPTER 9

In the days following, Astera found herself with all the time and lack of distraction she had been wishing for, and yet less able to conclude her poem than when her guests had been claiming her attention. She was on the last canto, which Mr. Millbanke had long been expecting, but she simply was not able to concentrate.

Every third line attempted was interrupted by the ironical gleam of Viscount Weston till she had to either totally put down her pen or seize the intruding lord and put him into her narrative—where, astonished and ill-at-ease and subject to her every whim, he finally permitted her to continue. And from that point on, she derived a good deal of satisfaction in writing.

Subsequently this tactic was expanded to inserting the emotions Weston had unleashed in her as well, which enabled her creativity to take such winged flight, she speedily concluded the canto, filling it with an emotional intensity not quite her usual style.

Upon reading it over, she was rather embarrassed by that intensity, yet felt it so suited the romance that, without allowing herself to reflect further, she hurriedly sent it off to Mr. Millbanke, and had only to await what, he had assured her, would be the most immediate publication possible. Indeed, at his last visit to Mayberry he had brought, for correction, the proofs of the first few cantos, which had been sent to him earlier, and had taken away the next two. And now the last as well was on its way.

The visit was concluded. The manuscript finished. Astera was left with nothing to do but remember—which she refused to do. For her guests, after exhibiting such reluctance in departing, would not be given vouchers for re-entry—even if just into her thoughts. Further, she forbade herself to have second thoughts on her manuscript as well.

Yet the uninhibited last passages kept surfacing in her mind, and often she found herself dreading the effect these sections would have on ladies like Miss Sybil Farnshorn! At other times, more resolute, Astera would gleefully look forward to the effect these very passages would have on ladies like Miss Sybil Farnshorn!

As to the Viscount's reaction she did not bother to wonder—above one or two times a day.

But whatever the general opinion, her part in *Idyll in the Isles* was concluded. And to make its finish more of a reality, she announced that fact to her aunt and her guardian. Both, accustomed to literary people, understood at once that she, in actuality, was asking for praise; and it was immediately given—although her aunt could never understand why she never expected others to praise her for finishing menus, firescreens, or even her principal vocation of overseeing the planting of the gardens. After all, one expected, having begun something, one would *perforce* finish it! Why her dear, dead brother and now Astera insisted on seeing what was natural as so meritorious always left her in a puzzle. But she obligingly patted her niece's hand and said what was expected. Lord Winthrop, always prepared to be gallant to ladies, went so far as to toast his ward at dinner and even murmur a "hip-hip." And then that was over as well.

The next day Astera rode Frolic hard for hours . . . and still had the rest of the day to get through. Fortunately, on her return from the stables a letter awaited. Quickly snatching it up, she was somewhat disappointed to recognize Cuffy's scrawl. But as she read, Astera's spirits rose prodigiously—her face was, in fact, quite flushed when she entered her aunt's chambers to convey the news: the Viscount Weston was inviting them all on his schooner for a cruise through the Greek islands. "The Greek islands!" she repeated a bit breathlessly.

Her aunt, however, put an immediate damper on the scheme. Neither she nor Lord Winthrop would like to leave England during the hunting season.

Astera did not plead. For after the initial joy, second thoughts occurred to give her pause. She reread Cuffy's letter. The invitation was to be sent by the Viscount directly to Lord Winthrop; Cuffy was just preparing her for it and urging her to accept because he himself missed her like "the-very-devil." Incidentally, the same delightful group that had convened at Mayberry was to be reunited.

The thought of spending any more time with Lord and Lady Marvelle, not to mention Sybil, was rather more than she could contemplate with equanimity. Therefore, she accepted her aunt's demurring with tolerable ease.

If it had been an invitation to any of the Viscount's estates . . . or even to his father's, the Earl's, famed Haddon Hall, she would have evidenced not even a momentary desire to comply, but the lure of the Greek isles had been an inducement indeed!

Of all the group she was the only accredited Philhellene (although the Viscount had stated that he too had visited there), so the destination must have been decided on to give *her* pleasure. It was perhaps an apology for his rudeness . . . his downright insults! Indeed, she wondered how he had the nerve to write to her at all after his exhibition at Mayberry! She would judge by the tone of his letter to her guardian, and moreover, by whether there was any special mention of . . . or *message to her* that could be construed as an apology! But, in any case, it did not signify, for they were not to go.

Slightly over two months later, Lord Winthrop, Miss Minerva Claybourne and Miss Astera Claybourne arrived in Greece after a stop at Italy.

Lord Winthrop had, it developed, urgent business in Rome and could very easily extend his travels from there to Athens. Nothing could be more convenient! What business Lord Winthrop had in that area was never satisfactorily explained to Astera, and, indeed, it took him an amazingly short time in Rome to conclude it.

Her aunt had been laid low, as she was each time they even neared Italy, the burial place of her Arthur. Once more she found herself unequal to a visit to the grave and once more Astera substituted, bringing flowers and messages which she resolutely repeated at the gravesite regardless of the people watching. But as the Italians dismissed her as *inglese* and the English tourists quite properly pretended not to hear, it was concluded with as little embarrassment as possible.

Since John Keats and Percy Shelley—recent poets she admired—were also buried there in the Protestant Cemetery, Astera paused before each of their graves. She was moved by the fact that no name was on the recent gravestone of the talented Keats—simply the message "Here lies one whose name was writ in water," and above that was carved the symbol of a broken lyre. Saddened by the death of those so early deprived of life, she looked about at the rows of low myrtle bushes and oleander trees that shaded the grove of death, and thoughts of those she, too, had early lost fell like shadows across her, spreading out, touching all she saw: broken columns, urns, rows and rows of white tombs and, at the edge, like exclamation points on these griefs—cypress trees, tall, straight, eternally evergreen, even in this death of winter. Slowly, unwillingly, she walked on, the cold of the place permeating her pelisse and velvet bonnet. A statue of Psyche at the end of the central pathway was the only other woman there—husbanded by all the poets and unfulfilled lovers about her. To stave off this abrupt eventuality, Astera was jolted by a need to be joined to someone.

Turning for a last look, she saw two graves in the distance, side by side, joined; and that seemed an answer . . . or a peace. Yet as she stared at them, in the blink of her eye, the joined graves changed to ones in a green English cemetery, and one was, she sensed rather than saw, hers . . . and the other, Viscount Weston's.

Abruptly turning aside, Astera almost ran out of the cemetery, no longer allowing her eyes to register any sights. And when subsequently that second grave would intrude—both as she gently described Arthur's headstone to her aunt, and later, while preparing to board ship again—Astera determinedly shook it off!

She was only rid of that picture when her sense of humor gave it some semblance of balance by envisioning the Viscount's shock as she informed him of their eventual resting place: his ever-mobile eyebrows would arch as he inquired politely, "Indeed, Miss Claybourne, and who shall initiate our joint demise—you or I?"

Thus her laughter wiped out all other emotions but incredulity. Of all men to have chosen for the honor of eternally resting with her! . . . That cold, abrupt, egotistical *dandy!* Heavens! Why, the man with whom she would be forever joined should at least have *feelings!* . . . or rather, have *had* feelings before becoming a grave man—not been that way to begin with! The only explanation for the delusion was obviously the sorrow of the place had temporarily disordered her senses!

Once out to sea again, it was not difficult for Astera to forget all depressing thoughts, for she was in her element in that element. Even Aunt Minerva felt well on board—as she always had on her previous sails. She attributed it to the salt sea spray, which she had heard was beneficial. It was Lord Winthrop who was finding it rough going, as he had from the beginning when they'd set sail originally from the Thames at Gravesend. The winds in the English Channel had him close to ordering them off at the next possible point of disembarkation. Yet when the opportunity shortly presented itself, for they were becalmed at Lulworth Cove on the south coast, and all were able to walk a few hours on land, he regained his control and stalwartly boarded again.

But beyond such nautical adjustments, the good lord was constantly subject to other rude shocks on the voyage, the first being that there were no horses on board. For all his fifty plus years, he had never been out of sight of his cattle, or, indeed, of land, for so long a period. Second, never had he to go so long without his pleasure of shooting at something. But being a man of resource as well as resources, he approached the captain and the two devised a way. Empty bottles were set up as target practice, and once, due to the fair amount of livestock on board, they used live poultry. A goose or fowl was put in the basket and hoisted to the main yardarm. The head wriggling above was the goad, and Lord Winthrop was pleased to discover that even the waves did not disturb his much-vaunted aim. He defeated the captain two out of three, and triumphant, and much praised by Minerva, was momentarily reconciled to this watery mode of transportation. Yet the time stretched out . . . and out. For the *Merry Wind*, the brig they'd booked, was more moody than merry, sailing at so slow a clip Lord Winthrop was once again snappish. Humming and stroking away his megrim, Astera soothed him. But at one such moment he allowed himself to slip and exclaim, "Why the devil did he choose so slow a tub!" Pouncing on that, his ward questioned, "Who chose it? Guardy, was it *Weston?*"

He was too sick to put her off and eventually nodded, but

prevented the possibility of his divulging more by rising quickly from the deck and retiring to his cabin.

Pacing the deck to cool her anger, Astera wondered again about the Viscount's interference in her life. But what in heaven's name had been his purpose in choosing such a tub of a brig, if not to assure their delay in arriving, for she herself had previously sailed on a schooner that moved along at a pretty clip.

But she had not been allowed any say in the arrangements. The same deaf ear had been turned on all her suggestions as had been turned on her objections: that she could not wish to be away from England for Christmas, that winter was not the most felicitous time for sailing or even traveling.

The rest of the party, Lord Cuffsworth, the Marvelles and Sybil and, of course, Weston, were to take the packet to Portugal and go overland to Gibraltar, where they were to be picked up by the Viscount's own vessel, the *Hawk*.

Not that Astera would have wished to be in such close proximity with Weston, but she could not help but imagine what the results of that close confinement with Miss Farnshorn would be. And when she'd said as much to her guardian, she had been surprised to see him greatly disturbed and very snappishly assure her that it was his understanding that Miss Farnshorn was not *that way* inclined! To which Astera could only throw up her hands and give up—either on her own understanding or on her guardian's.

More delays, so close to their eventual destination, for again and again they were becalmed, made even her aunt begin to consider a spasm and seek the seclusion of her cabin, or rather what she called her "cabinet," so small and close was it. Further, both her aunt and guardian again and again commiserated with each other on each day of the hunting season passing without them. Only Astera continued to enjoy the voyage, running to see the different outlines of land in the distance or seating herself at her usual station by the taffrail, pencil in hand, waiting for the muse to strike. (She did not—not once on the trip—

either because Astera was too excited to concentrate or because hers was clearly a land muse.)

One ignoble feeling in Astera did surface—an overwhelming envy of the sailors climbing up the ropes and seating themselves at the masthead. Nothing could equal that sensation, of that she was certain, and after having talked for a while with the first mate (a laughing fellow not above risking his captain's displeasure to please such a pleasing lady), it was arranged that she would change into sailor's garb and he would help her climb to that desired perch! A cap hid her bright golden hair and the sagging clothes her body, but nothing could dim the brilliance of her eyes and smile as she thanked the man. So eager, she even refused his hand and pulled herself up, up to where she could feel herself part of the ship itself at last—billowing, lurching, swaying with it across the blue above and the blue below. Only after did she think of her aunt's reaction if she had seen her up there, and even later did she consider the risk to herself or her reputation if her unladylike act became known, but since neither dire event occurred, that glorious moment proved worthwhile, for it stayed with her long after. Oft it would flash in her mind's eye when the cabin was too close or the thought struck that soon, too soon, she'd be having to deal with the Viscount again . . . *and his party!*

The same hand that directed their travels apparently was directing their settling in at Athens. A villa had been let for them on the outskirts of the town on one of the highest promontories, which had a direct view of the Acropolis. Not that that was remarkable, for that architectural wonder was so situated that there was a tolerable view of it from almost any vantage point. They were greeted by the English Resident himself, Mr. Hollis Smithers, and aided in every possible way, and every possible courtesy was extended—which soothed Lord Winthrop, whose title had accustomed him to expect pampering, a quality sorely lacking on board ship. Though the captain had been most accommodating, the accommodations had not. Nor had the mists and squalls shown any respect for class, dampening and rocking all alike, viewing *all*, if society did not, as in the same boat.

Athens had memories for Astera which she assumed would not disturb her. But once her aunt and guardian were settled, and it developed that the villa was going to run itself under the capable hands of an English-speaking Greek lady, Mrs. Corcoras, she was left with nothing to do but remember. The housekeeper was generally called "Kyria"—the Greek word for madam—by the Resident, the tradespeople and the help. Astera was urged to do so as well, and after a cozy chat, she did. Kyria's only fault was excessive curiosity. Not that Astera was all that high in the instep, but she was just not accustomed to being asked such personal questions by a lady of a mere half a day's acquaintance.

"You have been to Greece before this time?"

Astera explained about her earlier visit.

"You are pledged to some man—or you are looking about?"

Astera explained that she was neither, which shocked Kyria so much that she could do no more than roll her eyes in disbelief. "A young, beautiful girl like you with a Greek name and a love of Greece in her heart. It is impossible not to have had dozens, hundreds of men collapsing themselves at your foot!"

Astera had grinned at that. "You mean throwing themselves at my feet," she corrected, but allowed there had been one or two who had suffered a lack of balance in her presence, but the effect had not been permanent. "Also I had a very good-looking Greek man insist that I throw myself at his foot, but I resisted that . . . eh . . . position in life."

Kyria was instantly interested, and Astera, who would haughtily have refused this information to anyone encroaching enough to ask the particulars, under those shiny olive eyes instantly told her all about Andreas: that he was a sculptor, that he had known her father previously, or so he had introduced himself, and that he had been the first man to ever rave about the beauty of her face and form to the point that she'd almost lost her common sense and agreed to his proposals—of which he had made many, and of a diverse kind. But at the end, she had refused them all and returned to England.

"Where you met an English man who won your heart?" Kyria asked eagerly, wishing the story to have a happy ending, and Astera toyed with the possibility of mentioning the Viscount just to make the story come out right, but since it was not true and since in all probability Weston and Sybil would be arriving engaged, she curbed her author's enthusiasm and merely shook her head.

"Po-po-*po!*" Kyria intoned, shaking her head. "But that is sad. Better you should have run with this Andreas. You are old now. Perhaps you have come back here for him?"

Astera, astonished at that conclusion, assured her she had not, that as far as she was concerned Andreas Jason was only a memory . . . and actually a rather embarrassing one at that!

Kyria jumped up at the name. "Andreas Jason! But he is with Odysseus himself!"

While Astera knew that Odysseus was the leader of the Greek fighters against the Turks, it instantly became necessary for her to have the full particulars, and she soon was in possession of them. Odysseus, she was informed, was a man all women prayed to meet—wild, vengeful, full of fight and fire . . . and honor—and he had with him in the Parnassus Mountains the same kind of men from all of Greece, who stood ready to give their *all* to oust the "Infidel Turks"! And with that last comment, Kyria spat on the floor.

As a lady, Astera did not permit her face to betray her surprise, and she soon became accustomed to this one distressing action of Kyria's. Inevitably when the word "Turk" was mentioned, she would *spit*. In all other ways, she had fine manners that would totally please even her aunt. But since, Astera reasoned, it did not seem likely that her aunt and Kyria would ever engage in a conversation in which the Turks would be mentioned, she lived in hope that her aunt would never have to see this gesture of contempt.

Nor did she. Minerva Claybourne was very well pleased with

Kyria. She, it developed, also was quite knowledgeable in nostrums and even had some that would have surprised the ladies of London, but Minerva was more cosmopolitan—and when it came to nostrums, she would generally accept anything. But Astera could scarcely believe it when her aunt on the third day in Athens suddenly developed a distinct odor of garlic about her person. When questioned, Minerva agreed she not only had taken to eating a daily clove, but had one secreted in her bosom. "It strengthens the blood, it calms the soul and wards off 'the evil eye,'" her aunt assured her happily, and Astera was just able to suppress her laughter, but that restraint faltered subsequently upon noticing Lord Winthrop sniffing curiously and casting an astonished glance at Minerva as she tranquilly passed him by. He was too much of a gentleman to question the source.

On the fourth day Astera began to wonder why the rest of the party was not making its presence known, but she could not bring herself to seem anxious and ask. Finally her aunt, who had no such scruples, faced the evasive Lord Winthrop and brought it out in the open. "Well, we are *here!* But after urging us all this distance, where is that man . . . our 'delightful' host! Surely since they had no stop for 'business' in Italy, they should have arrived well before us. Every day I expect either the Viscount or certainly Lord Cuffsworth to pay us a call!"

Lord Winthrop's face grew a bit flushed as he mumbled something about "delay" and "all would come out right and tight" . . . and made his escape. Minerva was left to wonder, and Astera to conclude that this "lack of attention" was all a deliberate attempt at humiliation—even a retribution for her early evenings with Reverend Smallward when the Viscount was her guest. How else to explain the discourtesy of his delayed call—as if he had forgotten he had invited them at all! The possibility that they were of so little consequence that their host would not even recollect them was so aggravating, Astera had to pace her room for more than half an hour to rid herself of its effect.

But more thoughts in this vein would intrude. It certainly was a distinct possibility that the original invitation to them had been a mere courtesy, that they were expected to refuse and her guardian had not understood! All that explained why the Viscount Weston did not invite them along on his private vessel . . . why he made their exclusion so obvious!

Another possibility for their invitation could be that Weston was still uncertain of his feelings for Miss Sybil Farnshorn and by inviting all the original party, he made his invitation to her and the Marvelles less "particular"; and thus, less of a commitment! . . . while he had the leisure of the sail to consider!

It was just the kind of selfish device he would contrive. To have her poor guardian, who hated the sea, come all this distance just to lessen his own obligation! Although since Sybil and he had been traveling so intimately, it was probably a fait accompli by now, and the presence of others, totally unnecessary, and all three of them would probably be dismissed. Well, at least he owed them the cruise of the islands before rudely sending them back . . . and she would insist on his fulfilling his promise to the letter!

"Oh fiddle!" Astera concluded when still another day passed with no attendance. It was totally immaterial to her whether the Viscount paid a call or not, but neither her aunt nor her guardian deserved this kind of discourtesy. And when her aunt exclaimed that "his abandoning them there was definitely unworthy of a nobleman!" Astera advanced from chagrin to wrath. It was her aunt's further opinion that Miss Farnshorn was probably occupying his time; to which Astera testily replied that that lady could have the pleasure of *all* his time and *total* attention from now on, if he would just give them the courtesy of a call to at least explain their situation!

On the following day, the Viscount arrived prepared to do so, but Astera was so primed against him, she accepted his apologies with no more than a cold nod. Once or twice he looked at her with a puzzled expression, as he steadfastly conversed with her aunt. After exhausting their assurances on their comfort, Kyria's invaluability, the delight of the view, the comforts and discomforts of the journey, the Viscount seemed ready to take his leave when Astera stopped him.

"You are aware, my lord, are you not, that when I received you at Mayberry, my aunt and guardian stood in stead as host and hostess, so my presence was not totally required, but since we arrived here at your express command—"

"Command?" the Viscount interrupted gently with a smile. "Surely not?"

"Well, then at your request . . . oh bother! What I was trying to say was that you really should have been here earlier than this to at least explain the future arrangements. . . ."

Staring at her steadily, the Viscount asked softly, "What arrangements?"

"Why for . . . whatever! The cruise . . . or whatever plans you have for our entertainment. Obviously one could not make ones own plans for fear of conflicting. . . . I mean, well certainly Cuffy should have been here. I simply cannot understand what would prevent him . . . or rather who would prevent him . . . just to keep us in suspense!"

"There appears to be some confusion here, Miss Claybourne. At this moment Lord Cuffsworth, Lord and Lady Marvelle and Miss Sybil Farnshorn are still on the high seas, enjoying themselves hugely, I am certain, for I have given explicit instructions to that effect to my captain . . . and he has never failed me. As for myself, though I wished, shall I say, 'most ardently' to be at the dock to greet both Miss Claybournes, it was a pleasure of which I was unable to avail myself as I have been in the west of Greece until this very morning. I stopped merely to change my clothes so as not to embarrass such fine ladies by my dirt!"

Here Minerva, thus appeased, and, always gracious, interrupted. "You look very much as if you'd just stepped out of your own drawing room, my lord. And we appreciated Mr. Smithers deputizing." She then departed to consult Kyria—after inviting Weston for tea. Left alone Astera realized with a flushed countenance she had not asked him to sit and he was obviously waiting for her to do so. She made the necessary gesture.

"Thank you, I confess I am rather tired from my travels."

Another period of silence between them.

Still not appeased, Astera touched on another sore point—the choice of the *Merry Wind*. She mentioned her own earlier swifter travel on a schooner, and then said pointedly, "Whoever chose our sluggish little brig was certainly not concerned with our comfort!"

"Really?" Weston replied innocently, refusing to acknowledge it as being his selection. "However a schooner with its additional sails, which might lessen the time of the journey, would perforce require additional crew to handle them . . . and surely that would encroach on any privacy a lady might possibly have in so limited a space!"

"I have found," Astera snapped, "that whether on land or sea —one gentleman can be just as 'encroaching' as several!"

He refused to rise to that bait, just remained blandly surveying her as if he had forgotten the exact location of her eyes and lips. In response, Astera critically surveyed him, then with a slight smile, she pointed to his cravat, it having attracted by its excessive exuberance. "Does *it* have a Greek name in honor of the country?"

"It does, of course. It is called 'Nike' and symbolizes not only my respect for that statue, but my victorious objectives here in Greece."

Assuming that was meant for Sybil, Astera could not understand why he was looking at her as if he meant herself, except that it was his way to want all women, as Kyria had suggested, "collapsing" at his "foot."

"Why are you not traveling with . . . I mean . . . on your own ship?"

"You have not been attending, Miss Claybourne, did I not explain I had business in the western part of Greece which required that I arrive earlier? I was fortunate enough to have some influence with the admiralty and joined their HMS *Corona* on its way to join the Mediterranean fleet."

"What business?"

"That is a singularly personal question. Do you feel we stand in such close relationship that you could—"

"I just meant . . . could it be the same 'business' that brought my guardian to Italy?" Astera broke in suspiciously.

Viscount Weston was saved from an answer by the entrance of Kyria, who greeted him (as she did anybody of more than two hours' acquaintance) as an old friend! She had both tea and the bitter Greek coffee accompanied by a spread of delicacies that would have fed an entire ship's crew. When Lord Winthrop entered, they all sat down and made a good meal of it, during which several facts were then cleared up. The *Hawk* had been delayed (and, indeed, had not started out till the *Merry Wind* had well departed) and was not due for at least a week yet, and when the rest of the party arrived (this to her aunt's question) they were not to share this establishment, he would not stand for her being cramped. Rather, arrangements had been made for a private villa for Lord and Lady Marvelle and her sister "somewhere near but not *too* near. At first I had considered placing them in Sounion—"

"Ah, that is some distance!" Astera cried cheerfully, and Weston could not help but smile as he continued. "Yet . . . it would not serve, as it would be too out of the way . . . for the . . . eh . . . antiquities," he finished with an innocent air.

Astera, disappointed, missed his sarcasm in her anxiety to persuade him to reconsider Sounion, claiming there were a good many things to see there. "There is a temple belonging to Athena Sounias which is quite a breathtaking site . . . and sight. And there is delightful swimming just below."

"I do not believe either of the Marvelles or Miss Farnshorn would wish to avail themselves of either of those treats . . . but you, I gather, have?"

"Oh yes, rather, I went with An—" catching herself quickly she exchanged a look with Kyria, who dramatically rolled her eyes at the slip while making a lot of distracting clatter, giving Astera time to smoothly alter her words. "With . . . *an* . . . other lady. Lord Byron scratched his name on the column, and

I had to persuade An . . . Annette to refrain from doing so as well. I have the greatest dislike of people who deface antiquities."

"And I for people who *li*—ke their own name so much they must see it everywhere they go."

"Then we agree," Astera said cautiously, not sure what that emphasis on "li" was meant to stand for . . . or the sudden flash in his eyes.

"More and more each day," he finished gallantly, and Astera, relieved, gave him her first welcoming smile.

"But Lord Cuffsworth?" she suddenly remembered. "Where is he to stay?"

"With me."

Astera frowned. He had put her in the position where she had to ask about *his* lodgings. Could they both plan to stay with the Marvelles? She could not bring herself to ask it. And smiling, as if aware of her dilemma, the Viscount took his leave without clearing the matter.

The next day he arrived to take her driving in his curricle. On the way there, the Viscount smiled at Astera's attitude—as if they were in actuality to see the Parthenon in the pristine shape it had been in in ancient times, surrounding the forty-foot gold and ivory statue of Athena with the onyx eyes and pupils of precious stones, instead of the rubble the Turks had left and an empty stone base.

But somehow when they arrived, enough of the Acropolis remained to be overwhelming. Both having been to the Acropolis before, they were prepared for the steep climb on the slippery, marble-strewn road, but Weston was not prepared for a lady to race ahead, visibly demonstrating her excitement at seeing old "friends"—pointing out *that* temple . . . and that statue . . . and almost jumping in place as they approached the Erechtheion with the Ionic columns of Greek maidens. As usual with Astera, the Viscount was not certain whether he approved, but he did enjoy. And then she began telling him stories her mother and father had so often recollected—of their walking hand-in-hand across the interior of this same Parthenon and pausing before this very center niche (that once held the golden goddess Athena) and pledging to that goddess their first child. That's why she'd just escaped being called Athena—although that was given her as a middle name—but the dedication held, so standing here was rather like reliving her baptism, and she could feel her mother and father closer to her here at this moment than she had in years!

Embarrassed by her speech and the emotion on her face as she looked around her, Weston next felt a totally unexpected sensation—that of wanting to make it up to her for the loss of her parents, wanting to take her hand and retrace her mother's and father's steps, now, as the high noon sun split itself through the ring of columns to reach and warm them, now, in this moment of ancient quiet—to hold her hand and make some kind of pledge himself. Astera was wearing a large straw hat, and the sun reflecting off her golden hair made a blaze of rays that extended out onto the hat, so at times, when she turned and looked up at him, her face seemed a piece of the sun itself, surrounded by rays and all inner-lit with a similar sunlike intensity —whereupon, damning conventions, Weston took her hand, and they walked silently through the Parthenon. She started at the gesture, and after a wondering look, accepted his hand and the walk. Her acquiescence and her silence he felt indicated she shared some of his feelings of the moment, and further that they had at last, for that brief moment, crossed over the bar of misunderstanding and formality. And thus, they walked and shared. And the softer, warmer bond between them lasted till at her doorstep he softly reminded her that he was to come to dinner that night. Sighing, Astera had whispered, "But which one of you shall attend tonight, my lord?" and not waiting for his response, she slowly entered the villa.

Riding back to his lodgings, Weston wondered at her question and whether there were indeed two of himself. First, there was the Viscount, and then there was Weston. And Astera appealed to the latter and appalled the former. And she disconcerted both Weston and the Viscount by seeing that split before he did. Indeed, it crumbled a great deal of his own self-image—to think that young girl should have such a perceptive understanding of himself—and left him a bit aloof, even downright wary of her when he arrived that night, which again confused Astera, and had her brooding in turn. Luckily, the Resident, Mr. Smithers, was there, and he had quite a lot to say. In the course of which it came out what the Viscount's mysterious business had been earlier in Greece. Astera was astonished.

"But you are here to help them!" she exclaimed; and the Viscount demurred, explaining that he was here at express request of the London Greek Committee to overlook the situation and determine on a loan for the Greeks to aid in mounting their fight against the Turks.

Mr. Smithers was not very optimistic. "They are so split, so many factions: Prince Mavrocordatos ruling the West, and here Odysseus Androutsos, who controls the East, but who spends most of his time in the Parnassus Mountains attempting raids that turn out to be mere skirmishes! Centralization—under *one authority*—would be the answer, but it is the question of who would be that authority."

"You cannot deal with a man who is descended from the Klephtes and believes the answer is ambuscades and rock-fighting," Weston said disdainfully. "Mavrocordatos, I have spoken to. And the Prince very sensibly believes in liberating the outlying islands first—that means controlling the Turk's source of *supply* and making this a naval adventure, breaking the Turkish blockade and releasing the Greek fleet now lying idle in the islands. That is the solution that I believe in as well!"

"That could very well be because you have a naval background yourself, my lord," Mr. Smithers replied. "I myself feel there is *something* in Odysseus that could do the trick!"

"*Tolmiri psyche,*" Astera answered. At which they all looked up in surprise—not only that she had taken part in this discussion and answered in Greek, but that she earnestly continued her point. "Spirit . . . the daring spirit or psyche of Greece— that's what Odysseus has, and that's why the Greek people will follow him, for they themselves are a daring people who like sudden raids and 'do or die' situations, not long-ranged committee plans. Get two Hellenes together and you have an argument, get three and you have not a deciding vote, but *three* different arguments. They will only unite under the motion of a charge . . . or the drama of a spirited leader!"

"And how do you, Miss Claybourne, know so much about this mountain leader?" Mr. Smithers asked with a just barely tolerant smile. The Viscount was too surprised to engage in any questioning.

"Well, I have talked to the people here and I sense their feelings. They lift their heads up when the name of Odysseus is just mentioned. There is a reverence there that can be . . . well, harnessed. As for the Greek situation, I have been aware of it for many years, both in my previous visit here and at home. Part of the monies sought by public appeal and brought here are mine. I believe in their liberty enough to back them both financially and with my heart."

"Not enough people have enough heart or monies then," the Viscount answered coldly. "For no more than twenty thousand pounds was collected—not counting the monies from the Society of Friends and not counting the sums from the Americans. That is why they will have to float a loan. Daring spirit is all very well, but supplies win a war."

"I do not agree," Astera claimed hotly. "It is supplies that can just be wasted, but spirit can win without supplies—with rocks, if need be."

"Rather an emotional approach to the situation, I fear," Weston continued in his languid tones that were more denunciatory than a loud rebuke. "Miss Claybourne is prone to emotional outbursts, I have found. It makes one wonder whether your poetry might not be equally out of control."

Flushing at that personal rebuke, Astera tried to keep her own voice very calm as she replied, "There are certain situations when emotion is not out of place, my lord, that is if the people are 'human' enough to feel them, and not given to cold, practical decisions in their lives—not considering other people's feelings because the very word 'feelings' is foreign to their natures. And then, they are often surprised to find themselves rejected . . . and disliked."

Here Lord Winthrop gasped, as even he realized she was referring to the Viscount's proposal and her rejection. Aunt Minerva did not know which way to look—a spasm was definitely beginning to form, for she recognized that look on Astera's face, and nothing was going to stop her now. Only Smithers, unaware of the double meaning, and the Viscount remained calm.

"There *is* something in what she says," Mr. Smithers innocently contributed.

And suddenly both the Viscount and Astera laughed. Astera tried not to meet his eyes, still too angry with him to acknowledge they had the same sense of the ridiculous, and forced herself to politely listen as Mr. Smithers agreed about the English not taking into account the emotions of the Greek people, not that he would go so far as to say feelings were foreign to the English people. In fact, he had the pleasure of just recently having met an Englishman *and a lord* who was known for some "very definite feelings," and that was Lord Byron.

The conversation instantly turned from politics to this fascinating subject. Astera eagerly wanted to know where the poet was, and Mr. Smithers, pleased that Astera had acted as he expected—the mere mention of that name had her, as it did all other ladies of either Greece, England or indeed, all other European nations—instantly intrigued.

"Miss Claybourne perhaps would be interested to know," Weston put in here with a slight smile, "that Lord Byron is also of the opinion that Mavrocordatos is the solution for Greece, and, according, he is stationed in *western* Greece or Missolonghi this very moment and awaiting supplies to further the cause."

"And that is whom you went to see!"

The Viscount bowed. "He is one of the men I consulted on this financial matter; and I found him to be very much a practical person who refuses to budge until the supplies and armies are of sufficient strength and *unity* to make a difference."

"Then I appear to be totally routed," Astera replied good-naturedly and Weston hesitantly returned her smile. As usual she had surprised him, taking defeat so "sportsmanlike," and he wished now he had been less particular in his attacks.

Astera, however, did not feel it was a defeat, and her argument on the importance of the emotions and the Viscount's lack of heart was not noticeably altered by the conclusion that Lord Byron's thinking was similar to his *strategically*—for hadn't she heard Lord Byron preferred the unemotional *Pope* as a poet? He was, after all, of the "older generation," and in his personal life he probably, from all she'd heard, did not as totally eschew emotion as Weston did. In any case, while still annoyed with the Viscount for his cold veneer and deprecating manners, she was somewhat more impressed by his being involved in the Greek cause at all! It did say something about his character that he was seeking a loan rather than risking his life for it, but that was better than nothing.

Yet the opportunity to demonstrate this more cordial attitude toward her host did not arise, as for the next few days the Viscount neither paid a call nor invited Astera to any more outings. His time was taken in making preparations for the arrival of the *Hawk*, which had apparently picked up a good wind and was due to land shortly—several days ahead of schedule. They would dock at Piraeus before midweek, he informed Lord Winthrop in a note, and the old man was pleased, anxious to renew the friendship with the Marvelles. Both Astera and her aunt could just look at each other as they half-heartedly agreed.

Imagining him so absorbed with assuring his "intended's" comfort that he could take no time for them, Astera felt herself neglected and annoyed with the Viscount once more. Unwisely, she let slip her feelings to Kyria, who often had the kind of simple solutions to problems that made Astera either smile or shudder—usually both.

"He is adding a woman into the stew, you must add a man!"

Astera smiled. "Whom do you suggest . . . Mr. Smithers?"

Solemnly Kyria walked round the marble-floored patio, stopping to peer in the distance at the Acropolis (as if an answer were carved on one of its columns), and finally she turned, with a slap of her hand on her thigh. "*Andreas!*" she exclaimed in triumph. "You bring in a man who loves you to push aside the woman who loves him, yes?"

"*No!*" Astera responded, astounded. "I would not dream of doing anything so dishonest. I have no feelings for Andreas—actually, I'd be afraid to see him again, it was so difficult ridding myself of him before. Besides, it has been almost five years—he won't even remember me. And, in any event, I am not interested in preventing a union between the Viscount and the woman he loves . . . . if he can love."

Kyria merely shrugged; and the next day as Astera was ready to go for a drive, she noticed that Kyria's son, Panos, her usual escort, was smiling broadly and excitedly gesturing toward a handsome man sitting nonchalantly in her curricle.

Astera stopped, stupefied—just staring—and then barely whispered his name, but he heard it, turned and jumped out to bow before her. It was Andreas.

CHAPTER 10

The same black curly hair, the same open-throated blouse and tight breeches, but he was taller than she remembered and broader. And while he could have gotten more muscular, she could not see how he could have grown—it was just that she must have somehow reduced him in her mind to more comfortable, conformable proportions; and now again his impact was making her tongue-tied.

"Asteroula mou," he murmured, using the diminutive of her name, which was often done affectionately in Greek.

"But how are you here?" she asked in surprise, and after he handed her into the carriage and seated himself next to her, he responded to all her questions. Kyria had a friend who had a friend who knew him, he laughed, amused by the Greek twists and turns. And thus, circuitously, he had gotten the message that she was here in his country again, and through the same route, going from person to person, he finally came across Kyria herself, and they had a discussion. And *here he was!*

"Indeed," was all Astera could think to say. Both Lord Cuffsworth and the Viscount would have been surprised at how silent she was, but Andreas, jumping out and showing her things that had changed and kissing her hand and embracing her in his joy at seeing her again, had a way of silencing her thoughts as well as her words. She just was able to respond when required . . . and occasionally ask a question. Such as, was it true he had fought with Odysseus in the Parnassus Mountains?

"True as God's will! I fought and was wounded. Two musket balls were ripped by my head, and one landed in a fig tree, and one in the man next to me, and since then, I eat figs every morning in gratitude!" Astera laughed with him. "And the man was an Englishman, one of the many foreign oppor— eh, many very able soldiers who have joined us, wandering about in rags; he was a Mr. Sands—a member of the Animal Guards himself . . ." ("Horse Guards," Astera corrected, giggling.) "Whatever," Andreas continued. "And I have lived in my clothes for six months, and my gun at my side, and often the Turks do not come, but when they do, they are 'finished,' and I have roasted a man over a fire and smelled him for days after. Ah, but I have lived through torture and terror, my *kukla*, my little English doll, and *always* I think of *you*. In the caves, I have scratched your profile on the walls and drawn stars around it and called your name in moments of my agony . . . in moments of my loss—for I have loss a great many loved ones, men and women, but you, the one I love most, were never there. . . . Now, like a gift from the stars, you come back . . . now you are here!"

"I am here with a party of friends and gentlemen," Astera put in quickly.

"One of these gentlemen is yours!" he gasped, pinning her with his beautiful dark eyes—daring her to admit that betrayal.

She was not up to that. "I am not engaged," she hedged uneasily. Then recollecting her independence, she continued in stronger tones. "But Andreas, you know you have not a single reason for sounding like that. We were not right for each other several years ago. There is even more of a distance between us now. I have come here because I still love your country—not *you*."

Andreas turned his perfect profile from her and brooded. "Ah Astera," he moaned. "You are so English! So direct! You always speak *too much*. And what is distance, if one can travel over it and return? If a woman comes back for love of my country . . . love of *me* cannot be far behind!"

"It is very far behind," she laughed.

"I do *not* believe it. You are older now, and not so afraid. You were a child then—not in Greek terms, it is true, but *English women* need more maturing. Now I can see the difference in your eyes. They laugh more and fear less. If love were to call you now, you would rush forth. Yes?"

"Yes," she whispered. "If love were to call me now I would . . . but . . . *but*, I do not hear even a single sound from its direction."

"Hard-of-hearing as well as hardhearted," he scoffed, and Astera laughed at his tragic face.

"What are *you* doing back in Athens then . . . does not Odysseus need you?"

"I am Greek, therefore I give up my life for Greece, but between times I must come back to Athens and continue my career, yes? Now, under the express orders of Odysseus himself, I am engaged in making a statue of him to be remembered . . . and to inspire the people to the cause. When I have concluded it, I shall perhaps die in the mountains, and like a goat, lie out there till the sun bleaches my carcass to look like a statue myself."

"A very moving thought," said Astera, smiling.

"Exactly what I think myself!" And in delight that they shared the same thought, he embraced her.

She resisted him but, caught up in his emotions, allowed one kiss to pass between them, which seemed to satisfy Andreas that she was once more in love with him, and confuse Astera as to her own emotions.

He was on the point of taking her to see his studio, which she refused, and they stopped in the square to heatedly discuss that when a friend of Andreas' called out. She was introduced and was not attending to their animated conversation, which was in more rapid Greek than she could assimilate, when, all of a sudden, one specific word struck her and she interrupted: "You are a *designer*, Kyrios Stamnos?"

Andreas jumped in to puff up his friend. "All the ladies, Greek and foreign, they come to him . . . well, not so many foreign, because he cannot speak English, but he is very fluent in French, having studied his styling under the great Roy himself!"

Here Mr. Stamnos interrupted his friend. "*Leroy!*"

"Ah yes, Leroy—whatever," Andreas agreed complacently. "A designer of le royal airs, eh?"

"Indeed? Perhaps then Mr. Stamnos could do something for *me?*"

Mr. Stamnos was delighted, and in her half-Greek and his half-French, they understood each other quickly. Money being no object, there could be no objection that could not be overcome, even time . . . which Astera implied was very limited. Could he not come up with outfits for her that would if not transform, at least improve her? He could! And even had one or two originals already made up (needing few alterations) in case he ever met a woman who had all the perfection required by these outfits!

"In other words—money." Astera smiled and refused to be won over by both men's reassurance that it was her beauty that inspired them both.

"She never believes that," Andreas said disgustedly. "She is *English*. She would rather have you praise her horse!"

Astera laughed loudly at that and assured them she would not stop them from praising her all they wished as long as the transformation was made. Quickly Mr. Stamnos jumped into the curricle. An *"embros!"* from Andreas; a "spring 'em" from Astera; and they were off to his place of business, each congratulating each other on the fortuitous meeting.

Since so much time was required to be devoted to her transformation, Astera had had to enlist the aid of both her aunt and Kyria. Nothing could have delighted or interested either lady more, and they eagerly did their utmost to deflect all questions from both Lord Winthrop and the Viscount when he finally made his appearance. Astera decided she was not to be seen till the big welcoming dinner Lord Winthrop had scheduled for the Marvelles and Sybil in two days' time. Till then she was unavailable for rides or even brief meetings with the Viscount. And to a very long letter of his informing her of the full particulars of his preparations (since she'd seemed so annoyed before at not being *fully* informed), she returned a short, formal reply.

Mr. Stamnos and Andreas, while showing her designs, proudly proclaimed the entire Regency style a *crime*—since it was stolen from their ancestors. Not only were the high waist and airy lightness of the robes an imitation of Grecian fashion, but even down to the heelless slippers . . . and up to the headdresses such as the Minerva bonnet with its plumes and the Psyche knot. So how could she fail but be successful if she were to be dressed by the originators themselves!

These were much-needed reassurances, for in her heart Astera was nervous about the transformation, having had such a disastrous first attempt when Sybil had turned her into an obvious ugly duckling. At least Mr. Stamnos and his aides were all so enthusiastic and complimentary that she knew the results had to be an improvement. (One she hoped worth all the wasted hours standing for fittings and viewing yards of materials and laces and frills and furbelows . . . and all kinds of accessories.) Andreas was often present to add his artist's eye, which, even Astera had to admit, was unerring: "Not *that* color, Mitsos, she will look like a dead cypress tree!" "That line is too severe, she is a sparkling girl needing *simple* . . . not serious . . . *soft* . . . not silly!"

It was further decided to change her hair as well as her wardrobe, and Astera closed her eyes as the scissors cut away locks that had grown there since babyhood! And for her skin, an almond and lemon speciality, devised by Kyria, had almost eliminated the one or two offensive freckles that Sybil had noticed on her nose and décolleté, while crushed almonds and honey had concurrently purified its texture, and almond oil had softened her hands to ladylike feel. Andreas even devised a special scent for her from the subtlest spices. "No flowers for you, my girl—you have too much life to lie about in a garden waiting to be sniffed. . . . You are for running on mountaintops and need basil that grows there, and a touch of resin from the pines for 'might' from the Olympian peaks, yes? . . . But wait! I correct myself. Perhaps a touch of crushed carnations for the crushing effect you have on men—like me!" The results were surprisingly pungent yet pure. Astera wore it cautiously and was pleased by the reaction.

She was ready not a moment too soon, for the *Hawk* had docked, and all the members of the party were resting and preparing to be reunited that night at Lord Winthrop's. Her guardian had invited, besides Mr. and Mrs. Smithers, two other Greek officials and their wives, and, at Aunt Minerva's suggestion, both Andreas Jason, a noted sculptor, she informed him, and Mr. Stamnos, a designer. While acquiescing to a sculptor, Lord Winthrop was afraid a designer would smell distinctly of "shop," but on Astera's pleading that he was "her designer," my lord, always maneuverable, agreed.

Lord Cuffsworth had rushed to the villa where Astera was staying almost on docking and was instantly received by Miss Claybourne—unlike the Viscount, who on that very day, on having his card sent up, merely received a reply from Kyria that Astera was lying down and would give herself the pleasure of seeing him that evening. However, when Lord Cuffsworth's card was delivered, Astera instantly descended to cry joyfully, "Cuffy, you're here!"

Grinning and hugging her, Cuffy shouted in delight, "I say, am I? I can't quite believe it. I thought I'd never hit land again, but was sentenced to spend the rest of my life swinging in the breeze with Sybil. By Jove, that's punishment! I told Weston, by Jove, take a trip with the gal first before you marry her . . . and he agreed to do so!"

"Then he is still toying with her affections and unsure of his own, I see," Astera answered grimly, and while Cuffy was about to disagree on the harshness of her verdict, he was suddenly stopped cold.

"Astera?"

"Yes?"

"Do something different?"

"Yes, Cuffy. Lots of things different."

"Well, you know, you always looked dashed good to me . . . but now, now, I say, you look smashing!"

"Don't tell anyone, will you? I've had a designer, well, you'll see tonight, and I want it to be a surprise for *everyone!*"

"Oh yes, rather!" Cuffy agreed enthusiastically, promising not to breathe a word.

So Cuffy and her aunt and Andreas and, of course, Mr. Stamnos were the only ones prepared to see the new Astera. She had delayed her entrance till all were present and waiting impatiently for her arrival. Andreas had been introduced to all by Lord Winthrop. Mr. Stamnos was somehow forgotten, but Andreas instantly repaired the omission, taking over and praising him to Sybil and Lady Marvelle, mentioning that Mr. Stamnos had confided in Greek just moments before how overwhelmed he'd been at the sight of the two sisters . . . and so forth, till they were very well pleased with him. Not forgetting self, Andreas was suggesting a statue of Sybil to the Viscount—having somehow gotten the impression that that was the way the wind was blowing from a discussion with Lord Marvelle —but the Viscount merely shrugged and told him coldly that if he were here seeking commissions he "had much better apply to the lady herself!" The situation threatened to get a bit awkward when the door opened and Astera appeared.

She was gratified to have left them all speechless.

Her golden hair had been washed with camomile till it shone like the sun, and it was lifted up in a Greek goddess style with silk ribbons threaded through, releasing strategic ringlets at her temples and over her ears—as well as several longer ones covering her lovely neck.

Her face was whiter than ever, and yet her dark eyes were burning with such intensity one could almost feel the heat. But it was in the dress that the most obvious change had come about. Completing the look of "à la Hellène"—as Mr. Stamnos dubbed it—her dress was of the softest spun silk, and it clung to her figure in a way that if it did not have an occasional drape would have been near indecent. Also rather daring, and true to the goddess motif—one shoulder was left bare. Further circling the high waist were the same silk ribbons as adorned her hair. And both ribbons and dress were in the exact same *golden* shade, so that it seemed, when she stood there, posed at the door, as if a goddess had stepped out of the hot Greek sun to welcome them to her homeland.

The Viscount caught his breath at the familiarity of her appearance, and he realized with a jolt that *this* was how he had often seen her . . . in her moments of poetry reading, when she had raced by him on her horse, and the other day at the Parthenon when the sun had flooded her fiery body. Thus, he was surprised and not surprised. Wanting no one but himself to hand her in to dinner, he stepped forth eagerly, but was prevented by Andreas, who had quickly leaped up and rushed to her.

"Ah, the goddess Astera! Your humble worshippers are waiting to pay their homage!" And he bowed long and low before her, which had her laughing and telling him not to be silly. Turning to indeed welcome them each to Greece, she found herself going from the lecherous, interested eyes of Lord Marvelle, to his wife's cold glance, to Sybil's fury, and last, last, she shyly cast a glance at the Viscount—only to see his face looking disapprovingly at her and Andreas!

Momentarily deflated, she bravely approached him and directly asked his opinion. Languidly he replied that she seemed to have gone "quite a bit overboard on things Greek," which had Sybil letting out a sigh of relief and had Astera in that moment she'd hoped to be in her glory—totally devastated!

Unable at the last minute to alter Kyria's table arrangement, Astera was forced to sit as that good lady had planned—between the Viscount and Andreas. Whenever she spoke to one, the other listened in. It was decidedly awkward, but basically Andreas monopolized all conversation, and the Viscount was repressively silent. After dinner, there being no harpsichord delivered yet for Sybil to play, she volunteered to sing a cappella— a suggestion, of course, accepted with alacrity by Lord Winthrop. And somehow, there they were, after all the transformation, and all the miles traveled and time gone by, sitting in a saloon with Sybil, in her usual elegant blue, singing a love song to the Viscount, while Astera was helping serve the tea! It would have been much better if she had spent her time—as she'd originally planned—at the newly discovered excavations in nearby Agora. When Cicely Marvelle joined her sister in a duet, Astera could only philosophically reflect that no matter how much things changed, eventually one was always back where one began.

After a round of applause for the ladies, Andreas took the floor to invite them all the next day to view some carvings in several Greek museums, but Lady Marvelle explained she had seen quite a bit of "those things" when Lord Elgin brought them to *her* . . . and she saw no reason to travel all this distance to see what "one could have perfectly well stayed at home to see." Lord Marvelle agreed. Andreas, never at a loss, suggested viewing temples—*they* could not easily be transported and would have to be observed on the *original site!* "There is one particular one in Sounion which is like nothing one could see in London!"

"You haven't seen Nash's work, old boy," Lord Marvelle put

in complacently . . . and was just stopped from repeating Prinny's exact instructions to that architect by his wife's pronouncement that she could bear "no more talk of *buildings!*"—especially antiquities, which she had seen enough of from her window to last a lifetime and would "*not* travel to Sou— whatever . . . or any other place to see *repeats!*"

This was echoed so heatedly by Lord Cuffsworth and Sybil that Andreas was finally brought to a stand.

A moment of silence followed which the Viscount stepped in to fill: "Sounion, did you suggest? Is that where you attempted to scratch your name close to Lord Byron's and Miss Claybourne reprimanded you?" he asked smoothly, and Andreas, delighted that Astera had told the story and indifferent to the trap, quickly acknowledged it to be so.

His suspicions verified, Weston sent such a look of distaste in Astera's direction that she nearly protested audibly. And then she wished she had, as well as mentioned her aunt's presence on that occasion, for in the interim, Andreas had gone on making it seem as if they were alone and telling tale upon tale of that excursion—how she had lifted her skirt to dust Lord Byron's signature and caused quite a commotion—and other personal remarks which had Astera ready to sink.

Mr. Smithers again came to the rescue. "I was just telling Miss Claybourne the other day, and perhaps the other ladies would wish to hear, that Lord Byron is quite near here in Missolonghi, and that I have had the pleasure of seeing him."

Again this proved a successful ploy. No other topic would now interest them. Lord Marvelle, it developed, was more anxious than even his lady to really meet the disgraced lord. "By Jove, wouldn't that be something to tell them back home. Fellow's not received back there. But it would be quite unobjectionable to see the cove in a foreign place, what? And what stories we could tell, eh, Cicely?"

Cicely, or Lady Marvelle, agreed it would be of all things great, and Sybil too wished to meet him. Somehow they had gotten the impression that Mr. Smithers could arrange that, and were disappointed when he had to backtrack and admit he did not feel he could make the introduction and so forth. There was a general silence till Andreas broke in with: "But I shall introduce you! I shall take you all to Missolonghi. . . ."

The Marvelles were again excited, and Sybil was speaking softly to him when it developed that Andreas had never met Lord Byron either. "But I have explained to you all during dinner about how close I am to Odysseus."

"If you're going to tell us the story of roasting the men like goats once more . . ." Cuffy warned.

But Andreas was continuing. "Odysseus is in control of this entire east of Greece. A note from me to him; and we shall have a note to Lord Byron before the month is up!"

"That, unfortunately, Mr. Jason," Weston interrupted dryly, "is both too vague and rather too far off in the future, for as I explained at dinner, we shall be sailing again within a fortnight. Thus, obviously, your invitation need not be put to the test."

Andreas sensed the challenge and responded typically. "You imply *I* cannot arrange this! I, Andreas Jason, of whom Odysseus said, 'One more such man as you and I shall win Greece's freedom in a week!' "

"Greece is bereft then that you did not have a brother!"

Andreas, suspicious, nevertheless took it as a compliment. "Yes, that is so! Two of me would have done it. With Odysseus making three, of course. But now, it will have to be done more slow . . . and *after* I have finished my statue." But the sadness left his tone at a sudden notion. "Perhaps the ladies would like *instead* to see my studio. It would be to me as if the muses themselves had stepped into my humble working place, and when"—he looked deeply at Sybil and then carefully, almost equally as deeply, at Lady Marvelle—"and when you have left . . . you will have left your images in my heart!"

Lady Marvelle twittered and allowed she would very much like to see his studio, and Sybil softly concurred. Lord Marvelle put them back on the track.

"But if we're to see Byron, by Jove, we've not got much time."

Both sisters recalled to their original wishes began urging the project once more. Even Aunt Minerva surprised them and herself by agreeing she would very much love to meet the man. And, amid the general declamation, Astera wistfully said she too would think it a marvelous moment.

"Then I shall arrange it," Viscount Weston said softly.

"You!" Andreas scoffed.

"Oh yes!" Astera exclaimed, clapping her hands. "I forgot *you* have met him. *You* for certain could do it!"

The Viscount bowed at the compliment and, ignoring Andreas' protestations as much as he did the Marvelle's exclamations, calmly announced it would be set up before the end of the week. Thus having lost face, Andreas sought desperately to reclaim his position and talked incessantly of his statue of Odysseus on which he would value Lord and Lady Marvelle's opinion. Not unsusceptible to that compliment, they both agreed to give one, and an appointment was made to visit his studio on the following morning. Seizing the moment, Andreas mentioned that a small bust of Lady Marvelle would not be amiss to show the world "the perfection of English beauty," and as that was listened to with favor and one for her sister as well suggested, Andreas was in spirits again.

The commissions were finalized on the following day as the Marvelles and Sybil and Astera and the Viscount walked through Andreas' studio. Astera was surprised to discover herself impressed by the statue of Odysseus—larger than life she was certain, till Andreas maintained reverently that was how the man appeared to all who saw him.

It was Viscount Weston who questioned the possibility of completing even such small heads as were being envisaged in the limited amount of time the ladies had in Athens. And there was a momentary consternation over this, till Andreas assured them some simple sketches today and perhaps the next would be all he'd require, and then they could go off on their tour of the islands and return to find the pieces finished. Both sisters and Lord Marvelle were relieved, the Viscount suspicious, Cuffy indifferent, and Astera amused as she exchanged a glance with Andreas which clearly told him she recollected his shortcut stratagems: Andreas always had several "prepared" heads of gods and goddesses, with the features just suggested, in readiness—thus whenever a certain lady or gentleman desired to be immortalized, he simply made a few identifying touches and the thing was complete. When Astera got Andreas off to the side on the pretext of questioning the marble in a certain piece, she reprimanded him gently; but, as usual, he found nothing wrong with this practice.

"Bah! So anxious are you English to assume you are one of the Mount Olympus elite, it would not even be necessary for me to make any definite changes on my goddesses and gods. It is my *own* artistic integrity that urges me to cut a nose here and add a scowl there. For one English gentleman who had very little time, I took a full figure of Paris—substituted in place of the apple in the outstretched hand, a snuff box—and he assured me 'it could not be more like!' These ladies, I suspect, are also of that persuasion. One Aphrodite and one Athena . . . no, too old for that . . . ah, one Hera! Both with the alteration of slightly snubbed noses and smaller eyes, and *telione to zitema*— nothing else will be required. And I get the husband too. So larded over is he, I will not use my Apollo, but perhaps a Bacchus, eh?"

"Shameful!" Astera whispered, but she had to laugh, and Andreas, so pleased with himself and his wily plans and coming commissions, laughed loudly with her.

Both were observed in this intimate moment by a coldly reproving Viscount. Sybil was addressing him, but he was not attending and answered perfunctorily, which had her all a-flutter till Andreas approached and, with several well-placed sighs while drawing each feature, soon had her in a tolerably composed mood to not only continue the day but wish not to depart from the studio till every angle of her face had been reproduced.

Astera and Cuffy were meanwhile on the balcony looking over the Attica plain and the blue Grecian sky. She was dressed today in a heather-pink velvet day dress that fit her figure as if molded and a dashing velvet suggestion of a hat that added just a touch of insouciance that seemed to accent her natural liveliness. "Charming" was what Andreas had said at first sight, and Weston, who had been prepared to utter that very word, on finding himself superseded could only look at her in silence, which again disappointed Astera.

It was maddening to see her so perfected by another! Very like having discovered a gold vein and anticipating the secret pleasure of exploring and bringing forth the munificent results only to discover a poacher scattering golden nuggets round and making claims on *his* property. And it was this very chagrin that had engulfed Weston into such a prisoning silence, he could not break out of it. Rather was he just able to follow her about with his eyes, as she flitted from person to person—flirting with Andreas and then Cuffy and then even laughing at the sudden compliments of Lord Marvelle.

Time and time again he felt his emotions declining in a declension of rage from exasperation to irritation and finally, past all participle of help, to cold wrath. Yet he continued to draw near her, seeking his own pain, following Lord Cuffsworth and Astera out to the balcony, where he was in time to hear Cuffy reproving her for her familiarity with "that Greek fellow" and was at last released to add his own admonition.

"Oh fiddle!" Astera dismissed them both. "You're both worse than my aunt. Andreas is perfectly harmless. He may not have your gentleman's code of behavior—although from some of the stories Lord Marvelle has been telling us that code is not very dependable—but Andreas has his own ego that protects him. He would never force himself on a lady who was unwilling. He prides himself too much on his ability to make them willing . . . eager even. Look at Lady Marvelle. I have not seen her so animated, so sparkling, since the day she attempted to transform me!"

"And are you not in danger of being made willing?" Weston replied testily.

"Well, if I am . . . then it is my lookout. Why—what would be the danger? Andreas has always been anxious to marry me."

"A man like that can promise and not be in earnest. Are you so much of an 'innocent' that you cannot understand that!"

Astera was diverted by the Viscount's slight loss of composure. "Some men even propose marriage and even perhaps go through the ceremony and never are in earnest! You might live with them for twenty years and never find an earnest emotion in them!"

"Are you speaking generally or under the assumption that if one does not run around kissing women's palms and rolling one's eyes one is not capable of emotion?"

"To have a genuine emotion," Astera continued airily, "one must be willing to risk throwing conventions to the winds . . . one must be able to go beyond the importance of surface matters, such as dress, which as you can see"—she pointed to herself—"can be assumed at will. One must be able to want a person with all their true emotions, and not decide by how well one plays a part. Andreas does not have a social position; he is not 'noble,' but he is committed to his cause. He risked his life this past year, he has been wounded; he risks his heart each time he attempts a work of art. He fails and seems at times a fool, but he has *attempted*."

"This is your opinion of that man! And your opinion of all English gentlemen! Speaking of seeing only surface! If you continue to equate the genuineness of feelings by their surface show and their ungenuineness by their restraint, you shall, I daresay, deserve to find yourself in a position where you've lost all hope of a respectable alliance! But what else should one expect of a lady who writes for publication, but that she would prefer a man who sculpts for commissions!"

No longer amused, Astera whirled on her heel away from Weston, throwing back that she'd had enough of his advice and his concerns in her affairs. "Since I've had the misfortune to meet you, everywhere I turn I find myself the victim of your managing. And do not be deceived that I am not aware of your manipulation of my guardian. This entire junket I am certain is to fulfill some objective of yours!"

As if surprised with himself for having betrayed any emotion, the Viscount was once more firmly in control. "Indeed," he drawled, "this trip is to assure two objectives of mine—first that we all have an enjoyable time in Greece and thus I repay my obligations to Lord Winthrop, and second, conclude my own interest . . . for Greece's liberation."

"That is a noble cause," Astera continued, catching the cue from him and trying to calm herself down as well. "But in the land of such splendid statues—of Phidias and Praxiteles—can you really be so scornful of artists and poets here in a land where Socrates and others have claimed a poet has in him the divine madness to achieve a truth otherwise unattainable!"

"Yes, in this land where the 'divine' Plato expelled poets from his ideal Republic as a menace to civil order—because an artist can 'at best decorate life and at worst threaten *morality*.' "

"Your *morals* shall suffer no danger from mine, my lord! Nor from any written word . . . or piece of sculpture!"

"As you have given very little evidence of their respectability since you arrived in Athens—rather the reverse—one would have to seriously question them and *you*."

"No, I say, W*es*! Astera's morals like everything else about her are dashed top form!"

Both the Viscount and Astera turned in surprise at Cuffy's interjection. They had in their intentness forgotten his presence. Trying to collect herself, Astera looked round her and then, putting her hand out to Lord Cuffsworth, she attempted to wipe the anxiety from his face.

"As usual, Cuffy, you are there to defend me when needed. And to bring me down to reality."

Cuffy bowed at this tribute. "Delighted," he murmured. "That is . . . certain you don't need defense. Wes don't really think you are that bad. Do you, Wes?"

The Viscount, still out of humor by the exchange, could just manage to assure him and to bow coldly to Astera before finding Sybil to join her in the admiration of her sketch.

The days in Greece continued with Astera and Viscount Weston staying apart. Neither was prepared to again experience the discomfort of another such meeting. Astera was too busy finishing up fittings for her extensive wardrobe, which somehow had begun to include all manner of "essentials" that went way beyond the travel outfits she'd first thought would be sufficient. Spring was approaching and certainly Astera would wish that season's outfits to bear the same stamp as her winter ones. Who else but Mr. Stamnos and Andreas had a true version of her and could so well translate it? And as for evening wear—there was some talk of the Resident's giving a ball for all the visiting foreigners—something for that should be planned. And hats . . . and reticules and fans. The sum, when she received it, was staggering; and she had to apply with dread to her guardian. Thankfully Lord Winthrop thought the expense well worth it and was even willing to basically take over the whole amount— which Astera would not allow. Her aunt, as well, had several dresses designed by Mr. Stamnos—but finding them too young and not in the "usual style admired by Arthur," she refused to wear them.

As for Lady Marvelle and her lord and sister—all were totally occupied by their sittings for Andreas. All were to have busts. Thus, the meetings between the two groups declined and were admittedly limited to occasional dinners—pushed for by Lord Winthrop. Sybil and her sister were pleased to discover that Andreas had not suggested a carving of Miss Claybourne, and they took that as a compliment to themselves, which praise— considering Astera's improved looks—was much needed by both ladies. But while silenced on Astera's appearance, the sisters continued to make remarks about her manners. She had been observed sitting comfortably in the kitchen with Kyria and even going shopping for food in the markets with that Greek *servant*. And if their ears did not deceive them, that . . . that "Kyria" addressed her as "Asteroula" even when serving—and Astera had not reprimanded her! Indeed, had not been aware of the solecism, till Lady Marvelle tactfully pointed it out—at which point she merely informed them that "Asteroula" was an affectionate way of saying her name, and she was rather honored by the feeling! Weston, when informed of this, continued in his recent habit of refusing to join them in criticizing Miss Claybourne, but rather just looked black and distracted for a few moments.

Astera, even in thought, distracted Weston more than he could explain. In her presence, it was unbearable. Therefore, he did not attend any of these joint dinners. His excuse was his preparation for the trip to Missolonghi. Since he did not wish to trust his *Hawk* through the Isthmus of Corinth, he arranged for two small Ionian vessels to take the party from Piraeus through Corinth (avoiding Patras, which was under Turkish control) and continue to Missolonghi. However, in the interim, Lord Winthrop was taken down by an intestinal disorder, and Miss Minerva Claybourne, although anxious to meet the legendary Byron, elected to remain to give him her most devoted care. She would have prevented Astera's going as well after being told by Kyria that Missolonghi was "very unhealthy place—full of swamps and sickness and rain," but Astera was determined. Another loss to the party: Lady Marvelle, for Andreas, up to this point, had been too occupied with sketches of Sybil to get an adequate supply of hers. Further, Andreas did not believe it would be safe for himself to go into the *western* part of Greece where many people would be prepared to end his life because of his association with the rival Odysseus! At that declamation, Lady Marvelle *insisted* he remain behind, and she would stay as well, and they could devote themselves to the study of her face. Andreas was delighted to do so.

Lord Marvelle, however, could not resist the opportunity of meeting that demon lord. He would go—he owed it to his friends. He would dine out on the episode for months after their return! Thus, the party to Missolonghi was now to consist of Lord Marvelle, Astera, Lord Cuffsworth, Sybil and the Viscount. Five in all—plus of course Sybil's maid and Lord Marvelle's valet. The Viscount assured them that there was no need for either servant on such a short trip, that they would be just staying overnight and returning the next morning, but the two were adamant on not advancing anywhere without the administrations of their Rose or Fineus—respectively.

And somehow it developed that both these servants and the luggage would be joining Lord Cuffsworth and Astera on one boat, while Miss Farnshorn and Lord Marvelle and the Vis-

count were to go ahead in the larger of the two. It had been
Lord Marvelle's suggestion and surprisingly the Viscount, not
wishing to be in Astera's presence for so long a time, had
agreed.

They came together at Missolonghi. Cuffy was filled with
praise of the trip. Astera, as well, had thoroughly enjoyed it. "By
Jove," Cuffy exclaimed to Weston, "did you know all the
fighting and such that took place along this same route? There's
a gorge filled with skeletons of an Ottoman cavalry group still
astride their skeleton horses—about five thousand ambushed
and slaughtered by the mountain Greeks, and the bones are still
there bleached white! And other such wizard stories. Chap had
long moustachios that went up and down at each exclamation
and, stab me if I could stop myself from laughing—though Astera was cross with me for interrupting the flow. She was busy
translating, and it appears he was in some of these *very*
skirmishes, and after a while, didn't those moustachios begin to
look good to me! Might grow 'em myself—what? Cause a sensation on Bond Street! Told us lots of Englishmen are here joining in the fighting and wearing them as an insignia. Some capi-
tal story about an 'Englisher'—he called him—given flack for
wearing those moustachios by his home regiment who clipped
them and sent them by mail to the officials objecting—or some
sort of protest . . . didn't get it straight 'cause Astera kept interrupting to point out some dashed bit of a rock or tree till I told
her what I thought of views and stuff. But, that aside, it was top
drawer!"

Weston testily exclaimed that he, however, was particularly
fond of scenery and should have wished to have seen some of it,
but Lord Marvelle, it appears, was not a very good seaman.

"By George, yes," said Cuffy with a grin. "And his wife's another. You should have been with us on the *Hawk*. He was sick
all over the place. Was he again?"

"Yes," Weston said shortly. "And it is a good thing we both
brought a change of clothes."

"Ah . . . thought you was wearing something different. Better let him travel back with his valet. Come aboard with Astera and me. We had a grand time!"

Somehow Cuffy could not understand why that last was too much for Weston—why he simply muttered and turned on his heel to rush preparations for the carriages to take them to Lord Byron's.

CHAPTER 11

It was raining, and they were told it had been raining for some days. Rose rushed up with her parasol to keep the drops off her mistress, but Sybil—whose coquelicot ribbons on her bonnet were not the only things beginning to droop—was finding Missolonghi a place of "monstrous discomfort!" In this she was joined vociferously by Lord Marvelle, wondering what kind of place Weston had brought them to! Cuffy began enjoying himself by pointing out the rivulets of water in the streets as the curricles splashed on, which became even more enjoyable as it brought squeals of dismay from Sybil about her shoes and Lord Marvelle, his boots. There was an inordinately large puddle before Lord Byron's house, which was established on the margin of the shallow, slimy sea waters. Not only were shoes and boots ruined but hems and breeches as well as they leaped their way across mud and dust to enter the house.

Inside appeared to be more of a barracks than a private home, for it was filled with soldiers. Further, swords and Turkish sabers, dirks, rifles, blunderbusses, bayonets and helmets . . . and yes, even trumpets were hung on all the walls, but particularly so in the receiving room or sala where they waited, the suspense rising.

More delay. There were several Englishmen in uniform— young adventurers who, along with the Germans and French, had attached themselves to Byron's group as sort of a chosen guard. He also had had a personal bodyguard of fierce Souliotes (they were told by the Englishmen present), but those same Souliotes had mutinied a few weeks back just as Lord Byron with two thousand troops was set to launch an attack on Lepanto. Actually when he'd given the order to march, his own Souliotes had refused! In fact, they had murdered one of the young volunteers from Germany and reduced Byron to such fury he had nearly had an epileptic fit. Turned out they'd been bribed by the other Greek faction to prevent the western Greek forces from gaining ascendancy. In the end, Byron had had to bribe the Souliotes himself so they'd leave off guarding him. But the planned attack was suspended—which was a good thing for his visitors or there would have been no one in Missolonghi to visit!

Flabbergasted by all this information and the red-capped Greek soldiers who kept passing by and staring rudely, Lord Marvelle and Sybil appealed to a friendly Scot, Dirk Mackensie, who assured them that the Souliotes were actually *Albanian*, and anyway, no longer here—that these were authentic *Greeks* and friendly . . . of a sort. But since they looked just as fierce and foreign, neither of the two were reassured. And considering the weather and the damp and Lord Byron's keeping them waiting, both members of the ton were beginning to suspect this would not be the tea party they'd been supposing when suddenly the floor began to shake!

It lasted but a few seconds, but Sybil was on the floor, Lord Marvelle and several recent adventurers from England found themselves nudging each other aside in their fright to get out of the door and windows. Cuffy was jumping up jubilantly saying, "An earthquake!" The Viscount had gone quickly over to offer assistance to Astera, who merely laughed and assured him she was accustomed to them from her last trip. He bowed politely and assisted Sybil from the floor.

In a short time a pretty little girl of eight or nine years, with large black eyes, ran by—only to be spat on by a Greek soldier. "Turkish," Dirk, the tall, bony Scot, interpreted. "Lord Byron released some Turkish prisoners and sent them to friends, but Hato there wanted to stay with us and begged so prettily. All women want to stay with our lord-poet. He plans to give her to some English lady—perhaps you?" He turned his prominent eyes toward Sybil, who shrank back at the suggestion—while Lord Marvelle leaned forward over Byron's interest in this "little girl." And all the time Hato continued to run around the room, indifferent to people's reactions to either her nationality or sex; she only stilled when Lord Byron himself entered and gave her a pat on the head.

At first view of him, Astera had to own herself surprised. Lord Byron was dressed in a military jacket, and it, as well as the rest of his attire, was so ill-fitting and so rumpled, he made a marked contrast to the Viscount, who even in these circumstances could not be mistaken for anything but an English lord on Bond Street. Nor was the poet as tall as she imagined him, and frankly, he seemed slightly under the weather. As if anxious for one not to notice his lameness, he walked in hurriedly with almost a skip and was soon sitting down with one foot concealed behind the other. He greeted the Viscount as a good friend, and they discussed the news of the loan; and he was polite enough to pretend to remember Lord Marvelle when he claimed acquaintance, say some gallantries to Sybil about a bit of "English beauty," and then turn to Astera.

"You, I am the most afraid of," he said in his low, distinct voice. "I've been told that you are a rhymster like myself, and there is nothing more frightening to a man than a beautiful woman who commits her impressions to paper!"

Astera laughed and assured him he had nothing to fear from her. To which he allowed he'd been written and written over by many a woman and man, and no longer feared for himself on that score. But that he feared, indeed, for his susceptibility to an intelligent woman—"especially one who speaks Greek, reads my works and further has a name that begins with A!"

Astera laughed at that conclusion and soon discovered that Lord Byron liked nothing better than to laugh, so she relaxed and began to be playful with him. Most of all she wished to know the significance of her name beginning with A. "Is it just an alphabetical predilection or is it the phonetic sound that appeals?"

With a smile from his full lips, the lord assured her seriously that as fate would have it, most of the women he'd ever totally loved had names that began with an A. "One was an unfortunate connection, but the rest I can only speak of with gratitude. There is my daughter, Ada, and previously my natural child, Allegra—who has left us. Most close to me, my half-sister Augusta. There! Is it not alarming for a Philhellene to meet, in the midst of this war and treachery and sickness, a young English girl named *Astera*. Would you not think it meant something in my stars?"

As he spoke Astera was no longer aware that one gray eye was larger than the other, nor that the beautifully molded face and dark hair, made darker yet with oil, were showing the effects of age with, respectively, extra lines and the onslaught of gray. . . . She was aware only of his soft, seductive voice, and she gave him one of her heartfelt smiles that had him looking up in surprise to Weston and whispering, "But you did not tell me about this young lady's beauty!"

"Is it from . . . him . . . I mean from Viscount Weston that you heard about my writing . . . and *name* . . . and such?" she asked quickly.

But Lord Byron, exchanging a quick helpless glance with the Viscount, assured her that he needed to be told by no one—that he had dreamed her, and there she was! Here Astera eagerly mentioned his own conclusion that dreams became a "portion of ourselves," and he, delighted to have that poem so well recollected, was discussing it with pleasure when Sybil interrupted.

"My lord would do me a favor—as one English person to another?"

Lord Byron was instantly all attention.

"I would request you order that man to stop staring at me. It is odious."

All turned to see a Greek soldier gazing in her direction.

"*Stamata*," Byron ordered and waved him out. He then

apologized for the manners of the locals. "In his defense I daresay he has probably never seen so lovely an English maid and was just committing her features to memory."

Sybil sighed and complained she'd found herself much harrassed by Greek men . . . and, indeed, by all nations of men.

"It is a problem you must learn to bear . . . as I have had to learn to accept the attentions of ladies."

Sybil didn't know how to take that, but Astera laughed, and Lord Byron turned with glee to her.

"You must have heard how harrassed I am by the fair sex?"

"Not only heard," Astera put in, "but *read* about it . . . and read about it in your own works."

Byron agreed he had not been sufficiently modest; and Astera asked him which did he prefer the attentions of, ladies or reviewers—which had him laughing and agreeing there was a similarity. "They either stroke you or spear you, and neither know when to leave you alone."

Fletcher, Lord Byron's manservant, came in with some refreshment, but it was sparse, and Lord Byron, taking just a bit of arrowroot, claimed he was not in the best of appetites, although seeing Astera . . . and, of course, Miss Farnshorn, had done him a world of good.

They were about to depart when Lord Byron handed a small volume to Astera and wrote something on the flyleaf, and as Astera whispered something, he laughed and plucked a few hairs off his head and placed them also within the book. They were continuing their private talk in the corner by the window for a good while, when he leaned over and kissed her lips—once, gently—and then stepped back.

The Viscount was no longer smiling when he took his leave of the lord, but Byron shook his head at him. "You have a whole life to enjoy her . . . I shall probably never leave this place, you know. It was . . . like kissing adieu all the beautiful women I have known . . . all the women named A— ah!"

And Weston had relented and promised to renew his efforts for the loan, and they laughed over the large quantity of trumpets the London committee had sent as supplies, "as if the

Greeks could blow the Turks down like the walls of Jericho!";
they spoke further of Byron's own monies being used for
supplies, and he dryly concluded it was better playing "at nations than gaming at Newmarket!" A few more polite phrases
to Lord Marvelle and Miss Farnshorn and . . . the visit was
over.

Astera was too busy reading the flyleaf of the book and stroking her relic to listen when Sybil on the first leg of the journey
back to Athens remarked about "the unseemly way Miss Claybourne had put herself forward" during the visit, but they had
given passage to Dirk and since he seemed very assiduous in his
attentions, Miss Farnshorn soon forgot Lord Byron's inatten-
tion.

That night when they rested on land, Cuffy and Dirk and
Weston were the only ones not anxious for their beds. Dirk especially was delighted to have a new audience for his many
tales, all falling under the general heading of "Dirk's Successes
in Love and War."

At one time he interrupted his monologue to ask the gentlemen if Miss Farnshorn were committed to either of them. And
when Cuffy volubly assured him to the contrary, and Weston
quietly eschewed any connection, he relaxed and concluded:
"Then she is just the kind of lady with whom I should wish to
start a flirtation! *So English!* Not like these Greek girls who are
so quiet one moment and the next, like earthquakes, they've
knocked you off your feet. Fatiguing—all that, what? Byron
warned me against Miss Farnshorn, by the by, before I left—
seems she reminded him instantly of a certain nemesis of his
who was always remarking on how the "boys followed her" and
"how many men admired her"—things, he said, one forsooth
would not expect to prate of after sixteen or so. But I'm a lazy
fellow and rather like a gel like that 'cause I know exactly what
she wants without having to bestir my brains!"

After a few more judgments on several other people from
Byron to Mavrocordatos to the Greek serving girl passing, he retired, much pleased with the discussion, leaving Cuffy to consider why Weston had made no effort to disabuse Dirk of

Sybil's availability. But since his friend was no longer pursuing Astera, he felt it not his place to question the status of his latest flirt. Wes's entire attitude in Greece had been a puzzle to Lord Cuffsworth. Witness now, this normally confident, cheerful man was sitting morosely staring at the fire, not even aware that Dirk had left . . . and, indeed, had had to be poked several times during the discussion to force a comment out of him.

Disgusted, Cuffy chided, "You're as silent as Astera. Can't get a word out of her either!"

"It seems only poets and Greeks can awake that lady," Weston murmured bitterly. And Cuffy, considering how worried he'd been by Astera's spending so much time with Andreas and her moonstruck reaction to Lord Byron, could not but sadly agree.

As if in proof of the Viscount's pronouncement, Miss Claybourne on the return trip sat on deck holding the book of poems against her chest and staring sightlessly toward shore— whether she was thinking of the poet or of Andreas waiting for her, Cuffy could not tell, but he definitely regretted traveling back the second half alone in her company rather than joining Dirk and Sybil and the Viscount. (Lord Marvelle was there but thankfully spending the trip in the cabin with his valet.) Thus, there was no one with whom to converse! And Cuffy liked a bit of chatter. By Jove, he was even tempted to try out his Greek on the sailors, but after a few attempts which had them grinning and nudging each other and bringing him water or tea whenever he tried to ask "What's new . . . or *Ti nea?*" his conversational conviviality deserted him.

Two days following the return from Missolonghi, Astera, after reviewing Byron's poems, was in despair over the reaction to her *Idyll in the Isles*, since by now it should have had its baptism by the critics. Another thought that overset—why she had not received an *answer* to her letter to Mr. Millbanke, asking about the reaction, and asking for a volume of her work. She would have liked to have had one to send to Lord Byron to reciprocate for the one of his he had given her, according to the old custom of "from one author to another," but then he had said something about his publisher often sending him new authors to provoke him "to write a new *English Bards*." Recollecting that and flushing, Astera was relieved that she had not had her work with her, because so anxious for his opinion had she been, she just might have dared—and embarrassed them both.

She recollected with gratitude, however, Weston's having paved the way for her, since he it must have been who had either written or, in his first meeting, mentioned *her* to Lord Byron—so perhaps he was coming round on his prejudice against women publishing. Certainly some change must have resulted from just seeing that the great poet himself had not treated her as beyond the pale!

But Astera was mistaken. And part of the Viscount's chagrin and silence after the meeting with Lord Byron was that while it was indeed *he* who had informed the lord about Astera's writing, he had been relying on that poet's reputation for savaging new writers. He'd heard of his reaction to Keats and a good many others—none had been exempt from his acid tongue. And so Weston, inserting a few judicious phrases in his letter arranging the second meeting, had hoped to prepare Byron to meet a "lady poet," and further recollecting that lord's problems with another lady writer—Lady Caroline Lamb—he fully expected him to discourage Astera if not destroy all such ambitions in her forever! And to have found him, instead, *pleased* with her, and even going to the extent of giving her a copy of his poems with a complimentary dedication "to a fellow poet" was exactly what he would *not* wish! In fact, Lord Byron had gone so far as to speak of wishing to see her work—to which Astera had had the good grace to imply she would not dare expose her minor efforts to his great light—and he had laughed and replied that while his publisher had often sent him trash, he would look forward to receiving one of hers as one looked forward at night to seeing the shine of the other *"asteria,"* or stars. A few more hours there alone with that man, and the Viscount was certain Miss Claybourne would have become the latest on-dit about the "mad, bad and dangerous-to-know" lord. Thus, he had rushed them out, refusing Byron's invitation to stay the night with an embarrassingly inane remark about the "damp of the place," which, rather than making Byron laugh as he expected, brought a surprisingly dark look to that lord's face as he agreed that it was doing no good to his constitution, that, by the by, he had recently been quite ill and was not totally well yet—which doubtless explained why Byron had made no effort to keep Astera. For the Viscount was certain—the slightest effort on the poet's part would have had her easily encamped in Missolonghi for the duration of Byron's battles. Certainly if she had so little taste that she was responding to Andreas, Lord Byron would have been at least worthy of winning her. In other words, the Viscount was tortured by questions of Astera's virtue and found himself fluctuating between these jealous fantasies and convictions of her honor. Therefore, since their return to Athens, he had—in his attempt to lessen Andreas' influence—hoped to rush them all aboard the *Hawk* for the Greek Isles trip, but Lord Marvelle's reaction to sea travel and Lady Marvelle's absorption with her bust and Sybil's flirtation with Dirk left them all very pleased to remain on land.

As for Astera, Viscount Weston tried to avoid her, for when she was in a room his thoughts could not attend to other objects or discussions; it seemed she concentrated his whole senses. In fact, even when she was *not* present she had somewhat that effect on him. The devil take her! Here he was spending so much thought on her while she was probably content laughing with Kyria or Cuffy or writing some more doggerel . . . or off with Andreas!

And, indeed, during the following week, the Viscount would have been proved correct on all of his conjectures, including the last. Astera and Andreas, having finally managed to elude Lady Marvelle for the day, were together.

It was March, and Astera could sense spring coming. She hoped they would be here for Greek Easter, which she recalled was a momentous event, everybody out roasting lambs and joyously celebrating the resurrection of Jesus, but that had been in the Parnassus Mountains where presently there was much fighting going on.

Andreas was walking with her in the garden and both were looking for signs of new life and Andreas was telling her all about his fighting with Odysseus for the hundredth time. They had reached the point in the story when the musket ball had whizzed by him to hit an Englishman, when Kyria came running in with a package.

"From England—all the way this comes. And so big. What could be in it?" Her olive eyes were revolving with curiosity, and Astera assured her she could remain while it was opened. Andreas too, like a child, was anxious to open the package. It was this characteristic that had first attracted her so much—this enjoyment of the little things of life and the demonstrating of one's feelings—so opposite to the Viscount, who would have bowed and left her her privacy to open the package. Instead, it became more enjoyable by their joining in—even though all three began getting in each other's way, cutting the same cords twice and quickly tearing away at the brown paper, and laughing when the package fell and opened by itself! They all stared. The look of disappointment on Kyria's face when Astera picked up five books could only be equalled by Cuffy.

"Just books," the lady moaned. "Nothing pretty . . . nothing important."

"Yes, books," Astera said softly, stroking one and then another. "But very . . . very pretty, Kyria . . . and very, very important. For you see, it is *my* books."

Kyria was instantly impressed. "You write all these?"

"Well, I wrote a book, and these are several copies of it." And she was lost in the pages and the wonder. Now she had a volume to send to Lord Byron—and the thought terrified as it excited her. Andreas was carefully examining one—ohhing and ahhing—which could not help but gratify Astera. In fact, he was more overcome than she. And, as he was always looking for an occasion for a celebration, he instantly proclaimed this as one, suggesting a party for all to come and honor her!

Kyria was caught by the idea. A celebration! *She* would personally arrange everything. Everyone was to come and see how brilliant and beautiful was her Asteroula!

Although pleased by the fuss, Astera hastened to assure them the *last* thing she wished was the Marvelles and the Viscount present to ruin her moment. Rather, she was sufficiently happy to spend it with the two of them. And both were so moved by this tribute, they joined her in shedding a few tears. In another moment, Kyria was off arranging at least a small party with celebration cakes for the three of them and "the good aunt," who would wish to be present. And to that, Astera glowingly agreed.

There was a letter included—containing several favorable quotes from one or two periodicals. Realistically, Astera sensed Mr. Millbanke was trying to show her the best possible response, but she would not quibble over his generosity. Time enough when she was home to read the scathing criticism which was certainly awaiting there.

But for this moment she would just enjoy the "well phrased" and other quotes, which included one that spoke of her passages as having "such an amorous intensity one overlooks the deficiency in rhyme." Well! That brought her up short and made her laugh—imagine how hard-pressed Mr. Millbanke must have been if he had to include that one!

And thus absorbed in pleasant and nonpleasant thoughts, she was only dimly aware that Andreas was complimenting her still, and that he had been holding her hand for some time, but she made no protest, feeling it was a thing of the moment—a sharing of her excitement—and did not realize the impropriety of walking around the pine-fenced outer edge of the garden alone with Andreas till he embraced her. Hoping it was just another expression of joint good feeling, Astera was gently disengaging herself when she realized, with a sense of panic, that he would not release her.

"Andreas!" she called sharply, but his lips were occupied in making a winding trail of passion from her neck to her chin, murmuring Greek endearments and groans. The disconcerting thing was that he did not seem to be aware of her protests, either verbal or physical, or rather, he was so intent in his own emotion that he was unaware it was not being reciprocated! Screaming in his ear caused him momentarily to lift his head, and his hold loosened just enough for her to wrench away.

"Andreas, you know it is rather wrong of you to take advantage of my distraction this morning!"

"Wrong! Have not you distracted me for all these years and have not you finally driven me *past distraction!*" he gasped in fury. His shifts of mood from joyousness to fierce anger had not been previously taken to heart by Astera, but now she was wary of his strength and tried calming him down with talk of the party and his sculpting . . . but he was not diverted.

"Ah, why did you come *back* if it was not to see *me* . . . why did you come to torment—if only to run again? You think my heart, it is so hard that you can stamp all over it, and I will not feel! That I can see your face—"

"Andreas!" Astera cried out, trying to prevent his working himself up. "Now be calm. I did not come back to *you.* Recollect now. I did not get in touch with you. We are friends . . . and I tried to help you by bringing you commissions with the Marvelles and not mentioning your ready-made goddesses, did I not? And I brought your friend Mr. Stamnos business—"

"My God, what is all this talk of business! Are we ledgers that you try to add and subtract and balance on me? We are *people* and I speak to you of my *heart* and you answer—"

"I speak to you of my friendship . . . because that is all I have for you . . . and you are very well aware of that . . . so please do not enact me this unseemly scene of tragedy—"

"You are so cold, you are so . . . so . . . so *English!* Where are your emotions, your feelings, that you could treat a man like this?"

In exasperation Astera sat down on the marble bench and looked up at him resignedly, just managing to keep her voice patient. "Andreas, you are *not* in love with me. I do not feel love from you. . . . Why, I feel more from one glance from the Vi—" she caught herself as she realized what name she was about to mention, but not in time.

"Now I understand," he fumed. "You are after this . . . Viscount, and he is too interested in that Sybil. So you use me to get his interest all wet, correct? You *use me*, Andreas Jason, to play with, while you prefer that tall stick of a man! *Me*—who women have rightly called 'Hermes' . . . and 'Apollo' . . . and have begged of me a lock of my hair to sleep under their mattress . . . and, and pregnant women to put under when they labor, to have such sons as *me!* And *I* am not enough of a man for you? Or is it that my title—the title of a *man* and *warrior* and a *Greek* is not enough for you! Because you prefer to be a Viscountess!" Catching his breath and her hand in one more attempt, he exclaimed in a softer, more cajoling tone, "But . . . then, perhaps you do not know *how* I could love you. Once you did, you could never refuse me . . . never deny me . . . you would beg for me . . . as *I am begging to you now!*"

Seeing him move suddenly, Astera assumed he was going to get on his knees, but it was she who was pulled to her knees and flat down on the marble bench. Their extremely intimate position and his intimate kisses surprised her into a momentary feeling of excitement, but almost immediately she struggled so decisively, they both rolled off the bench, and, thus entwined, into the bushes.

"Why are you children playing in my bushes!"

Minerva Claybourne's plaintive tone had Astera quickly up, followed by a somewhat slower and more reluctant Andreas, who had to lean for a moment against an accommodating giant pine tree. Ignoring them, Minerva rushed quickly to inspect her bushes.

"Quite an effort to get these shaped just as I wished, I can only hope they have not come to any harm. Rolling about in them, indeed! Astera, shall you *never* grow up?"

Astera quickly apologized. Andreas stiffly bowed to the lady, but unable to do or say more than that, he made a quick exit. At which point Minerva Claybourne smiled at Astera and whispered, "It seemed a rather fortuitous point to interrupt, child. But I expect it would be best not to be alone with these foreigners. They do not have the control of an Englishman."

Too startled to do anything but nod, Astera, picking up her

books, retired to her room to mull over and gasp at the afternoon's events: at her aunt's control just when one expected spasms; at Andreas' unreasonableness and passion, and finally at her own disordered emotions—half frightened, half delighted . . . and lastly, totally shamed. To have been caught rolling in the bushes like a scullery maid showed a want of dignity that she was positive would have given the Viscount a disgust of her —if he had seen! And then she wondered what it would have felt like to be rolling in the bushes with the Viscount, and that image of him in such a situation was so incongruous—with his correct manners and concern for his clothes—that she could do nothing but laugh . . . a bit ruefully.

Andreas Jason did not recollect the scene either with humor or embarrassment—rather total fury. While cutting the last expression lines on Lady Marvelle's Hera statue, his hands began to shake and he made several glaring mistakes. "*Sto diavolo!*" he cursed and walked to his window to stare out at the square and seethe. To control his trembling hands, he fingered his *komboloy*, the worry beads going, clicking away, in soothing monotony. The beads were dark like Astera's eyes and her *heart!* And like the Viscount's black heart as well! All *blackguards,* these English, amusing themselves in his country—stripping it bare of its glories and then coming here to take its land as payment for this so-called loan! Pretending to be seeking his country's freedom and wresting total control over his land instead. Just as they had already done with the islands of Zante, Corfu, Cephalonia, Ithaca and Cythera . . . and made them all a protectorate of Great Britain! Ah, they would "protect" them all right—as the Viscount would protect his Asteroula! . . . And there was nothing he could do . . . as there was nothing Greece could do. You fought and freed yourself, and *there* were the English—swooping down, taking all the credit—sending men who demanded, under the guise of unity, that the Hellenes abandon their own several authorities to be "unified" under them. Those *English*—sending *poets* and *fops* and *egotistical ladies* who felt their *titles* gave them a closer connection to the

Greek gods of antiquity, not realizing that they were Greek gods and Greek goddesses with Greek characteristics that gave the meanest Greek scrubwoman more of an authentic connection with the Olympian elite! Certainly more than those who knew only the *status* of the gods and none of their *stories* of fighting . . . loving . . . *revenging!* Yes, revenge! And he, in true Hellenic style, would revenge himself on all the English, especially on the Viscount with his "loan" and his desire for his woman!

The question was, was there a wily way to revenge himself? A way worthy of the original Odysseus—a way where the people's own faults would lead to their fall . . . and one could sit back and watch the destruction . . . like shoving one small rock from a Parnassus Mountain peak on the Turks below and watching that one rock gather others to it . . . and others, till your enemy was totally, gloriously crushed! And the sweetness of it was that you had just exerted yourself to the extent of pushing one rock! But it had to be well-placed! . . . And no one was as good a placer as he—no one else recalled all the rock slides caused by earthquakes in those mountains and thought to use the *very nature* of the place to defend itself against intruders, as Andreas had! And now he would use the *English nature* to rid himself of *their* intrusion.

And then he recollected another relevant stone. When Astera had first left him, he had used his talent to sculpt his revenge by doing a full-figured nude statue of her in marble. And after he devoted so much loving and bitter attention to that work, it developed into the most triumphant piece of his collection, becoming dearer to him than the memory of the original Englishwoman. For that statue would always be his and always the same—with the same half-smile (just enough to intrigue a man) and yet never quite breaking out into laughter (to bedevil a man). But most of all, he loved his "Asteroula" because she was dumb and because he could keep her hidden away in his back room, covered over, as he had kept his feelings for the real Astera—hidden and covered over.

Yet to be honest, he'd almost forgotten her. In fact, two years ago he had married a mountain girl who had fought beside him and lived with him in the caves till she died abruptly in childbirth. As a result, Odysseus himself ordered him back to Athens to forget his loss. And then, like a bolt from the heavens, Astera had appeared to him again, so it seemed to him that the saints were trying to make it up to him for what they had so cruelly taken away. Andreas was certain of it when Astera gave herself over to him completely for a transformation, listening to his every suggestion with total trust. And he had sculpted another goddess out of her. And then, she had turned away from him again, using her transformation for another man. He had planned to show her the statue on their wedding night when Astera and "Asteroula"—both his creations—became one with their creator. Well, now he had returned to his mountain ways —in all aspects. And this sculptured rock would be the rock in his plan of revenge. He would let it loose to work what destruction it would.

Lady Marvelle arrived. And after paying him both in pounds and praise for her bust, she sat down to collect *her* payment—a tête-à-tête. While dutifully kissing her arm, Andreas judged this an opportune time to begin his plan.

Rising abruptly, as if overcome by passion, he urged Lady Marvelle to leave, or he could not be responsible for the consequences. However the consequences were exactly what she had been waiting for, so she remained expectantly present.

Pretending to be getting himself in order, Andreas walked into the inner room where he kept his finished statues, pulled off the covering on "Asteroula" and calmly waited there long enough for Lady Marvelle to become alarmed. Then, with just the right amount of volume to indicate distress and yet still be heard, he groaned.

Lady Marvelle was instantly at the doorway. One moment she was putting out her arms to him, and the next, they collapsed as her eyes bulged out. "Miss Claybourne!" she cried, aghast.

Pretending to be horrified, Andreas made blatantly inept attempts to cover the statue, and yet the cloth kept falling and revealing and revealing.

"It is not what you think. This time I have not seen her. It is from before—that is, this time my heart has been won by another English lady—not that I mean to suggest the word 'lady' could equally apply to you both!"

"I should think not!" Lady Marvelle snapped. "But I knew it! I thought as much when she read us 'indecent' poetry. And subsequently, I found a statue no bigger than my hand in her room, and she said it was of her Greek—"

Lady Marvelle's eyes shot open wide. "But it was you. A statue of *you!*"

As Andreas could recall no statue of himself, he made no response at all to this point, but simply moaned and pleaded that she not expose his Asteroula. What could the poor girl do if her disgrace became known!

Lady Marvelle assured him she would not breathe a word. And after accepting a few passionate kisses on the arm and hand, Lady Marvelle, too anxious to spread the news, did not prolong that moment, but was quickly, gleefully gone. Andreas sat back and picked up the *komboloy* again—his face had the same satisfied expression it was wont to wear when he'd unleashed a rock on the mountainside and could hear it turning into an avalanche. The rock had been thrown.

The next afternoon the avalanche continued to build as Lady Marvelle arrived with Lord Marvelle and the Viscount. The purpose of the visit was for all to see her bust. And when it was sufficiently admired, and the one of Sybil as well, they had the servants carry the statues out. (Lord Marvelle's bust had already been delivered and was proudly perched on the mantelpiece in preparation for its being shipped home.) While casually walking around the studio, Lady Marvelle made a great pretense at sudden hunger, requesting Andreas procure for her some of those delicious "honey cakes" he so often served and which the other day he did not have. She held her breath that he had not bought any in the interim, or that he would refuse to be accommodating, but Andreas was only too delighted to do her errand.

The moment he departed, she invited them all to the interior room to see "some really exquisite pieces." The Viscount, with his usual (of late) glum demeanor, exclaimed that he had quite enough of that man's work and would wait in the carriage for the rest. But before he had reached the door, Lady Marvelle had quickly acted, stepping into the interior room and screaming.

Lord Marvelle and Sybil were there before the Viscount, and more outcries were heard. By the time Weston had straightened out the cause of their alarm and had looked up at the brazenly nude statue of Astera standing before them, Andreas was back with profuse apologies that the shop was closed—and then, horrified by the exposure, he cursed fluently in Greek and English, which had the ladies ready to depart and Lord Marvelle handing them out.

Alone with the Viscount, Andreas made an exaggerated show of slowly covering over his beloved.

"You think I believe this—this trumpery piece!" Weston said coldly. "I'm aware of your little game of changing statues to fit their sitters, and if you imagine I believe Miss Claybourne posed for more than a few distinctive lines in the face, I will as little buy that as I would buy the blasted thing itself!"

"You may indeed buy this—as long as I keep the original, my English lord." Andreas smiled. "I do not care what you believe. I do not have to prove to you that Astera is my woman! For in a short time now it shall be known to the world—because she has written it out . . . in full particulars . . . in this!"

And dramatically he whipped out one of the volumes that had been delivered to Astera. "You see, it has her name. And it is called *Idyll in the Isles*. Look into it. You may have that copy. I have a good many . . . and I have the memories of the original moments. For I am the *idyll* she had here in my Grecian *isles*. *I* am the man she came back to . . . to carry on with our idylling about. You see? *My* woman. A woman of passion, you know, unusual for English. Or perhaps you have already discovered that?"

At that, the Viscount neatly threw him a leveler and walked

out, leaving a startled, cursing Andreas on the floor, surrounded by his statues—who had formed a sympathetic huddle around him.

Some of the avalanche had backed up and hit him, but Andreas was not too concerned, for the sound of the gathering rocks ahead and the tortured look in the Viscount's eyes promised much destruction directly below! He picked up *Idyll in the Isles*, tossed aside by the Viscount, and called his man to immediately deliver it to the Viscount's accommodations, where it would be waiting for him on his return from escorting the ladies. The Viscount would find, as he had, that it was exciting reading, Andreas thought with a smile; and he turned back to carefully cover up his "Asteroula" once more. She had done her job well.

CHAPTER 12

Returning from a morning spent at the Greek museum, Cuffy was complaining to Astera about having had such a "dashed awful time" and how all these statues had been leering at him . . . and at least at Madame Tussaud's the figures wore sensible clothes and seemed more likable, but this had been like walking through "a dashed cemetery" . . . and the ilk.

Astera was laughing and trying to soothe his sensibilities by assuring him she would never invite him along again, when Kyria did not help matters by bringing in as the refreshment Greek black coffee, which Cuffy also despised—claiming that Kyria had probably been digging a pile of dirt and mixed in some hot water and had the nerve to serve it to people—and Astera was hushing him and reading several delivered notes at the same time when she sat up in alarm.

"Good gracious!"

"Whatever's the matter?" Cuffy asked, coming close to her in concern, but Astera was opening the next note, and that seemed to startle her even more. She was almost faint by the time she'd opened the third and last, and then she just put all three in her lap and gazed ahead, stunned.

"Well, are you going to tell me, or am I dashed well going to pick 'em up and read them myself!"

Recollecting Cuffy's presence, Astera whispered, "Guardy and my aunt have apparently left Athens for a few days of business, but they do not say where and why. This first note from Lord Winthrop is filled with excuses and promises of early return, and my aunt's is totally uncomprehensible, about "standing by Lord Winthrop in his hour of need" and assuring me Kyria would take care of me and that I must stay in the house and wait and hope for the best! But the last, that is the worst, because it is *not* undecipherable! It is from Viscount Weston, and he informs me that my guardian has been taken *ill* and my aunt is sailing with him tonight to visit this special physician, but he does not say where! *Ill!* Oh, dear heavens!"

In her extreme agitation, Astera dropped the notes as she jumped up to walk about the room and then had to find them again and read them and sigh, and then murmur at the third one. "He is to be here at six and that is in half an hour." Yet she sat fixed in astonishment till Cuffy recalled her, whereupon she continued, "Listen to this, the Viscount says he shall escort me to a vessel if I 'wish to accompany them.' Certainly I wish! There is nothing that could preclude my attendance. Surely I could be of some use to my aunt if not to my . . . my guardian, but I must not think of that now! The time advances . . . I must talk to Kyria!"

And Astera was off. Cuffy carefully sat down and read the notes. She was right about both Lord Winthrop's and her aunt's. Both incomprehensible—and written under a great deal of emotion. But Wes's communication while neat and controlled did not make much more sense. If Winthrop were ill why not bring a physician here? Why the sudden rush? And why did not they wait for Astera, and take her with them? Her aunt's note claimed they had no idea where she'd gone for the day and whether she'd be back in time—which could answer, but there was something smoky. Cuffy could feel it.

Astera was back and snatching away the letters. "Cuffy, why are you staying? I mean, this is hardly a time for a visit! I've got Kyria packing a few necessities for me, and I'm off!"

"What does that Greek lady say besides 'po-po-*po*,' which I could hear from down here?"

"She verifies that my aunt and guardian had a very serious discussion this morning, and then rushed out . . . that the Viscount was here with them, offering his assistance. But she could not make out what the problem was. And, imagine, Cuffy, they did not pack anything. And yet apparently they had time, since the boat does not leave till after six. Unless that was a later decision, for Kyria says that the Viscount's letter was delivered just an hour ago. So that must mean . . . they rushed off to a physician and finding the results . . ." her voice faltered, ". . . desperate . . . they must needs seek relief elsewhere, and the Viscount obligingly offered to sail them . . . there . . . to get further opinion or immediate aid. Oh, Cuffy!" Astera sat down and suddenly broke into tears. "I am so frightened for them both, I cannot think. Shall I have Kyria pack clothes for them? I've had her add overnight attire for my aunt, but if Lord Winthrop is ill, what shall I pack for him . . . and I am so distraught!"

"No need to get into a pet," Cuffy assured her. "If Wes is in charge, he'll handle things all right and tight. Bound to take care of clothes and such. No need for you to bother. Mean . . . very good at managing is Wes. He'll tell us the right of it when we see him!"

"Oh Cuffy, are you going along?"

"Am I coming along?" Cuffy repeated, dazed. "I dashed well am! Not going to leave you in the suds—all drippy the way you are."

"But you have no necessities . . . no robe . . . no . . ."

"Never saw such a girl for worrying over nightwear," Cuffy interrupted in disgust. "Wear Wes's . . . now just let me think . . . something here bothers me."

"And what about the Marvelles! Are we to go off and leave them?"

Cuffy nodded happily. "Very good idea. Go off and leave them permanently."

"Oh Cuffy, how can you make me laugh at such a moment! I mean surely we must inform them."

"Nothing to inform them," Cuffy insisted. "Don't know anything yet. Wait till we know *what* to inform them."

With that bit of sage advice Astera could not cavil. And so only Cuffy was at her side when the carriage arrived and the Greek driver explained to Astera (in speech almost too rapid for her to understand) that his instructions were to take her and no one else to a dock. When that was translated, Cuffy cried out that he damn well better be included and made such gestures that the Greek shrugged philosophically and drove them both off, accompanied by shouts, prayers and kisses from Kyria.

It was almost dark when they reached the dock, and Viscount Weston was there to rush them aboard. He seemed undisturbed by Cuffy's presence or by Astera's frantic demands to be told the worst, and with calm assurances he informed Astera that her aunt awaited her on the *Hawk*, if she would just follow that sailor. Cuffy was detained by a whisper and a conspiratorial shaking of his head, from which Cuffy understood he would be told the worst privately and anxiously waited behind. At which point the Viscount signaled him into another waiting carriage for the revelation.

Meanwhile Astera, anxiously keeping the seaman in sight, crossed the plank onto the deck—taking only the briefest glimpses of the famous *Hawk* as she hurried on. Before, it had loomed large in the moonlight and menacing, but perhaps that was due to her dread of what awaited her on board. Now all she saw were quick glimpses of conventional equipment: four guns on each bow . . . a netted canopy, tops manned . . . tackle gliding through a seaman's hand. Evidently all preparations were well away for sailing. The wind was up. They stayed for her.

"*Glighora, koritsi!*"

Astera started at the seaman's urging, and he turned it to English, "Rush, rush . . . lady," till she began almost running; her alarm was so high that when he opened the door of a cabin and stepped back for her to enter, she unquestioningly dashed in.

It was deserted.

Assuming she'd been brought to the wrong cabin, she turned back to protest, just as the door was slammed shut and locked in her face. Although her heart began beating in panic, it took her a further moment to accept what had happened. Then, enraged and breaking out into tears of fury, she pounded on the door calling out in Greek . . . in English . . . for Cuffy . . . for her aunt . . . and finally for the Viscount—demanding his presence!

To all, the response was silence—except for the creaking of the boat. She was imprisoned.

It was a night of torture in which Astera had imagined every conceivable possibility while pacing the cabin, knocking down some of the Viscount's library and sea instruments, realizing that somewhere behind all this agony—it was he. As it had always been he!

And when she became aware that they were afloat and out to sea, she once more went running to the door and pounded. Then to the portholes, which revealed the moon on the black Greek sea below. And as the night wore on, all vestiges of land disappeared and left just the black sea. A lamp had been lit in the cabin, but it was beginning to flicker. She moved it from the draft of the porthole, reluctant to be in the dark. Sometimes she stared around. The cabin was larger than those she was accustomed to on board—about seven feet by seven, equipped only with a narrow bunk bed and a small desk and an even smaller chest, so while not much, there was some room for pacing and pace she did, from the door, which she pounded, to the porthole, where she looked for signs of help. And back to pounding on the door. And back to the porthole. And back and forth.

Pounding and looking. Till her hands began to hurt, and she sat down wearily, with a sob, on the bunk.

Were they all in on some kind of plot? Her aunt? Impossible! Cuffy? He had been as much surprised as she by the letters . . . and further, he could never have carried a deception off— there was just not that much deceit in him! But there obviously was in the Viscount Weston—deceit and trickery. And heavens! The cold, calm way he escorted her from the carriage—as if he were handing her in to a social dinner!

Approaching his desk, she, without a qualm, opened the top drawer. Maps and papers there, which she quickly perused, but they were of no assistance to her predicament, no mention of their present destination, nothing! So she picked them all up and threw them out the porthole!

Feeling significantly better by this one act of retaliation, Astera looked about the rest of the cabin for further objects to dispose of. There were several books, which she was quick to also consign to a watery finale. Scott's *Life of Swift* made a swift adieu and Colonel Hippesley's *Expedition to South America* had its last adventure. That anthology was there as well, the very volume which had been so useful to the Viscount at Mayberry—first for setting up Cuffy for ridicule, and then, with the assistance of Romeo's speech, making a cake out of her!—*that* was thrown out with such force, she knocked herself back on the floor and felt dazed for the next few moments and had to lie down on the bunk.

It was not till dawn that she moved from that position, but her thoughts had roamed—to the deck of the ship . . . back to Athens and her aunt and guardian . . . back to England and Mayberry and back to the bunk in this cabin. There was the sound of the lock being turned, and she was up and at the door before it was fully opened. But it was only the same sailor who had brought her here. This time he brought her portmanteau which Kyria had so hurriedly packed. And some food on a tray and a basin of water. Judging him too occupied in putting all those necessities down, Astera felt free to make a rush out the door, but there was another man there who blocked the exit, and between the two, not taking into account that she was a lady, they delighted in pushing her back into the cabin's very center and indicated the food. When she cursed them in Greek, they broke out into laughter, as if she had done something amusing. And then the door was locked again.

Alone once more, Astera went back to her position at the porthole. She was as uncertain of where she was as of *why* she was here! But worst of all, *how could* she be here! How could a gentleman, like the Viscount, have brought her here and treated her thus! Hadn't there been moments of some feeling, of even respect between her and Weston—especially of late. Hadn't they had moments when they had some communication . . . when she felt an understanding unlike any she'd ever felt with . . . say, Andreas . . . and, even Cuffy (although Cuffy was so dear to her). And *how*, considering that, could he be so vengeful as to put her through the torture of this night . . . the concern for her aunt . . . the alarm for her guardian . . . the fear for herself!

Of course, she'd never understood his determination to include her in his life. After her initial rejection, she constantly assumed he'd want to be rid of her forever—as she had of him. And always he'd come back . . . or arranged for her to have to go to him.

Could it all be revenge? Was the fact that she'd turned him down so *unusual* and so *unsupportable* to him that he'd been unable to rest till she'd been put in a position of equal humiliation . . . and after attempting that through words . . . and his society ladies, had he still wished for more . . . had his hatred . . .

At that last word this theory instantly collapsed. There had not been hatred for her from the Viscount—she had felt quite the reverse! Hadn't she even boasted to Andreas that she'd known what real caring was because she'd seen it in Weston's eyes? There had to be another explanation!

Possibly her aunt and guardian *were* on board, and the sailors had misunderstood! Or the Viscount was not here himself to see what was being done!

On these faint rationalizations, Astera, refusing to be cowed, made a good breakfast and repaired her toilette and grimly waited. Explanations would soon come. As long as her aunt and guardian were in good health and spirits, she could take any other circumstance! As long as it related to just herself, she could do something . . . she always had—Viscount or not.

In an hour the same sailor opened the door. This time Astera was ready and had slipped out before he realized, but when he did, he only smiled and signaled her toward the deck, which made Astera pause. Upon concluding that she obviously had been *sent for*, she stubbornly slowed her pace to a more dignified advance.

It was almost high noon and the sun was turning the sheets above her to gold. Wings outspread, the *Hawk* was really flying! But she was not disposed to marvel at the craft. Grimly she looked round about and saw the Viscount at the rail.

There was a difference about him. But where the difference lay she could not immediately discern. And then she knew. His *dress*—of course. Of course, he was wearing a rough sailor's jacket that did not quite fit him . . . and there was no neck-cloth. No elegancies of any kind. Somehow that disturbed her more than if he had been carrying a musket. It suggested he had left behind the elegancies of life and of civilization, and her indignation and prepared demand-for-explanation momentarily were held back by a sensation of fear that was overtaking her. Furious with herself, Astera shook it off and advanced. She was not a girl who had gone through Europe with just a retiring aunt for nothing. She, who had calmly faced Turkish pirates and paid her way free, was not likely to quail in the face of a known and familiar enemy.

"Would you have the decency to inform me how my guardian is, and if he and my aunt are on this ship?" she called out from a distance.

Now it was the Viscount who advanced toward her. Yet the closer he came the more unapproachable he seemed. His face, a stranger to her—as in a nightmare when a familiar object suddenly changes before one's eyes to a fearsome one. Still undaunted, she repeated her question.

"We are alone," he responded in eerie, soft tones. "Your aunt is occupied in impeding your guardian's commission of a great folly—only matched by my own in asking for your hand. Lord Winthrop was about to suggest an elopement for himself . . . and Miss Farnshorn."

Astera started. The embarrassment of the notes now became clear. Her aunt's phrase "I am standing by Lord Winthrop in his hour of need" was now easily explained. It could have been nothing that required vagueness if he were ill, but subtlety, indeed, would be required if his senses were disordered! "Guardy and Sybil!" she whispered incredulously. "But otherwise he is well?"

"Physically well. And your aunt also. By now they have received the news from Lord Cuffsworth that I have abducted you."

"Very obliging of Cuffy to carry that information," Astera said, much amazed.

"He was not anxious to be obliging. I led him to a waiting carriage under the guise of being private with him while I explained matters. And when I did so, he, unfortunately, had to be restrained and held at bay till the *Hawk* weighed anchor. Amazing the way he refused to believe the truth about you. His Astera has not advanced beyond the playmate in the greens of Derbyshire . . . and therefore, he cannot cease playing childish games of hide-and-rescue with you."

Astera could not respond to the points made—so overset was she by the almost masklike face before her and the cold expressionless way he announced, "I have abducted you." Yet that calm voice continued making more pronouncements.

"You are rather talented at playing games, Miss Claybourne. You have had much sport with me all these months—appearing one thing on the surface while underneath . . ." The cold tones threatened to crack here, and she was aware that behind that veneer was an emotion of such fury it leapt and stormed in his eyes and worked around the corners of his mouth. Yet he mastered it and continued again in the same dead voice. "The games you have been playing with that Greek, that *Andreas*, have been ones you most enjoyed—did you not? Ones you boast of . . . to the world!"

It was quite like standing still and allowing a tiger to lick around your feet, needing equally as much nerve to continue in a conversational tone when she could sense the danger slipping closer every moment.

"I have not the smallest understanding of what you are saying! My lord, we have known each other for some time, and whatever our past feelings, surely, as a gentleman, you will explain yourself and your deed. That much decency must—"

"*Decency!*" he roared. Her attempt at keeping him at bay was totally overset by her use of that one word which released him from all bonds. The fury now in his face was unrestrained: "You jade! You conniving strumpet! How dare you use that *word—decency!* How does it not stick in your throat or die of shame on your tongue!"

Astera stepped back hurriedly as if she would flee, but he held her by the wrist. Never having seen him as out of control, she cried, "You are not yourself, my lord!"

"But *you* are *yourself* at last! Unmasked at last. Not an independent lady, not the free, high-spirited, unfettered, unclipped woman you pretended to be, but totally false and conniving. Not demure but debased. Not lacking in decorum but denying all decorum and *decency*. I make you no offer of marriage this time . . . to be refused or accepted. You are not to be given such an honor!"

"Honor!" Astera exclaimed, wrenching away, her anger pushing out the last vestiges of fear. "If you'll recollect, I have again and again refused the honor of any association with you! And I do so again. Dear God, if there was the smallest chance that my feelings might have changed towards you, this . . . this criminal act has ended that forever!" Her eyes were flashing from a full night of terror and worry. "What do you mean by so terrifying me! *And* my aunt! And guardian! By what right do you claim to

do so! Return me at once to port, before the whole world dis-
covers what I have learned: what a depraved—if not deranged—
man you are!"

Her anger seemed to cool down his. And he was back to his
collected self as he languidly leaned against the rail, smiling sardonically and marveling at her. "Yet *another* face, Miss Claybourne? One of outraged virtue is this one? Well done. My
applause and congratulations. But as for your concern for the
'whole world's' opinion, surely you are aware that a substantial
part of it is at present reading about your illicit liaison with that
other poseur—that Andreas. He has revealed all. And speaking
of revelations"—he smiled coldly—"your nude statue has caused
quite a commotion. Lady Marvelle and Miss Farnshorn, however, inform me they are not surprised, because you had a nude
statue of that man at Mayberry! And lest this private exposure
is not enough, I have had the pleasure of reading the most intimate details of your affair in *this!*" And contemptuously he
tossed her the edition of *Idyll in the Isles* sent him by Andreas.

She picked it up. "I thought there was another one," she exclaimed, pleased. "How did you get this?"

"Your *agapetikos*—your lover—boasted of it while revealing
your statue, anxious to make a profit out of the showing."

"Did Andreas charge you for a view of my . . . eh . . .
statue?" Astera laughed, for imagining that scene—especially
the Viscount's shocked expression—was too much for her.

Yet that laughter seemed to finally convince Weston of all he
had been accusing her, and his face once again was white and
taut. "By George, it is true," he whispered furiously. "I still had
hopes there was some mistake . . . that Andreas had hood-
winked you . . . I even considered forgiving and taking you
some place where we could be married to save your name and
reputation, but now it is obvious you are totally corrupt! You
find your lover's tricks—*amusing!*"

"Heavens, if I did not find people such as you amusing, I
should have long since been reduced to a quivering, weeping
woman, which I assure you, both of us would detest! And as for
Andreas, yes, he has always been entertaining," she continued

matter-of-factly. "He is a wily Greek. Do you know those statues are all, if not forgeries, at least juxtapositions? I posed for *no* statue for him—nude or not. Not even a sketch. Nor is Andreas my lover, but like you, another *rejected suitor* who revenged himself on me."

She had the pleasure of seeing him start at that and quickly carried on in the same vein. "But as an English woman, I regret to say even *he* would not go as far as you have done—*you*, one of the first gentlemen of England. No, not even Andreas would be so ruthless . . . so depraved . . . so . . . so . . . *unkind*."

In two steps the Viscount had caught her by the arms and pulled her close to him. "You think I do not wish to believe what you have just said . . . that it was all a lie of that Andreas fellow . . . and even that Lady Marvelle lied when she told me subsequently of frequently seeing the two of you 'together' on arriving for her sittings. But there is *truth* in the poem! The hero *is* Jason—a *Greek* and further, a *sculptor!* And the passion is *true*. It drove me mad when I read it. You often asked me to show my emotions. You demanded I hold nothing back and let my feelings take charge. Well, I have done as you requested. For all the times when you smiled at me as if you could reach my heart—and did reach it—and then rushed away from me. For all the times of showing how much passion you could feel—in the readings, in our discussion . . . in our journey through the antiquities, I shall show you passion now. I have been in a rage of passion for you for months, and only my respect for you has kept me in check. You wished that respect would be gone. You wished exposure of all feelings . . . naked emotions. Well, now you have it, because now, you deserve it!"

While Astera was struggling away from him the book of poems fell and distracted Weston, and he instinctively bent down, but when she instinctively made a motion to retrieve it, he grimly held it aloft out of her reach, and at her demand for its return, coolly threw it overboard.

Astera winced as she watched the volume arching in the sky and heard the splash. "Why would you do such an unnecessary cruel thing?" she gasped.

"You have the tendency to select the most inappropriate word!" he said with a bark of laughter. "I *cruel* for throwing away trash! And what would you call your actions? Is it not cruel to be false? To pretend one thing and be another! To gather a collection of men: Cuffy . . . that Greek . . . and even that degenerate Lord Byron. And I stood by and watched you with your smile and wit weaving your little spell till he was beguiled into pulling a fistful of his hair to give you as a pledge. Dear God, a woman who could entice that jaded poet-lord would have had to be experienced indeed! Yet still I wanted to continue to believe he saw, as I did, the honesty in you and that *that* was what attracted—not the corrupt actress. Well, I daresay, we have done with playacting now—both of us—and let us at last have the honesty to admit our feelings and act upon them. I ask you now to cease your pretense as I have ceased my gullibility about you, and whatever you are, I shall accept you . . . and let society be damned!"

He gave her no time to further refuse him, stopping up her mouth and protests at once—kissing her again and again. And then, even then—when they were breathing as one and senses beating as one—she enraged him further by continuing her pretense of innocence with her trembling and cries to be let go!

"There is no place you can ever go again without me," he whispered. "You shall be mine in earnest . . . with no reserve. For as God is my witness, nothing shall save you now!"

He was about to lift her and carry her into his cabin when Astera cried out in pain and sank to her knees, falling hard on the rough deck where she emitted groan after groan.

Instantly Weston was down beside her asking if he could be of assistance . . . if he could suggest a palliation of her distress! And she whispered there was a vinaigrette in her portmanteau . . . if he would get it . . . or better still give her "the privacy of the rail"!

"You are ill . . . *mal-de-mer!*" he exclaimed incredulously. To which she just hurriedly gestured him away. His training as a gentleman was too intense for him not to retire.

At the rail Astera began swiftly searching about for another ship. There was none. But a rocklike mass was within swimming distance . . . one of the little islands, perhaps uncharted . . . perhaps large enough for a fishing stop. Deciding to risk it, she cast one look backward at the lord, who was properly keeping his head averted and, choking back a laugh, she leaped into the sea.

CHAPTER 13

The sound of a splash turned the Viscount quickly round. Astera was nowhere at the rail. Assuming she had fallen over, he rushed forward, vaulting the rail and plunging into the sea. Calling her name, he dove repeatedly. And then he saw her! In the distance! She was swimming strongly away from him. With renewed rage he realized that she had not fallen—rather she had *jumped!* That entire scene had been just another subterfuge. Now his strokes were propelled by anger. And it developed into a race—very like the one they'd had on horseback in Mayberry. Once again she had the advantage of a head start, but once again he had the advantage of clothing. Her skirt dragged at her, working like an anchor; and once, twice, she seemed to sink and give up, but the sound of his voice and his coming closer spurred her on, and that determination had her pulling ahead till she smashed into a sunken rock. She was looking over her shoulder at her pursuer, but even if she had been staring ahead, the submerged rock would have come up abruptly on her. She sagged. The lukewarm water pushed her down and rose over her head. Bubbles of air exhaled into its density. Her hair floated around her. Unconsciously she was about to replace the breath in her lungs with a full measure of sea, when she was lifted by the hair above the water. Her lungs took in fresh reviving air. And then she was floated, held easily along the top of the sea . . . and finally put down on the rocks.

When Astera sat up and looked round, the island she had

spotted from the *Hawk* was smaller than she'd assumed. No larger than Mayberry's drawing room and dining room put together. Weston was watching her anxiously.

"You're safe!" he whispered thankfully.

"Am I?" she asked calmly. "It was from *you* I was escaping, my lord."

Guiltily and annoyed by her composure, he turned away, staring at the *Hawk* retreating into the horizon, and said crisply, "A simple no would have been sufficient. This"—gesturing at them on the island—"this was quite unnecessary."

Stunned at the sound he heard coming from her, Weston looked at the wet, bedraggled girl before him and realized with a shock that she was laughing at that. And then glancing round at their whereabouts and the awkward position they were in and all she'd been through, and realizing that she could *still laugh*, he began to marvel at her and joined in the laughter as well.

"Dear God, I am sorry," he whispered at last, humbly. "I do not know what possessed me. All these days of reading that *Idylls* thing . . . and my feelings for you . . . and the knowledge that you did not want me."

Thus, the mighty Viscount—totally humbled. Astera never thought she'd see it.

Touching him gently, she smiled ruefully and answered, "I expect I should not have asked you to unleash your emotions! I did not readily perceive you would be so obedient! Andreas also attempted to display his unleashed emotions to me, and when I refused him, I saw how disagreeable lack of restraint could be as well. I daresay one should strive for a happy medium or, as the Greeks so rightly say, *Pan metron ariston.*"

"Then he *was* lying about the two of you? For revenge? Yes, even as you say it, I know now you are telling the truth. All I had to do was look at you again to see the truth, you are so clearly representative of it!"

He sighed deeply, shaking his head at himself. "But I stayed away feeling such misery—more than I ever recollect experiencing in my life—why, the sound of your name alone and the poetry in your book went through me like a knife. And I constantly kept seeing you vanishing from me into other men's arms, and I knew I simply had to prevent that happening."

"But even if it were the truth, you know," Astera said practically, "you had no right to demand an accounting. I never committed myself to you."

"Yes," he nodded, wiping the wet hair from his eyes. "There is *no* excuse for me—none in all God's heaven—but that I could not bear to have Andreas have you. And then when I saw you sinking into that sea and thought you were gone," he groaned, "I would have given anything—given you to Andreas even—just to have you bright and smiling for one moment. . . ."

Astera, pleased at his contrition and grateful for his rescue, still was not beyond another reproof for all he'd put her through. "You should have had more confidence in my intelligence! I saw through Andreas the very first time. Actually he was just around to give you a little discomfort . . . and me . . . a little entertainment. But I could always hold him in check. However, I must own I never expected he would go as far as to sculpt, well, what you said. Of course, being an artist, perhaps he did not think it an insult?"

"His comments about it and *you* were quite unmistakable and foul!" Weston exclaimed, regaining a bit of temper for the first time since landing on the isle.

"Then he was more of a scoundrel than even I imagined. I thought, you understand, he was just after my small independence and future inheritance."

"I acquit him of that," Weston choked, his spirit sinking again, "if any of the emotions you transcribed in your poems came from him."

"Oh no," she replied cheerily. "I just used him as a model in the beginning, and then gave him feelings and thoughts he probably would eschew. And later, I gave my hero some of *yours* as well. I was not particular from whom I took my passions," she teased. "Do you recollect that time we raced back to the stables at Mayberry and you were not chagrined at my win, rather, told me I rode 'like the blazes!' Well, *that* was in it—in the part where the heroine and he race across the seas on the backs of the two dolphins. Also, I took from you those icy gray eyes, and that's why I had her retaliate by turning him into a piece of crystal . . . till the warmth of his . . . eh . . . 'passion' melted him free, you recollect? That imprisoning of you was most satisfying." Lost in the delightful task of explaining her poem to a reader, she was unaware of the startled expression on his face as she continued, "Further, his charge of her being 'more a trickster than a goddess' was also what I would call pure 'Westonian.' With these clues it would probably be enlightening for you to read my poor effort one more time—one never knows when one may find oneself."

Weston grabbed her to him, sensing a reprieve from his agony in these statements. "Then you care for me a bit . . . there is as much of *me* in there as him?"

Astera pulled away from him and responded sternly, "The word I would use is *cared*. Past tense. Since I have been abducted and terrorized, it is not too surprising that you have sunk quite below reproach with me."

"Are you jesting or in earnest?" he whispered tormented. "For I fear you are justified in what you say. And yet if only you would give me a chance to recoup your esteem . . . that is, if I could in some way reestablish myself with you."

"You can," she exclaimed, rising and looking about. "Get us off this rock."

And Weston stood up, laughing with her, attempting still to continue the topic, but she forestalled him by agreeing that although their feelings were "most interesting," it appeared they were in somewhat of a desperate situation, and it really did "behoove us to attempt some solution."

Ruefully Weston nodded. "I can only hope that my crew is not so addlepated as one would assume and will return to seek us out. Or failing that, I daresay, we should make some attempt at attracting attention from another vessel. This is not exactly a forsaken spot. We should be seeing some—" The words were no sooner out of his lips than they heard, "Ahoy, there!"

Weston turned and peered into the distance. A small caïque was approaching.

"At your service, Miss Claybourne." The Viscount bowed as if he had single-handedly materialized the ship from the mists.

"That voice," Astera began. Weston and she were exchanging a glance of incredulity when the sound came again, and they both shouted, "Cuffy!"

Lord Cuffsworth it was, stepping out of a craft so small as to leave one in doubt as to whether it could safely hold them all.

"I say, not quite the place to take a lady, is it, Wes?" Cuffy asked amiably as he stepped ashore, sliding a bit on the rocks before straightening himself out. The seaman with him secured the boat as best he could but began making ominous sounds and gestures to Cuffy—who shook him off and turned to Astera.

"Came to rescue you. Thought I'd have to board the *Hawk*, you know, and settle with this fellow for a bit of underhanded play. Quite prepared to do so. Right now." And he lifted his hands and made rather weak fists in Weston's direction, much to the approval of the Greek seaman behind.

"That's quite all right, old fellow," Wes said languidly. "I surrender her to you at once. I surrender myself to you as well. In fact, we are delighted to see you . . . and most particularly your . . . eh . . . means of transportation."

Confused, Cuffy put his hands down and turned to Astera who readily explained, "Everything is quite all right. I believe the Viscount was playing some kind of prank on us both." Then coming closer and hugging Cuffy suddenly, she whispered, "I knew *you'd* always come to my rescue. Brought your greased sword along?"

Staring from one to the other, Cuffy shook his head. "Beats me what's going on, but, dash it, I'm not going to let *anyone* harm her. I *warned* you about that from the beginning, Wes. Want her to have anything she wants. Would rather it be me . . . but if it isn't . . . I'd be happy to stand by her even if she wants that Greek fellow!"

Astera hugged him once more. And the Viscount said softly, "You shame me indeed, Cuffy. I shall try to learn from you how to be worthy of her. But I'm still hoping she'll have me, old boy. And if not me, I hope you. But, by George, not that Andreas . . . not ever!"

"No, I say, *no* . . . if she wants him . . . she . . ."

"Excuse me," Astera said patiently, staring at the two fighting in earnest as to whom she would or would not have.

"I regret to point out some obvious facts . . . such as that I and Weston are standing here dripping wet . . . and your seaman is getting apoplexy trying to keep your caïque anchored. Further, I have no wish to *have* Andreas, so may we proceed to other topics?"

Weston, laughing, agreed with her, and they quickly entered the boat. It was a tight squeeze and only when the Viscount took over some of the oars did they make some progress.

Lord Cuffsworth demanded to know how they lost *their* ship, since they found *his* so incommodious, and Astera was perfectly willing to explain that she simply jumped overboard—which got a rousing cheer out of Cuffy as he sat contentedly back and watched Weston laboring. "Had a notion you'd know what to do. But had to make the push, you know."

Astera was thanking him once again, and then they had to hear his exploits; how he'd run about trying to find a way of following them and discovered he'd come away with no money and had to pledge his diamond stickpin to this fellow—who assured him he was very good at picking up a trail—but they had to change boats overnight, for the first one had sprung a leak and this one didn't seem as if it could go a much further distance.

"Precisely my thought," Weston was muttering. "But what I am most especially considering is why my Captain Diabolus has not thought to double back in all this time . . . and it is a topic on which we shall have some rather extensive discussions . . . ah, speak of the devil!"

Turning in the direction of the Viscount's gaze, Astera saw the white sails of the *Hawk* in the horizon.

"It appears that they've finally been hit by the realization that they've . . . lost something," Weston murmured, signaling the sailor to turn in the direction of the approaching ship.

They had safely boarded the *Hawk* and all explanations in Greek and English made, when Astera, back in the very same cabin that had so recently held her prisoner, was chafing over a new grievance—the Viscount's holding her in his arms to be pulled up the ropes, as if assuming she could not handle that part herself. Of course she was not dressed for a climb, but still, she would have wished some acknowledgment that she could have handled the task before he blithely swooped her up without a by-your-leave. He had the most "managing" ways! And after all, it was Cuffy who had fallen, and Cuffy he should have taken up in his arms! Quickly changing to the one extra dress she had brought along in her portmanteau—a singularly appropriate sea-green with white foamlike ruffles—she was looking forward to a good hot cup of tea, when she heard a knock on the door.

Both Cuffy and Weston were without. Cuffy was whispering nervously that they didn't wish to intrude but had to discuss a "delicate matter" and did not wish it to be overheard.

Gesturing them in, Astera waited with surprise as the two men seemed to have a hard time disclosing the matter. The Viscount made some allusion to her appearing like Aphrodite rising from the sea foam, and she, dismissing that gallantry, insisted they explain why both appeared so blue-deviled.

Needing no further encouragement Weston stepped forward and said boldly, "Captain Diabolus has the right to perform a ceremony, and it is our opinion that we should be married before returning to Athens. I promise you I shall do my best to make you happy. It shall be my life's goal to—"

"Wait a minute, Wes," Cuffy hotly disputed. "We agreed she had to be married, but I don't see why she can't marry me as well."

Fortunately Astera's sense of humor came to dilute some of the returning anger. "Are you suggesting I marry both of you? Shall it be a three-way service? Or shall I marry first one and then the other!"

"No, dash it, Astera. Mean you marry me *instead* of him. *Have* to be *married!*"

"Indeed," Astera asked, now her exasperation getting the upper hand. "And why do I *have* to marry?"

"*Compromised*, you know," Cuffy finished sadly.

"Oh, I see. Well, you have both done the gentlemanly thing and made your offers. However, I decline."

"Can't decline. Can't be seen in society after this. Everyone will know—"

"Cuffy, will you be quiet and let me handle this!" Weston interposed. Then turning patiently to Astera, "You certainly do not *have* to do anything you do not wish." ("Thank you very much," Astera threw in testily, but the Viscount was smoothly continuing.) "However, you would be doing me such a kindness to save my name from disrepute. I shall never be received if it becomes known I . . . eh . . ., abducted you. However, if we were married, even that great crime shall be forgiven."

Staring at him darkly Astera shook her head. "I am not as gullible as that. I am aware of the rules of society. A gentleman—especially a Viscount of your standing—can do about anything and continue to be received. The blame will undoubtedly be put on me. They shall just assume I led you on. Being a poetess would make it something one would expect from me and probably Lady Marvelle would be delighted to put in some good words for you, and some bad ones for me—about my previous character. No, my lord, I have no fears for you. You shall come out blameless. And further, since we are nearing the start of the new season, a whole batch of new young ladies—diamonds and such—will be on the mart and anxious to accept your hand, girls who shall be very conformable to your social position. New Sybils. Or . . . there is always Sybil herself, if you can tear her away from Lord Winthrop—which should not be difficult, and for which both my aunt and I should be most grateful. So you are free to go your way . . . and I to go mine!"

"There is no possibility of my allowing you to disembark unless you marry me!" Weston shouted, losing his calm again at her contrariness. "I do not give a damn about all the society girls in the world. You know it's *you* I wish to marry. And I'm asking you again, formally . . . with all the words you could possibly wish, Miss Claybourne, *would you do me the honor of granting me your hand in marriage!*"

Thus, the Viscount's second proposal. Astera had the unlooked-for opportunity of giving him a second refusal.

"I tried to explain to you once before that I intend to live my life *free!* I shall be responsible for my life, my career . . . *and* my good name!"

"You do not have a good name any longer!" Weston exploded. "I have taken it away from you. And the only reparation I can make is to give you mine in exchange!"

"You would not then be giving me *my name* back unsullied, just camouflaging it, which is dishonest. I have done nothing to be disgraced about, and I see no reason to act as if I did. Further, I would only marry for love . . . and a sense of wanting to be with one person for the rest of my life, because my life without him would be limited. Not to hide a disgrace . . . not to be *less* of a person, but jointly, the two of us to be *more.* . . . Oh bother! if you can't understand—"

"But I *do* understand, my beautiful girl, and that is exactly what I want," he pleaded. "If you would just give us the opportunity to share our lives together to . . . to . . ."

"*Don't* have to do it," Cuffy put in suddenly.

Both the Viscount and Astera, having momentarily forgotten Cuffy's presence in the emotions of their scene, turned to him in surprise.

"Been thinking," Cuffy said. "Know Astera. She don't like to be forced. Won't force her. We go back to Athens. Say we were all on the trip *together*. Say your aunt was with us. She'll stand by us. No need for Astera to marry anyone but whom she wants!"

"Perfect!" Astera laughed, clapping her hands. "Cuffy, you always have the most perfect solutions. Like the time I was worried about losing my father's edition of Homer's *Odyssey* . . . and you suggested I say he didn't write one!"

"And this solution is about as perfect as that was!" Weston

snapped. "Cuffy, I could give you a leveler for that! The lady was just beginning to consider my proposal!"

"The lady was not!" Astera laughed. "Besides, as you so clearly pointed out to me, I shall no longer be considered a lady after everybody reads my book. In any case, I do not care *that*" —she snapped her fingers—"for what the Lady Marvelles say. Further, I shall deny everything, as Cuffy suggests. And an on-dit shall probably help the sale of my book, and, in all instances be believed only by people who would have already not received me for writing a 'warm book' to begin with! Therefore, may we cease this chatter and let us all go have a good hot cup of tea and enjoy the trip back to Athens!"

Although Astera felt that was the last word on the subject, both Cuffy and the Viscount had a good many more to say, but since she was adamant and cheerfully hushed them both, and disconcerted the Viscount by asking if she could climb to the mast and challenging Cuffy to do it, the topic was quickly changed or deflected. However, the problem remained there in all their thoughts—especially in the brooding eyes of Viscount Weston. Cuffy was assured his idea would see them through. Astera was indifferent as to the resolution, rather enjoying the Viscount's despairing looks. Not that she wanted revenge for her hours of torment when imprisoned in his cabin, but it was a bit of a pleasure to see him so glum and so willing to do any-thing to please her and so uncertain that he could . . . and holding back his temper when she made unreasonable demands, like asking to climb the mast, all because he was trying so hard to prove to her that he would make an ideal husband.

In short, Astera and Cuffy had a grand time and Viscount Weston suffered all the way back. His only hope was Aunt Minerva, that she had already spread the news or that she could work on Astera's feelings enough to persuade her to a marriage with him. His one fear was that that might cause Astera to marry Cuffy instead, and he knew Lord Cuffsworth would be wrong for her. It would be like an attempt to perpetuate her childhood. She was so above that solution. But then, he real-ized, gazing despondently out at the sea, it seemed certain that his headstrong actions had as surely wrecked his relationship with her as if he had purposely run his ship aground.

Coming to stand next to him, Astera whispered gaily, "Well, we can henceforth at least no longer be enemies, is that not so, my lord? Lost on an isle together, as we were?"

But Weston stepped coldly away. "You shall someday discover, Miss Claybourne, that love is not something to laugh off. Though you write a 'warm' scene, it obviously does not come from the heart. Or you could not dash a man's hopes to bits and then think we could play at being children—like Cuffy and yourself. I played no games when I told you I loved you. I loved you when I thought you were immoral . . . I loved you when I thought you were a dowd . . . and I love you now, even *now*, when I realize you have no heart!"

And with that, the Viscount turned away and left her alone—a good deal shocked and subdued. And for the rest of the voyage home, Astera was uncertain how to approach him, so she did not. Only Cuffy was unaware of the tension between the two, and when Astera retired to her cabin, only Cuffy accepted her excuse of exhaustion.

CHAPTER 14

It would soon be Easter and Kyria was busy planning delicacies to tempt her Asteroula's palate. Miss Minerva Claybourne was also not eating. She had in fact retired with her maid into her room—which was not surprising, considering how many shocks she had sustained in the last few weeks.

First, Lord Winthrop, whom she had tried to stop, had eloped with Sybil Farnshorn. But halfway to a preacher, Sybil had been followed by the Scot, Dirk (to whom she had writ a very moving renunciation with explicit directives as to her whereabouts). Once met again, the two had run off together leaving Lord Winthrop to develop a severe megrim and be cared for by Minerva. Yet a little over a sennight later, Lord Winthrop received a tearful note from that same elegant lady, and after visiting the abandoned Sybil, the good lord announced that his original plans for marrying that "epitome of grace and beauty" would stand. A young foolish girl had let her emotions run away with her, but she was back to her senses and anxious once more to become Lady Winthrop. Lady Marvelle, of whom it was whispered that she had had a brief liaison with Andreas Jason, was now back to her husband, and both Marvelles and Miss Farnshorn were avidly planning, not a secret elopement for Sybil, but a grand wedding for which Lord Winthrop had had the audacity to ask Minerva to assist in the preparations. Was it any wonder the lady sought seclusion?

Then there was the problem of Astera. Thankfully, her aunt had been too distraught at that time to inform anyone but Kyria of what had transpired, and since Kyria had advised her to let the Viscount handle things his way, she had been quiet. Therefore, both Kyria and her aunt were shocked not on Astera's safe return, but on her *unwed* return.

Her niece's refusal of both Viscount Weston's proposal and Lord Cuffsworth's, and her further refusal to discuss the matter —even going so far as to shut herself up in her bedroom—gave her aunt, after wondering where she'd picked up that habit, a series of spasms never before equaled. Thus, both ladies were not receiving visitors. Both were in seclusion. And Lord Winthrop, too concerned over his coming nuptials, did not inquire as to either cause. Nor did he inquire about Astera's volume *Idyll in the Isles*, although he saw several on the library shelf and patted it gently as he would a good child. Even when Lady Marvelle warned him that it was a "salacious tale" which in all probability would soon have all of England astounded, he was still unwilling to attempt to read it. First, because he generally fell asleep over poetry—oft by the end of the first stanza— and second, because he was certain none of *his set* would ever be found with a poetry book in hand either—and if that miracle occurred, they would in all likelihood have the good sense to put it down hurriedly before their minds were the slightest bit affected! Further, upon Lady Marvelle's pressing him to do something about his ward's predilection for poetry, he concluded placidly, "the girl comes of that habit naturally. . . . Wouldn't dream of stopping her, any more than her divine mother. Hits some people that way, don't you know . . . but she sits a good horse!"

His solution: since the gel would still be living with him and his new wife, the soon-to-be Lady Winthrop would find a gentleman worthy of his "puss" to distract her thoughts from her pen! Sybil, in short, was to be Astera's chaperone. Sybil's face had frozen at that prospect, but Astera when informed merely laughed. She needed no assistance from Miss Farnshorn "in any area," she assured her guardian, and further, neither *she* nor her *aunt* would be henceforth living with the "soon-to-be Winthrops." Rather, both had decided to take a villa in Switzerland for a while where Astera would continue her work . . . and the air would be good for her aunt. Much shocked by this unexpected future, Lord Winthrop pressed them to return to England with his bride and himself, but Astera was firm. Attending that wedding was the limit of the attentions she would show either Miss Farnshorn or the Marvelles.

Astera felt she no longer needed a guardian, and, indeed, that she had not needed one for a good long time, and if Lord Winthrop refused to terminate his authority (as was allowed by the will), then she had both the substantial independence left her by her parents and her writing to support both her aunt and herself. In any case, living with her guardian had never been stipulated legally. She was much too old to continue to do so— her aunt would give her all the consequence needed. Actually Astera had long been wishing to live alone, and only her concern for injuring her guardian's feelings had held her in check and under his sway—which had resulted in a great many disagreeable occurrences, like the visits of the ton. Now she declared the time had come, and tried to help Lord Winthrop to accept his change of authority by stressing that henceforth he would have a limited amount of time since his every moment would have to be devoted to pleasing his new bride!

Not too pleased by that version of his future, and in fact, not having realized that there would be subtractions from his living arrangement rather than just a new addition, Lord Winthrop could do nothing but bow to that decision and forlornly accept a future without either of the Miss Claybournes.

Astera further demonstrated to him how she had already achieved an independent state by showing him the long-awaited letter from Mr. Millbanke in which it was stated that *Idyll* had been "well received" and sold a respectable amount of copies. Such gratifying news promised a well-charted life ahead! And Lord Winthrop was left to commiserate with himself over all the changes. In a matter of a few months Astera had changed from the hoydenish little child he loved so much and become a totally independent lady. She was certainly dressing the part lately. He would have to accept it . . . as he did his own new future as a married man. But, by Jove, things were moving too fast—before he had time to have things spelled out for himself! He wished to add stipulations to his and other people's futures before agreeing they should come, but all their futures were already approaching—unstipulated!

With matters so neatly and promisingly resolved in the house, it was surprising that all three members, Minerva, Lord Winthrop and Astera, were so grim. Astera directly attributed her case of the blue dismals to her impatience with her guardian's folly and the way it had overset her aunt. It was clear that in the last few years Minerva Claybourne had devoted too much of her attentions to Lord Winthrop. Perhaps she had even joined Astera in unwisely assuming that one day Lord Winthrop would take a chance and sue to supplant Arthur in her heart. But it was not to be.

So many things were not to be, Astera sighed, staring at the always blue, blue sky of Greece that was beginning to get on her nerves. The sea here was similarly blue, blue and still. No rough tides to shake it up. And there was a lack of trees in the horizon that also depressed. Too tranquil! No wonder the people were so anxious to show emotions to contrast with all that. Just as in

England in reaction to the more unrestrained nature one wished to seem calm or cold—like Viscount Weston.

Strange—with whatever topic her thoughts began, they invariably culminated with Viscount Weston. For instance when discussing the marriage of Lord Winthrop, *self* would intrude; and she would find herself wondering what it would be like if she were now making preparations for her *own* marriage to Weston. Such a perplexing man—seeming so cold and in control, and then demonstrating a total lack of control! And after that last, Astera devoted a good many hours recollecting his demonstration of his "lack-of-control"—till her face became flushed and she had to stop and apply some cooling cologne. But the thought that most overset was recalling Weston's final astounding pronouncement that *she* had no heart. Even though she had explained that she just did not want to be *forced or obligated* to marry him for society's sake—had he really assumed her not wishing to marry under those circumstances showed *no heart?* Had he not realized that now that there was no longer a question of compromise, and now that neither Andreas nor Sybil were in contention, he was free to come calling on her at last, openly and honestly . . . and that such a visit would be acceptable to her—if not even expected! But instead, he had made not the slightest attempt to see her. Rather, Lord Cuffsworth informed her, he was once again concerned in finalizing the Greek loan and had departed to overlook the properties the Greek government had put up as security. Obviously, his heart, Astera concluded from that, had not been as much involved as his pride!

Thus, neither of the Misses Claybourne were finding themselves in the mood to celebrate—certainly not the coming Winthrop-Farnshorn nuptials, but not even the earlier Easter festivities. Kyria was priding herself on having learned to make a proper English tea and was just serving a cup to the two ladies in the garden, when Miss Minerva Claybourne said something about, "She'll never know about his wanting a touch of camomile brewed in" and, catching back a sob, sought her maid for assistance back to her room—from which it had taken Astera a good part of the morning to extricate her.

Sitting glumly back at the delicate glass and iron table, Astera stared at Kyria.

"How can men be so utterly, utterly dense!" she exclaimed.

Kyria smiled. "Woman stupid-in-love too. I am looking at one. Why do you not answer that Englishman's note?"

"It was just informing me that he would be away for a while. There was nothing I could say to that!"

"Nothing!" Kyria exclaimed. "You could say, 'I will miss you,' yes? You could say, 'Come say good-bye in your own person,' yes? You could say, *'Don't go!'* "

Feeling teary herself, Astera just shook her head. "And I suppose you think Aunt Minerva has just to say to Guardy, 'Don't marry Miss Farnshorn—she will make your life miserable. Marry me instead and be happy as you've always been'?"

"*Vevea!* Better than to say *nothing!* Better than to stay in her room all the time and cry. Invite this Sybil here and tell her about the lord's problems with his stomach . . . his pains in the head . . . the way he gets tired at night and falls asleep over his brandy, maybe she will think twice."

"Ha!" Astera laughed scornfully. "She doesn't give a hoot whether he's awake or asleep after they're married, she just wants to be Lady Winthrop."

"Why not tell her he no longer is a lord—that he lost his *title?*" Kyria asked wistfully, and as Astera merely laughed mirthlessly and shook her head, Kyria continued doggedly, "Then say he has no *money.* It is all *yours!* Eh?"

"I could not do that. It would be dishonest. And I do not believe she would believe me. Lord Marvelle has probably checked into all that."

Kyria sat down and so forgot herself in thinking over the delicate problem, she took a hearty gulp of the English tea and choked. "*Thehé mou!* Makes you sick!" Washing away the taste with an entire cup of black coffee, she continued, "That pale girl she runs away with a young man, and Lord Winthrop angry. *Once* he forgives it, not *twice* I do not think."

Astera agreed but said the idea was hopeless, for Dirk had gone back to Missolonghi and had refused to respond to any letters. In fact, Astera sheepishly confessed, Lord Cuffsworth, at her request, had attempted communication and received quite an unequivocal response.

Still Kyria was not ready to cry defeat. As a Greek she philosophically regarded obstacles as just so many rocks to be climbed over—put one in her path, she just jumped it and proceeded on her course undeterred. "He gone. We find another." And then abruptly her olive eyes rolled about. "*Oupa!* We get *Greek* man. We get Andreas!"

"*No!*" Astera exclaimed. "The last thing I need is *Andreas* in my life again . . . after I assured the Viscount that he meant nothing to . . ." She stopped, considered, then dismissed that. "No," she said pointedly to Kyria.

But that evening when Sybil and Lord and Lady Marvelle had come to dinner (her aunt was still indisposed), and Astera had to listen to Sybil's calling Lord Winthrop "Robbie" and to both Marvelles discussing the estates and town houses they thought necessary for Sybil's full consequence, and seeing the constrained look on Lord Winthrop's face, Astera began to have second thoughts about the wild plans so righteously dismissed that morning.

Thus, when the gentlemen joined the ladies for tea, Miss Farnshorn was politely asked if she was interested in hunting. Permitting one or two feathers to ruffle delicately over just the thought, Miss Farnshorn decisively pronounced herself "against hunting." When questioned as to her reason, whether Miss Farnshorn did not partake of that sport for the same reason as Astera—that she "felt for the animal"—she looked blank and said she assumed the horse enjoyed running about, but *she did not!* In fact, she had had her finest riding habit come to grief by a gentleman's pushing her aside at the sudden appearance of a fox—preferring to view *that* rather than *herself!*

Commiserating with her over that gentleman's callous behavior, which apparently still rankled with the lady, Astera subtly invited Lord Winthrop to join them to explain the *joyous* side of the sport. He was delighted to do so—his delight extended to half the evening—recalling who had broken a neck over a rasper or come to grief over a fence . . . whether "does" or "jacks" were better sport. Sybil tried several times to introduce the subject of her wedding plans, but to no avail, till Lady Marvelle took charge and questioned the propriety of discussing hunting when a more serious topic lay pending—the marriage! Lord Winthrop was sputtering and forcing himself to rein in when Astera overrode all with an amazed, "Then *you* do not *hunt*, Miss Farnshorn!"

"I do not believe it is a feminine sport," Sybil allowed softly, looking for the approval from Lord Winthrop that remarks in that vein usually engendered from gentlemen, but this time he was silent. Astera, however, was not.

"Indeed? It is a sport many queens have felt feminine enough to partake in. My aunt, and I believe I cannot find anyone more *representative* of the *gentle qualities* of our sex, is a bruising rider, would you not say so, Guardy?"

"Oh yes, rather! Bang up to it. And likes a good story on it too. Pity she ain't here. Could have told you some about me I forgot. Dashed if she ever forgets anything. That's her problem. Ain't forgot her first love. Still mourning the fellow. I'm that way myself. Lost my heart to that young puss's mother—never thought to find another!"

"Till you had the good fortune of finding Sybil," Lady Marvelle put in, and Lord Winthrop hurriedly agreed.

"But Miss Farnshorn is not at all like my mother. I would say my aunt is closer to her, if not in appearance, certainly in her compassion."

Lord Winthrop eagerly agreed to that as well.

"It is not my understanding," Lady Marvelle snapped, "that my sister was in contest with Minerva Claybourne for my lord's affections." And as Lord Winthrop was horrified by that suggestion, claiming there was no such thought in *his head*, Astera smiled her gratitude at the heavy-handed Lady Marvelle. For putting that thought in Lord Winthrop's head was precisely the point of the discussion.

"Certainly not," Astera concluded, looking earnestly at her guardian. "Although anyone would be fortunate to *marry my aunt*—don't you think? Life with her, now that she has finally gotten over her first grief of Arthur's death, would be so *soooth-ing*."

Lord Winthrop agreed immediately to that as well . . . and was much struck by Astera's information that her aunt was no longer in mourning and was eagerly inquiring *when* her aunt had made that discovery when Lady Marvelle called out, "*Whist!*" and all adjourned for a few rubbers.

Astera's next step was to get her aunt into Mr. Stamnos' designs which she had previously eschewed. So insistent was she that her aunt, unable to withstand such force when her spirits were so low, gave way and wore them. At which point Astera overwhelmed her with compliments, and before she had recovered from them, Kyria was called in, and she, as well, was so prodigiously entranced that Minerva felt a youthful flush coming back to her cheeks.

The campaign was further extended to include Astera's sighing over Sybil's probable treatment of her guardian. She began by mentioning Miss Farnshorn's dislike of hunting; went on to describe the odious face that lady had made at Lord Winthrop's prize story of his favorite hound Sniffer; and finally, finally, Miss Farnshorn's refusal to take a cup of *camomile tea!*

Although distraught over the first two, this last had Minerva Claybourne at the point of exclaiming. And when Astera further mentioned that Miss Farnshorn, in fact, did not even wish to be told how to make camomile tea, she *did* exclaim, and promptly swore to save Lord Winthrop from such a prospect of "gross neglect"! Encouraging this mood with the proper exclamations, Astera led her aunt into donning a Stamnos dress for that very evening when fortuitously the three were to be alone. Though riled enough to wear the dress, Minerva balked at removing her lace cap.

"Very well," Astera said ominously, "if you are more concerned with the dislodging of your cap than the dislodging of Miss Farnshorn!"

Considering that a moment and after sighing deeply, Minerva timorously lifted the cap off.

The reaction by the good lord to Minerva, whose hair was the same exact shade as Astera's, could not but embolden her aunt even more. "Flabbergasted," was what he said . . . the same word again and again, and further he made gallant references to the two Miss Claybournes as appearing to be sisters. (Astera had thought to wear an old gown and her hair in a bun similar to her aunt's.) And when the three were seated after dinner around a good hot cup of camomile tea, he sighed in deep contentment, and, looking devotedly at Minerva, expressed the wish that it could "always be this way."

Astera needed no further direction and rather was so much encouraged that the second aspects of her campaign were put into immediate operation. Nothing more conniving or arduous was required of her aunt than to persuade Lord Winthrop to take her for an outing for the next afternoon, and thus leave the villa free for Astera. Nothing could be easier, for there was no more persuadable man than the gallant Lord Winthrop. It was the work of a minute. An "I should like above all things" and a well-placed sigh, and Lord Winthrop had the horses put to. Purposely not inquiring as to why Astera needed an unsupervised villa that day, certain that if told she would have to sink to her bed, but after threatening to do so in any event, and after putting on her new Stamnos design—in blue taffeta—Minerva began to feel young enough to enjoy the proposed outing.

All Astera had done, however, was to merely write two letters. One to Miss Farnshorn inviting her for a private afternoon luncheon and discussion on urgent financial matters concerning her guardian which she could only discuss in confidence—"*as one woman to another*." The second letter went to Andreas, inviting him for a private luncheon with her on the same afternoon.

When Sybil arrived, Astera was wearing a very sad face, wondering with a deep sigh if she should warn Miss Farnshorn of certain "financial embarrassments" that would befall her directly after her marriage!

Miss Farnshorn, suspicious, claimed she never concerned herself with monetary matters—that Lord Marvelle handled *all such issues* for her.

"Well, I could not betray one gentleman to another and, in truth, I did not wish to speak of it at all, even to you, but knowing how *I* should feel if I married *in good faith* and discovered myself to be a pensioner to another—"

"What do you mean, indeed, Miss Claybourne?" Sybil exclaimed, excessively alarmed.

"Why, you are aware, are you not, that the moment I marry, Lord Winthrop ceases to be my guardian. And Lord Cuffsworth and I are shortly to have an announcement."

Delighted to hear that Astera was not to marry the Viscount, for whom she still had a tendre, Sybil was not at all backward in her congratulations, but she could not understand how that concerned Lord Winthrop and herself.

Pretending to be very embarrassed—even using her hands to cover her face, as if in great agitation—Astera at last drew a deep breath and pronounced, "Well, the *allowance* I have been giving *him* would perforce cease. And certainly Cuffy and I should prefer to live *alone* in Mayberry. You must have noticed Lord Winthrop's discomfort the other night when you were discussing the plans for its remodeling. . . ."

"Why yes, I did, but I assumed it was . . . rather for the difficulty in *your* position, why he even said—"

"Quite right, Miss Farnshorn, your memory is quite exact. He even said it would be as *I* wished, did he not?"

Recollecting that very statement, and realizing the new interpretation that could be put on the situation now, Sybil paled. "But how is it possible? Surely Lord Winthrop's finances are such—"

"It was his injudicious way with his cattle, you know," Astera improvised quickly. "Ah, Miss Farnshorn, Miss Farnshorn, you must feel for us as I do for you! How often my aunt and I have tried to curb his throwing good money after bad, and yet, he continues to buy horses fit for hacks and attempt to race them. You recollect us discussing his horses—"

"I most assuredly do, but I was under the impression that he owned only one racehorse and that was rather a winner."

"Yet, Lady Marvelle did not know him as a winner. Do you not recollect *her* stating that *she* had not heard of the animal, and my guardian, in a somewhat flustered explanation allowed that perhaps it was some years before *her* time."

"Indeed, I did hear something like that," Sybil gasped, now convinced enough to be terrified.

"But I do not ask you to take my word on the issue," Astera finished as a topper. "I suggest you hold off the ceremony merely till you reach England and have an opportunity to check into the truth or falsity of these matters before you commit your *youth* and *beauty* to an old man's desire, which seeing the great *incentive*, forgivably, had him embroider his circumstances. But whatever you decide, Miss Farnshorn, I must request you cease making any plans for a stay in Mayberry, as I shall not find it convenient to have visitors in my home for any length of time. Perhaps a small establishment in *Bath?*"

"*Bath?*" Sybil exclaimed, that image too much for her to accept. "A small establishment in *Bath!*" she kept repeating as if unable to mentally pass that point of horror. And when Kyria announced Andreas' presence and even showed him in, Sybil was still stuck on the word—murmuring "Bath" again and again —and thus was somewhat shocked to feel her hand taken and kissed.

"Mr. Jason," she whispered, starting.

Andreas, immediately concerned, asked if she were well. Uncertain why he had been invited, but anxious to take advantage of any opportunity, he took Astera's cue and agreed to take Sybil for a walk in the garden, as she needed some moments to collect herself.

"You are so very talented in the garden," Astera said, grinning at Andreas. He rolled his eyes remembering his last attempt to seduce her there and wondering whether that was a hint or a warning, but sensing that Astera could not be concerned over Miss Farnshorn's reputation, he instantly realized what was demanded of him and named his price.

"There is a statue I have of you, my fair Astera, perhaps you have heard of it?"

Blanching but determined, Astera agreed that she would like to see it and purchase it, and that further, he could name the price. That being understood, Andreas bowed low and offered his arm to Sybil.

Astera was left alone in the drawing room—feeling rather guilty and even conniving—when Kyria opened the door in obvious alarm. Barely was she given time to wonder when Lord and Lady Marvelle were ushered in. "I told her that the Sybil lady went away," Kyria put in quickly.

Uncertain whether to accept or deny that, Astera did neither, merely signaling the two Marvelles to be seated. But Lady Marvelle was not to be fobbed off and the question of her sister's whereabouts was put once again.

To gain time, Astera repeated the question, as if uncertain what had been asked.

"Have you lost your sense of hearing along with your sense of decency, Miss Claybourne?" Lady Marvelle attacked, bristling. "I asked you *where my sister was?*"

Cuffy's voice in the vestibule had Astera up on her feet and hurrying toward the door.

"Cuffy," she exclaimed in relief.

Trying to catch the meaning in his friend's undue exuberance, Lord Cuffsworth looked hurriedly about and spotting Lord and Lady Marvelle, realized he'd pounced upon two very clear reasons. He made his bows and, assuming he was doing what was desired, announced, "Come to take you to that . . . eh . . . white tomb on the hill . . . the Parthenon," he said nobly, grimacing just a bit at the thought of the antiquity, but continuing bravely, "You recollect we had an appointment to give it a look over. Must toddle along before it gets any older!"

"Exactly so," Astera exclaimed, relieved, trying to hide her momentary giggle at Cuffy's description.

The Marvelles, about to lose their hostess, demanded to see Lord Winthrop, and on being informed that he and Miss Minerva Claybourne had also gone to see some antiquities, they

at first refused to believe it, but after Lord Cuffsworth obligingly explained, "In Greece, you know," they digested this fact
as best they could. At which point Kyria entered again to offer
Greek coffee—a beverage it was known Lord Marvelle detested
—but when he demanded tea, Kyria pretended not to know
how to make it, and when Lord Marvelle called her to account
for this fib, reminding her she had served it to them yesternight,
Kyria blithely explained she did not know how to make it with
"spilled tea," for her son, Panos, had dropped the tea container
and there were tea leaves all over the stone floor and the scullery
maid had thrown sudsy water on it to wash it away—and now,
none could be saved or served unless my lord liked to make bubbles.

"Make *bubbles? Me?*" an indignant Lord Marvelle expostulated, raising his quizzing glass and subjecting the grinning
Kyria to one of his longest looks. "Why the devil should *you* assume *I* would wish to make . . . *bubbles!*"

"Is fun," Kyria continued, unfazed. "More fun than tea . . .
but bubbles sometime get on your *crevice.*"

"On my what!" the lord was blustering.

"Cravat," put in Astera quickly, her face red from the effort
not to laugh.

Implacably Kyria pointed to the steaming brew on the table.
"Café," she said, clarifying there was no other choice. "Panos
only spill *some* of that . . . and it no soapy yet."

"Unfortunate," Astera put in hurriedly as Lord Marvelle was
beginning to turn an alarming blue in his indignation. "But
then Panos is regrettably always spilling something. I expect we
have nothing else to offer you, and indeed we should not detain
you a second further. Then too, Lord Cuffsworth stays on my
leisure."

There was a mulish look to Lady Marvelle's face. But as As-
tera was halfway toward the door, and Lord Marvelle demand-
ing to be gone, she could do no less than regally rise and follow.
Astera and Cuffy exchanged instant grins as they rushed ahead.
All four had just reached the door when it opened and revealed
Lord Winthrop and Minerva Claybourne, both complaining of

exhaustion and looking forward to their tea. They stopped mid-word as they almost collided with their visitors.

After a pause long enough to digest the meaning of the gathering and the meaning of the others' return—all began talking at once. Lady Marvelle's voice rose over all as she demanded to know the reason for Miss Claybourne's note to her sister! "Could Lord Winthrop see any reason for a 'private discussion on finances' between these two ladies?"

Astera sat down. Cuffy realized his friend was in a bit of a fix, yet could think of nothing more to say than a weak, "Must be going now," but Astera did not rise to accompany him out. She was in for it now, and she would nobly stay to take her punishment.

Recovering from his surprise, Lord Winthrop answered the indignant questioner that he could see no reason at all for his ward's discussing his finances with his intended, but he would be delighted to hear the explanation, and he faced Astera with such a sorrowful expression that Astera felt herself sinking even lower in her chair. She made the attempt to claim the note being misunderstood, but before those words were out of her mouth, Lady Marvelle triumphantly reached into her reticule and produced the very item under discussion.

Cuffy acted quickly, reaching over and intercepting it. Then he began studiously perusing the note with a great many "ah-ha's" and one or two "by Joves," before announcing it was *not* Astera's hand. And with an earnest expression he turned it over to Miss Minerva Claybourne, asking if she did not agree. That lady, clutching desperately to her vinaigrette, perused the letter and looked agonized at Astera, who, to spare her aunt, quickly came forth ready to admit all—just as Minerva, in one of her sudden acts of bravery, firmly proclaimed, "Though the hand is like, it is not quite like enough!"

"Balderdash!" Lady Marvelle exclaimed. "And who else, pray, would be writing under Miss Claybourne's signature!"

"Obviously a *master forger!*" Cuffy threw in sagely. "Lots of them about you know."

Astera choked back a laugh at that, but closed her eyes in defeat, realizing Cuffy's remark had instantly made their protestations lose all credibility.

Yet so incensed were Lady and Lord Marvelle they were unaware they had won and continued to dispute even *that* preposterous claim, when Lord Winthrop silenced them by turning a pained expression to his ward and asking for a "sensible" answer, just at the very moment that Kyria was announcing, "The Veescount, he is *here!*"

Astera could not quite stifle her groan. It would have been discomforting enough to confess her shame to the Marvelles and her guardian, but before the Viscount! Yet he was there, and after pausing long enough at the doorstep to realize something was amiss, he calmly raised his eyebrows in Astera's direction. But neither Lord nor Lady Marvelle were content to have her explain, and for once Lord Marvelle (still fuming over Kyria and his not having had his cup of tea) made the indictment: "Dashed if this *lady*" (he pointed to Astera) "didn't write a note to Miss Farnshorn suggesting something smoky in Lord Winthrop's finances—a fact she would impart *only* to Miss Farnshorn if she joined her alone at precisely three o'clock for tea. An unheard of hour for tea, you must admit, what? Miss Farnshorn agreed, much against our advice, and set off for this *early* tea . . . and private talk. We—Lady Marvelle and myself —arrived promptly at four to hear the explanation ourselves, and were told Miss Farnshorn had left—which, mark me, she would not do, since she expected us at four, and was *unescorted!* Further, Miss Claybourne suggested her note was misunderstood, and when Lady Marvelle, my dear wife, produced it, Lord Cuffsworth here claimed the note to be the work of a *master forger!*"

Weston was keeping his countenance with some effort. Looking at Astera's flushed face and Cuffy's desperate one, he reached slowly for the letter and calmly read it over. Upon completion, he unperturbedly announced, "Obviously another example of that man *Andreas'* work. Whether he is a *master forger*, Lord Cuffsworth, I cannot pronounce, but *I have seen* evidences of other of his . . . eh . . . *forgeries*. Therefore, I do not think we need put Miss Claybourne to the task of explaining anything remotely related to that disreputable man. I have found that taking Miss Claybourne's word without unnecessary explanation is the soundest policy, and I am certain everyone else agrees."

Astera's eyes widened as Weston was speaking. And in the end, as he was addressing her completely and privately, she could only send him a look of prodigious gratitude.

Taking their cues, Cuffy and Minerva and, with even greater relief and volubility, Lord Winthrop also agreed the subject should be dropped. Lady Marvelle, whose brief alliance with Andreas had caused some unpleasant talk, was not anxious to have *that man* brought into any discussion, fearing her connection might be recollected, therefore, she too announced that they were to leave—*at once!*

Impossibly but obviously so—the situation had been concluded. Neither Marvelle would stay for tea when Miss Minerva Claybourne innocently suggested it, only to be astounded by Lord Marvelle's exclaiming he'd be dashed if he'd be forced to blow bubbles in company!

"No need to do that, my lord," Minerva said soothingly, uncertain of his meaning, and then thinking she had it, saying helpfully, "A bit of camomile is just the thing for *that* condition."

As he caught her meaning, Lord Marvelle's mouth opened; and then in high color he expostulated, "There is nothing wrong with my innards, madam, but there's something deuced wrong with serving *sudsy tea* . . . and expecting people to swallow it . . . and sit around of an evening blowing dashed bubbles at each other!"

Here Lord Winthrop and Minerva exchanged alarmed glances. The Viscount, however, viewing Cuffy's struggling with himself, and the sparkle in Astera's eyes, raised an eyebrow in her direction, asking with a fond smile, "*Bubbles* . . . did you actually?" when Lady Marvelle, more up to snuff than her husband, announced they would no longer stay in a place where they had become general objects of risibility! She and her husband were actually halfway out the door and Astera was just drawing in one deep relaxed breath when Andreas entered from the garden.

All exits were once more suspended.

Amused by the shocked reaction to his appearance, Andreas bowed to them all—and, winking at Miss Claybourne, whispered, "A party, Asteroula?"

Seeing the man who had so ungentlemanly refused to run away with her when she offered herself, Lady Marvelle could not control herself. Forgetting her husband's presence, forgetting all, she screamed, "That man . . . *here!* All this time you"— turning to Astera—"*you* had him hiding in the garden? You and that man then are co-conspirators! Partners not only in *lewdness* but in heaven knows what. My question is—*What have the two of you done with Sybil!*"

Lord Winthrop, for the first time realizing there was some doubt about his affianced's whereabouts, anxiously joined in the questioning.

Andreas remained enigmatically still. Then dramatically running his hands through his dark curls, he looked at Astera and whispered wickedly, "Shall we tell them?" And when Astera turned weakly away, he faced Lord Winthrop and informed him solemnly that he could find his beloved if he directed his steps toward the garden, for that was where she had been when he left her. And when the old man began rushing, Andreas called after, "Look for her under the pine tree by the sundial, and the faster you move your feet, my good lord, the more of your beloved you shall see!" Hugely enjoying himself he turned to the rest of the astonished assemblage and asked, "Shall we all accompany him and see what a naked Sybil portends for *our* futures?"

But Lord Winthrop was long since away—and followed hard upon by Minerva Claybourne, who, vinaigrette out, felt her aid would be required. Lord and Lady Marvelle remained only to denounce the cursed fellow with Lady Marvelle pausing an extra moment to give her ex-lover a blasting look, to which he had the audacity to whisper, "*she* is very like you, my love, especially in appetite."

All that remained were the Viscount, Lord Cuffsworth and Astera. Andreas looked them over and observing they all bore similar looks of haughty disapproval, laughed again and sardonically responded to their thoughts. "Yes, yes, quite right . . . I am *not* a *gentleman*, but I am what is so much more satisfying— a *man!*" Then reaching over to take Astera's hand, he smiled mockingly. "Isn't it remarkable how you knew you could rely on my *in*discretion? Shall I see you at my studio to complete our agreement, *kukla mou?*"

And feverishly kissing her limp palm and bowing once more to the Viscount and then Lord Cuffsworth, he made a laughing exit.

Determinedly Astera stared at the Viscount. Trying to master his emotions, he returned her hard, measuring glance. She would not help him. And as their eyes held, Weston understood: he was being given a test. Wanting so much to give vent to his emotions *and questions*, he could hardly bear to acknowledge what she was asking of him, but clenching his teeth together, he nodded and said in a tight voice, "I have no questions, Miss Claybourne. If there is anything I can do to be of assistance, please do not hesitate to . . . request it."

Astera flashed him the deep glowing smile that always moved him and whispered gratefully, "Apparently there are moments for restraint as well as passion . . . and this is such a one."

"Apparently," the Viscount manfully agreed and made his exit.

CHAPTER 15

It was Easter . . . and the sound of church bells ringing, ringing, and the sound of children running from house to house exclaiming, "*Christos Anesti,*" for which glad tidings of Christ's resurrection they received cookies, red eggs and sweets. Kyria had supervised the baking of trayfuls of cookies in the shapes of crosses, twists or the letter S—all thoroughly sprinkled with sesame seeds. Further, cacophonous Greek religious songs came from her mouth as Kyria went about with a gold incense burner to spread the "breath of Christ" all through the rooms.

Astera's chamber looked down on the garden, and she had the grace to find it difficult to contemplate that view with equanimity. A deep sigh did not relieve her feelings, merely set her to coughing as she took in a lungful of the incense filling her room. Nevertheless, even the breath of Christ did not eliminate the heavy feel about her heart. She had been instrumental in creating the final rupture between Miss Farnshorn and her guardian. One escapade was forgiven, but two he found he could not countenance. Lady Marvelle had tried to fault not only Andreas but Astera herself for arranging the rendezvous, but her guardian would listen to none of it. Miss Farnshorn's state of dishabille had been all he waited to see, and subsequently, he would not even receive the tearful Lady Marvelle. Sybil herself had made no protest or excuses. She retained her serenity throughout the scene and in fact attempted to dissuade her sister from trying to cool Lord Winthrop's wrath with the placid statement that there had been a great deal of imposturing and she expected she had as much right as Lord Winthrop to dissemble. Which obviously meant her belief in Astera's remarks on Lord Winthrop's financial situation still held.

They left, and the engagement was terminated. Subsequent attempts by Lord Marvelle to see Lord Winthrop were rebuffed. Miss Minerva Claybourne had been so overcome by Lord Winthrop's narrow escape and entered so much into his feelings that soon it became obvious to Astera that Lord Winthrop had very few injured feelings remaining. He enjoyed Minerva's total attention—her concern, her seeing him suddenly as a romantic figure—and in return, he saw her as just the kind of *honest, devoted horsewoman* with which he should wish to canter through life. Recollecting Astera's remarks that her aunt was no longer mourning Arthur and appreciating the Stamnos creation of the "new Minerva"—it did not take above three days for the true situation to strike both of them and Lord Winthrop to make his second proposal to a second lady since arriving in Greece.

Her aunt's happiness and her guardian's should have been enough to justify Astera, but it was not. Her feelings were not relieved, not even after she confessed her stratagems and received just a small scold from two people too delighted by the outcome to cavil about the methods—although Lord Winthrop assured her he was very near to that conclusion himself and was merely looking for a decent way to end the position in which he'd found himself. Indeed, he exclaimed, he could not quite recollect proposing to the lady in the beginning—somehow it was understood by Lady Marvelle when she entered and found him comforting Miss Farnshorn after Dirk's desertion. In short, Astera had nothing to blame herself for—she had merely precipitated what would have resulted in any case, since clearly Minerva and he were *meant* for each other. Minerva on that point could not help but tearfully agree.

Yet Astera could not totally rejoice. Perhaps it was the dazed look in Sybil's eyes as she walked out of the garden, her dress in dishabille, and for a woman who prided herself so much in her appearance, the flaxen curls falling every which way were definitely pathetic and burned into Astera's mind.

Her only solution, Astera decided, was to visit Miss Farnshorn and discover if she could in some way be of aid, but a note to that effect had been sent back with an indignant rejection by Lady Marvelle. Attempting to learn Miss Farnshorn's situation through Cuffy proved equally fruitless. "Never interested in the woman . . . don't see why I should inquire about her now that we finally got rid of her. My policy—once you get rid of a cold, no point in looking to see where it went and call it back, what?"

As for Viscount Weston, he was still keeping away. Now, when she waited every day to hear from him, now, when she would have willingly explained, *once he showed her he needed no explanations,* he no longer seemed interested in one.

A sinking thought presented itself: that Sybil had gone back to the Viscount and explained the matter in her own way, and Weston had been horrified by what Astera had done, and, as a gentleman, sought to come to Sybil's aid. It would serve her right, if while trying to disengage Sybil from her guardian—who now assured her that he was tending that way anyway—she pushed Sybil into Weston's arms!

As for Andreas, she had used the good offices of Kyria and discovered how much payment he wanted for the statue. Upon hearing the sum, Kyria reported, "I fall on the floor . . . and from there, I bargain him down to my price."

Nevertheless, Astera sent him the full amount, and the very next day two workmen arrived bringing the life-sized (covered) "Asteroula." She was standing now in the corner of her room—a sad, abandoned creature that fit in well with the other Astera's mood. Kyria and her aunt, the only two of the household to see the statue, had insisted she have it destroyed, but somehow Astera could not. It was an eerie sensation to see a figure so very like herself, and she could not order her destroyed any more than she could cut her own wrists. After draping a Norwich shawl over the nakedness, Astera decided to keep her as a companion—since apparently she was going to need one, with everybody else pairing off around her.

Accompanying the statue was a cryptic note from Andreas:

Asteroula mou—

Into *this*, I have put all my heart and art. If there is more of the first and less of the second, it is no less worthy. Your generous payment enables me to pay my debts and depart for the Parnassus Mountains to deliver my statue of Odysseus and at the same time deliver my country. I take along however a memento of England . . . and have to thank you for that as well. *Zito!* Live Long! Live Happy . . . and remember a man who loved you with more heart than you ever believed. Andreas.

Astera had smiled at the note at first. Nothing appealed to her sense of fun more than Andreas' extravagances . . . and he *was* undoubtedly the most handsome man she had ever met. She had immortalized him in her *Idyll in the Isles,* and he, *her,* in this statue that was, she acknowledged, his best effort. No matter how many servants and relatives were shocked, she would keep it. And, of course, being made by a man accustomed to sculpting goddesses, it was rather flattering as well.

"Well, Asteroula," she said crisply, addressing the vacant eyes, "what do you suggest I do?"

"Asteroula" did not respond, and Astera sighed deeply. "You are not very helpful. I refer to my situation with Weston. Or are you too loyal to your creator to advise as far as other men are concerned?"

Silent still the statue stood, her face with the half-smile that now seemed rather enigmatic if not tinged with sorrow. Astera questioned the source, "Is it empathy for me . . . for Sybil? . . . for Greece? No answer—ever?"

Sighing again, Astera moodily turned away and back to the window.

It was April, and she recollected that the spring flowers would be popping up all over England. She thought of the daffodils . . . the crocuses . . . the green leaves just beginning on the trees. . . . She thought of the fields near Mayberry . . . she thought of the Viscount rushing up the marble steps of Mayberry to ask her for her hand!

There was no avoiding that man. Astera turned back to "Asteroula" and spent a few moments placing her new hat on the marble head. Kyria entered, as usual without knocking, and laughed at the sight.

"She is good for that. Keep her clothed and your aunt won't get the chasms!"

"Spasms," Astera corrected, grinning. "But she no longer gets them. She is happy."

"There are happy spasms too," Kyria philosophized. And Astera shook her head in dread.

"Panos says you want him take you to Acropolis?"

"Oh yes, I forgot. Yes, indeed, that's just what I wish to do today."

"Why you go there all the time? I don't like the place. The Turks would sit up there with their guns point down on us. Such joy when we threw them out of there . . . but they mess up the place, you know."

"It is still beautiful. You stand up there so high and see all of Attica . . . and all the sky seems at your feet . . . and when the sun comes down and colors it all like itself, all your other feelings are quite, quite pushed out by that one rush of Ah!"

Kyria shrugged. "It is pretty everywhere when the sun sets. Just as good here. There is like tomb."

"No! The Erechtheion was funereal, but the Parthenon is a tribute to women, don't you think? To a very independent lady —Athena. She was alone and unmarried and somehow always in control. Yes! I definitely will go to the Parthenon this afternoon, and I shall wear my new hat. It is made of straw and wide enough to protect me from the sun!" She took it off "Asteroula" and whispered, "Pardon me, ma'am, but I'm going to borrow your hat. You, I perceive, do not stand a chance of breaking out into those horrors—freckles! While I, alas, am that way prone!"

Kyria, affectionately shaking her head at the crazy English, joined in Astera's playful mood while helping her dress. "What say?" Astera laughed. "Shall I choose *this* gown? Very spring-like, don't you think? I shall cause all the tourists to stop and stare and wish to make a portrait of me, shan't I? But most of all I shall be a credit to Mr. Stamnos . . . and, of course, to *England!*"

"Po-po-*po!*" Kyria exclaimed, smiling. "But you are prettier than even *her!*" she said, pointing at the statue. "Panos, I will warn to stay close to you today or some Greek man will grab you and eat you up, for sure!"

Placing the wide-brimmed straw hat on her new coiffure (with upswept front and the back in rows of shiny, elongated curls) and tying it firmly under her chin with its pink ribbons, Astera was ready. Her gown was white in an airy muslin with pink embroidery at the hem, and her reticule was similarly embroidered in pink. "Yes," she mused, pleased with herself.

"Asteroula, I have outdone you—at last!" And with spirits high and nodding to the grinning Kyria, she floated off to the waiting Panos.

Several hours later Astera was tired of Panos. He had never been so constantly in her view. Every time she sought to go off alone and asked him to step aside, he would nod his understanding and then in a few minutes be right behind her again. She was no green girl that constantly needed attendance. Good heavens, although today she did not feel her age, at five-and-twenty, back home she would soon have to take up her aunt's abandoned lace caps. Shaking off that disagreeable thought, Astera skipped along the slippery marble floor. The steps up to the Parthenon were so huge, only a giant could have easily mounted them. Astera had to use one hand on the top step to lift herself up, and then repeat the procedure. It had been much easier on the day the Viscount had escorted her—somehow he had lifted her easily over. No! She would not think of that man—who had obviously stopped thinking of her. She would think of Greece . . . and Athena . . . and the Panathenian procession that once occurred here at this very spot . . . with rows of maidens dressed in their white dresses with embroidered hems. Ah, she had not realized how fortuitous her choice of dress, but, of course, they would not wear straw hats! Feeling the straw hat was an insult to the priestesses and to the sun—as if she wished to hide from them—in one liberating gesture, Astera doffed it and shook her curls free.

"That is better. . . . Now you seem to properly belong," a soft English voice said behind her.

Astera whirled. "You!"

Viscount Weston bowed. "Me," he acknowledged.

"How did—"

"A message from Kyria. She was afraid some man would abduct you; so I decided to do so before anyone else did . . . since I have had some practice in that area . . . as concerns yourself."

Astera laughed fully at that, but Weston shook his head. "I am not in jest. I have paid off Panos, and he has departed. Look for yourself."

Astera turned around and spanned the expanse of white. No Panos. "Then I shall have to rely on you for transporting me home," she said, undisturbed.

"That is exactly what I intend to do. Home to England . . . and me."

"You are in earnest!"

"Certainly. It has been the one object of my heart for almost a year now—to take you home to my parents as my wife."

"You know I have the greatest distaste for being abducted. The last time left much to be desired."

"You felt so too!" Weston exclaimed, much struck. "Indeed, that was my reaction as well. And as this time I shall not leave your side on *whatever pretext*, I expect it shall be more successful and . . . less wet."

"However, this time neither my aunt nor guardian shall so fortuitously leave notes that you can misuse."

"No, indeed, nor will they be required," Weston continued smoothly. "For I have the approval of both your guardian and your aunt *and Kyria* to abduct you at any time I should wish."

"And my approval is not to be sought?"

"My dear Miss Claybourne, one does not seek the victim's approval for an abduction. For an elopement, perhaps. But as a 'romantic' yourself, I can see you would not be satisfied with a paltry elopement. Abduction it must be! How else can I show you the depth of my feelings?"

"You would show me only the depth of your depravity!" Astera replied, still smiling, but now a bit unsure. "It would be of all things what I would most dislike. I urge you to abandon all such thoughts!"

"Well," the Viscount sighed deeply. "I myself have found it the devil of amount of trouble. I should much prefer to do things in the ordinary, British, civilized manner, if only one could get *you* to come down to that level."

And as he spoke he handed her down the Parthenon steps and was directing her over the marble stones toward his waiting carriage.

"I should run away again, you know," Astera warned softly.

"Yes, I quite understand that goes with the libretto. And we shall probably have to rely on Cuffy to rescue us again! And I shall have to stay away from you in penance . . . till I have proved that I am worthy and have taken all your good advice for my character in account. Did you see how very well I took Andreas' remark?"

"*Well?*" Astera laughed, as he handed her into his curricle. "Except that you petrified like a Greek statue! But yes, you were very good to accept instantly, without my even saying, that Andreas and I had no assignation."

"But you did have an arrangement?"

Astera colored. "I suppose I should tell you . . . since you have been so patient. But, in truth, I am afraid you shall be very much shocked. I arranged to pay him to . . . to . . ."

"Seduce Sybil?"

"Oh good heavens! I didn't mean him to go *that far!* I just thought he would get her interested in him a bit, so she would be willing to postpone her marriage to my guardian at least till we returned to England. . . . I had no idea that he would be . . . so precipitous!"

"Precipitous is not quite the word. However I understood your plight the moment I entered the room."

"And you were very kind to endorse my story . . . although by that point I scarcely knew what it was with Cuffy's additions. . . ."

"The master forger, eh?"

"Oh!" Astera crimsoned and collapsed in laughter as she recollected Cuffy's "master stroke," and was soon joined in laughter by Weston. "But I marvel how you thought to bring in Andreas," Astera continued, "and then when *Andreas himself* walked in!"

"Yes, that was a moment I do not wish to recollect, if you please."

"I had to pay him quite a lot—ostensibly for the statue of me which he has delivered!"

"That is another moment I do not wish to recollect! The

image of that statue burned a hole into my soul that still torments me."

Thinking of poor, innocent "Asteroula" waiting in her room for the return of her hat, Astera could not understand the Viscount's emotions toward her . . . nor did she think he would ever understand her affection for that marble self.

"Actually, I have her in my room, you know. She wears my hats!" Astera confessed.

"Does she indeed?" the Viscount laughed. "That has somewhat destroyed the intensity of that image!"

Smiling, Astera continued anxiously, "Do you blame me for oversetting Miss Farnshorn's plan? I have been quite concerned about her. I did not intend her to be so disgraced. But she and my guardian would really not have suited. He and my aunt, you know, have finally reached an understanding."

"Yes, I was privileged to be told by Lord Winthrop himself. And as for Miss Farnshorn . . . well, what can I say?"

"She has spoken to you?" Astera asked with dread.

"I have since spoken to both Miss Farnshorn and Kyrios Andreas Jason!"

Clutching the side of the curricle, Astera could just cry out at that and wait for him to continue.

"You are not aware then of the development in that area?" Weston asked, amazed.

Astera assured him she was not and was most anxious to hear.

"It appears that Sybil has at last fallen 'genuinely' in love with . . . Mr. Jason. The *precipitousness* of it perhaps . . . or the man's romantic nature. Certainly only a lady could explain why he does not give your sex—as he does mine—an immediate disgust. But be it as it may—it appears Lady Marvelle wished to hold your guardian to his pledge as nothing had actually been seen but Sybil's dishevelment, which Lady Marvelle explained away as her having fainted and been almost ravished. But Sybil would have none of it! It appears she never wished to marry your guardian at all. She too wanted *love* . . . and found it in the form of a Greek lover . . . whom she refused to give up.

And as for the Greek lover, he was quite prepared to accept her as a companion on his trip back up to the Parnassus Mountains. And, by the by, can you imagine Sybil living the life of a mountain woman, preparing the muskets for her man and cooking the goats over an open fire?"

Astera surprised him by not finding it amusing. Her heart lifted from its last worry. "Yes," she whispered, "I can. . . . I think she has finally grown an additional wing!"

Weston stared at her deeply. "You are a very, very unusual girl. You are happy for this couple? Are you aware that I put up quite a sum to get Mr. Jason to agree to *marry* her, and that *she* did not care whether they were married or not. Miss Farnshorn! And that she was walking around in his studio in a Greek-draped dress with her hair wild and her feet—bare!"

"Was she?" Astera clapped her hands together. "And I bet she looked beautiful! And happy."

The Viscount thought about it. "She did look rather well. Well, they are married. I stood up for her—for neither Lord nor Lady Marvelle would come near the couple. The Marvelles, incidentally, have accepted my arrangements for their departure from Athens—and since they both do not relish sea travel, it shall be a long journey (over land as much as possible) before they appear at Almack's! Mr. and Mrs. Jason have also departed for the mountains. Your aunt and guardian are to be wed upon return to England. That leaves, unattached and unaccounted for, of our original party—just you and me."

"And Cuffy!" Astera put in playfully.

"Ah, yes, Cuffy. What are we going to do with him? We shall have to adopt him and let him come and play with our children—what do you say?"

"I say that, as usual, you are too concerned with maneuvering others . . . and far, far . . . too precipitous!"

The Viscount checked his horses and looked soulfully at the beautiful girl at his side. "You are not going to really make me abduct you, Miss Claybourne, are you? Actually if that is the only way you shall accept being courted, I am quite prepared to keep on abducting you every day of our lives . . . up to our twenty-fifth year of marriage. But," he paused and said plaintively, "it would be rather repetitious after a while, do you not think?"

Astera, with an abstracted face and a slight "Asteroula" smile, neither agreed nor denied, at which point Weston softly asked her to look around. "That direction leads to your villa. And we can, as a good respectable English couple, present ourselves to your aunt and guardian and announce our engagement. Note however, this other way, it leads to Piraeus and my ship. Now the choice is unmistakably yours. I warn you, I do not mean to live without you a moment longer. There are limits to how much a man in love can be trifled with. Which way?"

And as Astera took a deep breath but still did not respond, Weston urgently took her hand. "Surely you must admit now to loving me—just a tiny particle of the amount I care for you? *You* who feel so much for even *Sybil* would not wish to leave me so distraught for the rest of my life—always looking up at the skies and shrinking from the stars for the pain they give me! *You* would not wish to doom me to a life of empty, cloudy, dark skies with all the stars gone from me . . . forever?"

"Oh stop, stop!" Astera laughed. "Very well, drive on to my aunt and guardian and announce what you will! We shall do it the proper English way—if you please. But you must understand that I will not have my wings clipped even to . . . to marry the man I love."

"What did you say?" Weston whispered, taking her into his arms. "About the man you loved?"

"Hold, hold, my lord! You have to understand that I shall not give up either my *writing* or my *independent* ways. I mean, I shall not change—if it is me you want, it has to be *me*—just as I am."

"I want you exactly as you are—writing, riding, running, laughing—totally impossible! And for your 'independent ways,' my girl, I quite count on them to assure our never having a moment's peace together!"

And yet when he reached over to take his kiss of acceptance, Astera had one more condition.

"No, first you have to ask me again . . . because I was not attending the first time."

Groaning, the Viscount took a deep breath and began yet another marriage proposal.

"Now, for the third time, Astera, my darling, I have the honor to ask for your hand in marriage!"

"And for the first time, Weston, my love, I accept."

Instantly she was crushed against the Viscount's impeccable neckcloth, which he had that very morning designed and named "The Leveler" in honor of the occasion.